FLIRTING WITH FELICITY

ALSO BY GERRI RUSSELL

The Warrior Trainer

Warrior's Bride

Warrior's Lady

To Tempt a Knight

Seducing the Knight

Border Lord's Bride

A Knight to Desire

A Laird for Christmas

This Laird of Mine

FLIRTING WITH FELICITY

GERRI RUSSELL

Published by Montlake Romance, Seattle

www.apub.com

Amazon, the Amazon logo, and Montlake Romance are trademarks of Amazon.com, Inc., or its affiliates.

ISBN-13: 9781477827222

ISBN-10: 1477827226

Cover design by Laura Klynstra

Library of Congress Control Number: 2014912339

Printed in the United States of America

"The most beautiful people I've known are those who have known trials, have known struggles, have known loss, and have found their way out of the depths." —Elisabeth Kübler-Ross

For Mom. You are one of those beautiful people, and I thank you for teaching me how to deal with life's ups as well as the downs. You are always my inspiration.

CHAPTER ONE

Never in her wildest dreams had Felicity Wright expected the day to turn out this way. *Never.*

Vern Barron Bancroft was dead.

On suddenly shaky legs, she entered the Bancroft Hotel's lobby and made it as far as the front desk before she had to stop and clutch the wood counter for support. The Seattle-based hotel bustled with guests, but Felicity only felt a sick cold in the pit of her stomach.

She'd been in the hotel's lobby at least a dozen times a day while working in its restaurant as the head chef. She'd taken her simple life for granted. She'd taken Vern for granted. Now everything had changed.

"You okay, Felicity?" Edward McMasters asked with concern as he came to stand beside her. He looked every bit the part of the hotel manager with his short, gray-peppered hair and his classic black suit. He nodded at guests as they walked past them toward the elevator that would take them up the seven-story building to their rooms. "That meeting with the lawyers took a long time. Don't tell me that cranky old man found some way to leave you all his bills."

Felicity stiffened, the muscles of her shoulders going rigid before she forced herself to relax. "Vern wasn't cranky. He was lonely." *Only two people came to his funeral this morning.* Not one member of his family had come to bid him farewell. And after the funeral only she had been present at the reading of the will. A will with only three beneficiaries: his caretaker, her, and a nephew. Did the man have any other family? She had no idea. She knew almost nothing about him, except that he'd lived at the hotel, dined in the restaurant each night, and liked her cooking. Felicity's throat thickened. She would miss seeing Vern at the restaurant each night. "Vern wasn't who we all thought he was."

Edward frowned. "What do you mean? Who was he?"

"The man we all knew as Vern Barron was really Vernon Bancroft."

Edward's eyes rounded as he looked around the lobby of the hotel named for its owner. Edward reached for Felicity's arm, whether to comfort her or to steady himself she wasn't certain. "*The* Vernon Bancroft? One of Forbes 400's wealthiest Americans?"

Felicity nodded, still dazed by the knowledge that her friend, her visitor each night at the restaurant and longtime hotel resident, was a billionaire. Vern had needed not only special meals for dietary reasons, but more attention than most of the other guests. As a result of their nightly chats, he and Felicity had grown close. But not once did he mention his financial status. And she'd never assumed anything more than that he was a lonely old man with sufficient funds to keep him in a place where he felt comfortable.

"Why did he call himself Barron?"

She shrugged. "Turns out Barron was his middle name. He obviously wanted his privacy."

Edward's grip tightened on her arm. "What did his lawyers want with you?"

"He left me the Dolce Vita—"

Edward gaped. "He left you the restaurant?"

"And the hotel." The lawyers had informed her she was now a multimillionaire, if she took into account the hotel property, assets, and income. Her heartbeat raced at the thought. Felicity quickly squashed the rising panic with a steadying breath. Vern would not have wanted her to freak out over his gift. He would have wanted her to accept her new fate and move on just like he'd told her to do last week after the horrible review she'd received in the *Seattle Gazette*.

"*Life is like that, Felicity. I've learned in my many years the only thing that works is to accept what happens and move on,*" Vern had told her.

No drama. No hysterics. That's what Vern would expect.

"Oh my God!" Edward's voice cut through the din in the lobby, bringing a sudden silence to the room as guests and staff turned to stare. "Are you serious?" he asked in a softer voice.

Felicity could only nod.

"What are you going to do?" Edward asked as the people around them resumed conversations.

"I don't know," she replied, her voice uneven as she looked around. She knew nothing about running a hotel. She only knew how to run a kitchen. And now all this was hers.

An aching sense of loss moved through her. It was three years ago when she'd first met Vern. He'd asked to see the chef and then challenged her to cook something for him that tasted good while still being healthy for an old man with diabetes and cholesterol issues. From the moment they'd met, something about the sadness in his eyes had touched her heart. They'd talked for a few minutes, and as they talked, he gave her what she would learn later was a rare smile. The man was lonely, and in her, that night, he'd found a friend. He'd been a friend to her as well, offering her fatherly advice even though she never asked for it.

Her breath escaped in a trembling sigh. Vern was gone. His advice at an end. The world seemed a lesser place. But in the end, he'd given her a piece of himself, his heart, and his legacy. Tears burned at the back of her eyes, but she refused to let them free. She would cherish that gift, and try to make Vern proud.

Felicity fixed her gaze on Edward and tried to smile. "Please tell me you'll stay on as manager while I figure all this out?"

The hotel manager's smile flashed white against his wrinkled face. "Absolutely, boss."

His words fell like a life preserver in the storm of self-doubt that had broken around her since leaving Vern's lawyers' office. Everything *would* be all right. She could learn how to run a hotel and make the owner's decisions for the restaurant. She could hold everything together, not just for herself, but for every person who worked at the Bancroft. They'd become her family. She had to be strong and clever. She had to work harder and find a way to be worthy of the gift Vern gave her.

Felicity frowned. "How did Vern keep you from knowing he was the owner?"

"He was a tricky old coot, I'll give him that. He would only ever talk to me over the phone," Edward smiled. "For three years, he pulled the wool over my eyes."

"He fooled all of us."

"That he did," Edward said. "But in the end, we can only respect his need for privacy. I know I do."

"I guess I do, too," Felicity agreed.

Edward studied her. "You okay if I leave you alone?"

"Of course."

"I gotta go tell Marie." Edward's hazel eyes brightened. "She's going to be floored by who Vern really was." He gave Felicity's arm a final squeeze, then turned to head toward the elevator to find his wife, who worked as the head of housekeeping.

Between Edward and Marie, the rest of the employees would know the news within the hour. Felicity doubted any of them would challenge her new status as owner. They were, after all, her friends. But then again, Destiny Carrow had called herself a friend when she wrote a horrible review about the restaurant.

During one of Felicity's nightly talks with Vern while he dined in the restaurant, he had reminded her that if she wanted anything in this world, she had to hold on with bulldog tenacity until she got it. She'd won and lost many battles over the years. This was only one more.

Excitement sizzled along Felicity's nerves. She forced her feet to stay firmly planted on the floor when the desire to do a happy dance overcame her. *She had a hotel. She owned her own restaurant.* She was now the boss of her own kitchen. Though she had never been fired before, that fear had lingered in the back of her mind for years. What would she do if she didn't have a job? How would she support her father and pay for his medical needs?

Owning her own hotel, she could never be fired or see her restaurant shut down as was often the case in the food industry. The Dolce Vita had had a better chance of surviving the ups and downs of the industry since it was attached to the hotel, but owning both the hotel and the restaurant would definitely increase the certainty of a job long term.

And, with a little more help from her staff, she might actually be able to do something for herself for a change, like shopping, or going to a movie in the middle of the afternoon, or going out on a date. A real date . . . that was something she hadn't done in ages. The possibilities swirled inside her as she turned and came to a sudden stop against the solid wall of a man's suit-covered chest. At the feel of his muscular form against her body, her stomach did a giddy flip. A woodsy, manly scent filled her senses.

"Are you okay?" The rich sound of his voice rocked her.

Felicity swallowed roughly as she took a step back. "Sorry!" She reached out to brush away any wrinkles she might have caused in his suit, then stopped herself as she realized touching him would only make things worse. She snapped her hand back and met his gaze. Eyes blue as the deep ocean focused on her.

Felicity let out a slow breath. The man was drop-dead gorgeous—his jaw strong and defined, his cheekbones high. And he had the tiniest hint of a dimple in his left cheek.

"Miss, I asked if you were okay." At her continued staring, an easy smile came to his lips. Lips made for long, hot kisses.

"My fault. I should've been paying closer attention." She was paying attention now.

She'd never had the time to indulge herself in the kinds of things other girls did. Her responsibilities were too many, her fears too deep.

But in her new circumstances, with this guy, she might make an exception. He was definitely something to look at. Her mouth went dry at the thought of the well-muscled chest beneath his shirt. But he was more than just handsome. Confidence shone in his eyes. And why wouldn't he be confident? The black pinstripe suit he wore probably cost more than her entire wardrobe.

The thought brought an answering smile to her lips. "Welcome to the Bancroft Hotel," Felicity said, with what she hoped was a mix of friendliness and authority.

He raised a brow. "You're with the hotel?"

Felicity stood a little taller, grateful she'd chosen her favorite black sheath dress for Vern's funeral and her meeting with the lawyers. The stranger's gaze slid down the clean line of her body to her sensible shoes and back up again. His gaze was warm, sensual, and inviting. Heat infused her skin as she nodded. It had been years, more than she'd like to admit, since she'd been this close to any male who had caught her interest. "Will you be staying with us for a while?" she asked with a catch in her throat.

"I'm not sure." His gaze left hers to search the lobby. "Could you tell me where I might find Felicity Wright?"

Her breath faltered. "You're looking at her. Why?"

His deep blue eyes searched hers with suspicion. "I pictured you being older."

A flush warmed her cheeks. "Excuse me?" Okay, so the man was incredibly hot, but why would he come looking for her? No one came looking for her unless they had a problem with their meal. But that would be easier to believe if the restaurant were open for business at that moment.

"My uncle recently died here. I understand you knew him."

"Vern Barron—I mean Bancroft—was your uncle?" The soft jazz that played in the lobby suddenly faded, and the lights dimmed as her own heartbeat pounded in her ears. *The nephew listed in the will.*

He nodded without a show of grief.

"His funeral was today," she said, stating the obvious as she assessed the man before her. Was he affected at all by the loss of his uncle? Or was he here to challenge what Vern had given her?

"My flight was delayed, or I would have been here for the services." A flicker of remorse darkened his eyes. "I'm going about this all wrong, forgive me." He extended his hand. "Blake Bancroft."

His deep voice rumbled through her with a devastating effect. As needlelike chills worked across her body, Felicity accepted his hand. The feel of his skin against hers caused another wave of chills to consume her. "Nice to meet you," she replied, fighting the urge to pull him closer.

What was wrong with her? Was she that out of practice with men? It had been almost a year since her last disastrous date and almost two years since she'd kissed a man. An eternity since she'd gone beyond kissing . . . She swallowed roughly. Oh, how she could savor this man. He was better than any sweet treat she might whip up in her kitchen.

He released her hand, and she suddenly went cold. "We have much to discuss, but not yet, and not here."

At his words, reality returned. Blake Bancroft stood before her. Vern's nephew. Fear and grief mixed into a knot in her stomach. He'd come to challenge the will.

"Vern's lawyers said the will was legitimate." She reached into her pocket and pulled out a folded sheet of stationery from the Bancroft Hotel that had been attached to the will. The lawyers had given it to her as if she would know what to do with the message: *"Take care of the Bancroft, Felicity. You'll know what to do."*

She passed the note to Blake. She had no idea what she was supposed to do. Last week her life had been simple. Her biggest worry at the hotel had been whether the special she served that day would be well received. Today, there was so much more. What that "more" entailed, she had yet to find out, but she was certain the man before her was not going to make things easy for her.

In that moment, Felicity had never felt so alone.

"You're stronger than you think, Felicity. You always have been. You're going to be just fine." The words Vern had spoken to her on the day before he died came back to her. She straightened. "I'm not sure what else there is to discuss, Mr. Bancroft. If you want to know more about your uncle's last days, then I'd be happy to talk with you. If you're here because of the hotel, then you can talk to my lawyers."

◆ ◆ ◆

Blake returned Felicity's note without reading it. He recognized his uncle's handwriting, but he really didn't care what the message said. He had come to Seattle to take over the Bancroft. An impassioned note from his uncle wouldn't change anything.

Blake swept a look over the young woman before him. When he'd learned his uncle Vernon had given away the Bancroft to one of the staff, he'd figured it was because the old man had had some kind of secret mistress while he hid from the world in his favorite hotel.

Fighting for what should have been his would have been easy if Felicity were everything he'd imagined her to be—a gold digger. Someone who would be easy to manipulate. Yet the woman before him didn't appear to be any of those things.

She appeared strong, in control, and determined to challenge him. Definitely not his uncle's type—if his uncle had ever had a type. Felicity's long platinum-blonde hair was pulled back in a no-nonsense ponytail at the nape of her neck. She wasn't beautiful in the classic sense, but there was an exotic quality to her almond-shaped eyes that captivated him. Those eyes narrowed on him now with suspicion. "Shall I direct you to my legal team?"

Blake frowned. The look wasn't the typical response he garnered from women. He shifted his gaze from Felicity to the lobby as he considered what to do.

A woman glanced Blake's way as she walked toward him in her high-heeled black leather shoes. Her smile was inviting, as was the generous amount of cleavage her tight pink dress revealed. He smiled at her and her eyes widened. She moved past him with a slight brush of her hand against his fingers as she slipped a piece of paper into his hand. No doubt her room number or phone number. He was used to this kind of attention.

Years ago when he'd first taken over as acting president of Bancroft Industries, the fame and notoriety that had come with the position bothered him. But over the years he'd become used to the unsought intimacy that people—especially women—pressed upon him. He knew it had nothing to do with him personally; it was his wealth. People clamored to touch him like he was a conduit for success.

Blake returned his gaze to Felicity. Her expression was emotionless, her wide brown eyes blank. No smile lurked at the edges of her full, unpainted lips. He could feel judgment radiating from her. "Look, Felicity, I think we both agree that there are things to discuss."

"My lawyers would be happy to talk to you."

A twinge of irritation moved through him. "It's better if we talk. You and me."

She looked at him, hard. "Why? What else is there to say?"

He thought for a second of something that might persuade her to at least give him a chance to explain his position. Losing the flagship hotel in their hotel chain would be a terrible blow to the corporation. Upon his uncle's death, Blake had always planned to use the old building to establish a new trend in green living. What better way to establish the hotel chain as a leader in the industry than to turn a broken-down, money-leeching building into something other hotels would strive to become? If he could revamp the Bancroft Hotel and remake it as a success, he would attract new investors for more expansion across the country and around the world.

Then Bancroft Industries would lead the way for its competitors. The Bancroft name would mean not only quality, but sustainability worldwide. Seattle was already a leader in the nation with its innovative recycling programs, but he wanted to do so much more. And that renaissance for his hotel properties had to start with their first hotel.

Truth be told, she wouldn't stand a chance against his legal barracudas. She had the will. He had the Bancroft name and a history with his uncle and the Bancroft properties that was undeniable. Her relationship with his uncle was something he intended to explore and exploit. "My uncle left you this hotel, and I'd like the chance to know why. Can we talk in the restaurant?"

"The restaurant is closed."

He gave her his most charming smile, the one he used to sway many a female his way. "Aren't you in charge around here?"

She stared at him, hard, and he knew she was considering his offer. "You're right; I do *own* the restaurant."

He didn't miss the jab. "So that's a yes?"

She leaned toward him, and for a second, just a second, he thought she was going to touch him. For some reason, the prospect set his nerves on fire. He was used to people touching him, yet with Felicity it somehow seemed different. When she pulled back, disappointment fizzled along his nerves.

She nodded. "Vern asked that I protect the Bancroft, and I intend to do just that." She drew a harsh breath. "This place is more than just a hotel, Mr. Bancroft. It's where a father can stop his busy life for a short time to go on vacation with his family, or where a husband can spend the night with a wife he's loved for years. It's not just a building. It's a special place—a gift."

The truth of her words made him feel a little sick. The Bancroft was special, but with his upgrades, it would not only be special, it would be a destination hotel for years to come. "Call me Blake, please." He waved her toward the entrance to the darkened restaurant.

They entered the Dolce Vita in awkward silence. He was hyper-aware of her as they walked—the way her hips gently swayed, the way she smelled of herbs and lemon, the way a stray tendril of hair had escaped her ponytail. He was tempted to smooth it back over her ear to keep it out of her face. He doubted she would welcome the gesture.

Once they reached the empty dining area, she stopped to flick on the lights, and then waited for him to choose one of the tables and sit before she asked, "So why do you want to talk to me?"

A slight wrinkle appeared between her eyebrows as she watched him. She was worried, even though she wouldn't admit as much to him. He studied that furrow in her clear, silky skin with something close to fascination. He could see the rapid throb of her pulse in her delicate temple. He felt a sudden urge to reach out and touch that faint thrumming, to run the pad of his finger over her silky skin. He glanced away hurriedly. Christ, what was the matter with him? For a fraction of an instant he had felt a hot thickening in his groin that could only be described as lust. "You've been at this restaurant for three years?"

She fidgeted and sat a little taller. "A little more than three."

"How long did you know my uncle?"

She met his eyes. "I arrived at the hotel as sous-chef a few months before he became a full-time resident here."

He sat back and crossed his arms over his chest. Her voice was soft, melodic, and he found himself listening to the soft rhythmic cadence rather than the words themselves. What color were her eyes? Brown, he'd thought at first, but now he was sure he'd caught a hint of gold in their depths. "When did you become head chef?" he said, though it sounded harsher than he'd intended.

"This doesn't feel like a discussion. It feels more like an interrogation. I keep waiting for the bright lights to come on and the good cop to come out to assist you."

"Making me the bad cop?"

He was rewarded with a quick grin before her lips thinned. "To answer your question, I took over as chef two months later when the head chef's elderly mother became ill and he had to move back to Italy." She reached for a bottle of water and poured them both a glass.

Blake swallowed hard and tried not to stare at the smooth column of her neck as she took a sip from her glass. She had a small freckle at the base of her throat, right where her neck met the arch of her collarbone. Suddenly, unexpectedly, he wondered how she would taste if he pressed his lips to the spot?

Desire slid down his spine. He studied her eyes; at such close quarters in the dimly lit room, they gleamed like beaten gold, shadowed and mysterious, giving nothing away about who she was or what her relationship with his uncle had been.

She'd had a relationship with his uncle. It was more than he'd ever had. In their final heated argument before Blake had been sent away, his uncle had told him the only purpose he had in Vern's life was as the continuation of the Bancroft line. He'd never wanted children, and he didn't want to raise Blake now that Blake's own mother and father were dead. The memory of that fight more than fifteen years ago cooled Blake's ardor. Slowly, he brought his eyes back to hers. "What *was* the relationship between you and my uncle?"

"I hope I was a friend to him during his final days."

"Indeed."

She stiffened, steel infusing her. "I cooked for your uncle. Nothing more. As far as the hotel is concerned, I was as surprised as you that he left it to me. But he did. And I intend to keep it, if not for myself, then for every person who is employed here who depends on the Bancroft to support their families. The Bancroft is their livelihood. I won't let you take that away." Her words rang with outright challenge.

"If you want to keep this matter out of the courts, I'm willing to make you a decent offer for the hotel and the restaurant. You'll end up with enough funds to purchase another restaurant anywhere you choose."

"That's not an acceptable solution," she said, her voice tight. The feathery curve of her dark lashes came down to hide her eyes.

"It's just a kitchen and a location, and with your growing reputation, it shouldn't be hard to get your customers to follow you."

Her eyes snapped back to his. "You can't just create something new, something different whenever you want to. A location is part of the magic of a restaurant." She shook her head. "What about preserving the historic significance of this place? What about the people who work here? Live here?"

"It's admirable that you care about their welfare." He smoothed his hand across the surface of the table. "And completely unrealistic. You can't save them all, the building included."

Her eyes went wide. "Why would you say that? Are you planning to tear down the building?"

He shook his head. "I understand the significance of this hotel to the Seattle area. I won't tear it down, but I do intend to do an aggressive renovation. The exterior will remain mostly the same, with a few upgrades. The interior will need to be largely gutted. I'll try to preserve as much as I can. The goal is to make the Bancroft a LEED-certified building and an example of what can be done to old buildings."

"I have no objection to making the Bancroft greener, but I will not sacrifice my employees' livelihoods to those efforts. You have no idea how hard it is to earn a decent salary in this business, one that can keep the employees above poverty level."

A flush came to her cheeks as she talked. The woman was certainly passionate about the people who worked at the Bancroft Hotel. "The people who work here can reapply for their jobs when the hotel's renovation is complete."

"And how long would that take?"

He shrugged and took a sip of his water. "A year, maybe two."

Her face became ashen. "No. Absolutely not. Two years is an impossibly long time to be out of work. I will keep the hotel, and I will fight you in every way."

He looked into her eyes and saw not only her distress but her strength—a combination he didn't usually see in the women in his world. Most of those beauties allowed the men in their lives to make all their decisions for them. Blake firmed his lips. They were the kind of women with whom he usually fraternized. The thought left him flat. "I expected as much," he said with honesty.

"The Bancroft must have some sort of historical protection. Isn't that what historical societies do—protect against insensitive men like you?"

Blake frowned. He'd been called much worse, but her barb still stung. "My uncle never filed for protection by the National Register of Historic Places or the local historic preservation program."

She sat back in her chair, studying him. "Did you love your uncle?"

Love him? "What kind of question is that?"

"An honest one. When was the last time you saw your uncle? Because I've known him for three years and I've never seen you." It was a question designed to hurt him, and it did. He couldn't remember the last time he'd seen his uncle. Four years ago? Maybe more? It was the day Blake had taken over as acting chair. His uncle vanished from his life that year.

Thinking about it all now made him feel disconnected. He had lots of people in his life. Lots. Blake gave her a disgusted look. "Now who's playing the bad cop?"

She shrugged. "Vern might have benefitted from having his nephew around."

"I had a company to run. A company he left to my administration. He knew what it took to make the hotels a success. Just as he knew what needed to happen to this hotel to take the company into the future." And that didn't involve pandering to familial relationships.

Bitterness brought a thin smile to his lips. He was thirty-four years old. He was a successful businessman in both national and international circles without his uncle's help. His uncle Vernon had found little use for an orphaned relative. He didn't need the woman before him to remind him of that.

At his continued silence, Felicity stood. "I won't back down, not without a fight. Take me to court, if you must. In the meanwhile, I suggest you find another hotel to stay in."

He stood, meeting her gaze across the table. "Am I unwelcome here?"

"We've never turned away a guest yet, but—"

"Are you a gambler, Felicity?"

Her eyes went wide. "Absolutely not."

"I am. I've gambled on many things in my life, and I'm willing to do it right now, with you."

Felicity startled. "What are you talking about?"

He wished for a crazy, desperate minute that they'd met under different circumstances. That Uncle Vernon was not the only thing that had brought their lives together. Or maybe he should be glad the old man had made their meeting awkward, allowing him to keep her at a distance, so he could sue her without remorse. But before things went that far, he had one last idea. "Uncle Vernon placed us in an odd situation. I'm willing to keep this out of the courts, if you agree to my plan."

She frowned. "What are you offering?"

"We each spend one day with each other. We'll start here in Seattle. You can show me why you want to keep the Bancroft as it is. Then, you'll spend the day with me, and I'll show you why I want the hotel and what changes I have planned. At the end of those two days, we'll determine if either of us has persuaded the other, or if we still need to take this battle to the courts."

He saw a flash of temper in her eyes. "Why would I do that? The hotel is already mine."

"A lawsuit over the ownership of the hotel will turn your life upside down and cost you every cent you have to fight me. The end result will not be in your favor." He shrugged. "At least this gives you a fifty-fifty chance."

Felicity's cheeks flushed, but indecision flickered in her eyes.

He held out his hand to her. "We each spend one day with the other. When we're through, we both must agree on who can best serve the Bancroft Hotel and take her into the future." And the extra days would allow the necessary time to prepare a lawsuit, if it came to that.

"But if we don't come to a decision, we've wasted two days of our lives."

"Are you worried about your powers of persuasion?"

"No," she said in an irritated tone.

"We've both wasted at least two days of our lives before," he said, then paused to give her time to consider. "Do we have a deal?"

She stared at his fingers for a moment before she accepted his hand. Her fingers trembled ever so slightly, telling him she wasn't as worldly as he had given her credit for a moment ago, but she was brave. Not many men stood up to him. And fewer women.

She pulled her hand back and offered him a polite smile. "I'll let them know at the registration desk that you'll be checking in, if that's what you want."

"It's what I want."

"All right. Until tomorrow, then."

He nodded. "Until tomorrow. When and where should I meet you?"

A smug grin replaced her smile. "Meet me in the lobby at five thirty in the morning." At his frown, she added, "My day starts early. I'll get Marie to cover the housekeeping meeting at the hotel for me, so we can head straight to the waterfront to buy seafood, then we'll go to the farmer's market to see what fruit and vegetables are available."

"I'll be there," he agreed, as she turned and walked out the door. The room suddenly grew cold and dark without Felicity's vibrant presence.

Blake dismissed the thought and reached for his water glass, wishing it held something stronger. He never mixed business with pleasure, but maybe it was time to break his own rule. Felicity was not his usual opponent. She was passionate and headstrong, an interesting combination. If he was going to win, he was going to have to use every possible advantage he had, perhaps including seduction. He could be very persuasive. He lifted his water glass to his lips, his mind dwelling on the possibilities.

CHAPTER TWO

Felicity walked the short distance from the hotel to her studio apartment two blocks east without seeing a thing along the way. Dear God, she was frightened. Not of Blake Bancroft, but of what he could undo. Just this morning, Vern had given her a dream and a future. Blake could take all of that away and more.

If he took the hotel away from her, she would lose her job and her income. Blake wouldn't keep her around to oversee the restaurant if he took ownership. Without that, where would she be? Where would her father be? She fisted her hands at her side. She would never go back to the poverty of her past. A siren screamed from the street below as she let herself into her apartment and shut the door behind her. Her "Pill Hill" location was affordable, but she did have to put up with the noise of ambulances all hours of the day and night as they rushed to and from the three hospitals located nearby. Usually she could tune out the noise, but this afternoon she couldn't.

Too strung up from her encounter with Blake Bancroft, Felicity paced the small confines of her home. She cast an anxious glance about the sparsely furnished apartment. She'd happily accepted her austere lifestyle, because of what else it enabled her to do: provide for her father. The memory of the car accident that killed her mother and left her father permanently disabled came flooding back. Only Felicity had walked away without any visible scars, but emotional scars were there, buried deep. Her family had always struggled to make ends meet before the accident. But afterward, poverty had swallowed her father and herself in an unending cycle of bills from her mother's funeral and her father's hospital expenses. At sixteen, she'd had to sacrifice everything normal teenage girls dreamed about in order to give her father round-the-clock care.

Another siren blared outside her window. Felicity stiffened, the muscles of her shoulders going rigid before she forced herself to relax. The man her father had been would never return, but she had to care for what was left of him.

Felicity frowned. She'd never told Vern anything about her past, not that he had ever asked. Still, some part of her wondered if his act of kindness went much further than giving a nice girl a restaurant. If he was as rich as his lawyers claimed, then he could've had her investigated. She'd tried to hide the truth about how poor she'd been in the past, but if someone were determined enough to uncover her secrets, it wouldn't be hard.

Felicity forced her thoughts back to the present. She would never know what had motivated Vern to do what he did. All she could do was accept what he'd given her and be grateful. And she was so grateful. At the thought, the skin on her arms tingled and the giddy elation she'd experienced earlier returned. She owned a hotel—a hotel that was well furnished, luxurious, and blissfully quiet.

As the full impact of her situation washed over her, she stopped pacing. *She owned a hotel.* She could move in there, rent-free, giving herself an instant raise. The experimental therapy her father needed but could never afford was now within her reach.

It all seemed like a dream come true, except that Blake Bancroft was in town to challenge her for ownership.

Her joy faded. There had to be a way to stop him, or stall him, or win the deal he'd set up between them today.

Felicity pressed her fingers to her forehead, as if doing so would help her think. What could she possibly show him that might make him back away from a legal battle? She didn't have any special skills besides cooking, and she didn't know enough about the hotel yet to teach him anything significant. She could use her cooking skills to her advantage, but what else was there? Was there a way for her to make him see that he couldn't make the changes he suggested?

What hotel owner didn't want renovations to a building they owned completed for free? But those changes wouldn't be free. Blake wouldn't do the restoration work then walk away. The price she would pay would be with her ownership, and her employees would be out of work. Felicity dropped her hands to her sides. Could she bargain with Blake to continue to pay her employees during any furlough that might occur?

Again, that meant giving up her claim on the hotel.

She stopped pacing and stared out her third-floor window that had a partially obstructed view of Puget Sound between two brick buildings. Two old buildings.

What was it he'd said about historic preservation?

Felicity went to her table and pulled out one of the iron and mosaic chairs. She reached for her laptop and turned it on. The first thing she did was to search online for information about Blake. What she found only made her more determined than ever to succeed. After that, she searched for information on the National Trust for Historic Preservation, then on the Seattle Historic Preservation Program. The process of applying for historic protection looked fairly straightforward, because she was the property owner. From her searches, it appeared the entire process from application to approval would take no more than six to eight weeks.

Felicity's teeth sank into her lower lip. Could she avoid Blake that entire time other than the two days to which she'd committed? Or was there some way to expedite the process? She had no idea who she should talk to about speeding up the process, but she was certain the lawyers who'd handled Vern's estate did.

Determined to succeed, Felicity printed out the application and filled out as much as she'd learned about the Bancroft Hotel in the three years she'd worked there. Edward and Marie were the two employees who'd been with the hotel the longest. She could ask them for more details about the Bancroft. In the meanwhile, she was determined to look online, on her own, to see what she could find about the hotel's past.

She learned the hotel had survived the Great Seattle Fire of 1889, but that the east wing had been rebuilt after another fire destroyed the kitchen area in 1993. Two presidents and numerous dignitaries had stayed there over the years. It had served as a Red Cross station during World War I and World War II, had a fallout shelter installed during the Cold War, and acted as a women's dormitory for a nearby university. The Bancroft Hotel had a long history of housing many local families as well as travelers over the past one hundred years. Some of those local families had been taken away from the Bancroft and sent to internment camps during World War II. One report she read said that a room in the basement still contained personal items the Japanese families left behind.

Felicity leaned back in her chair. Why had no one ever told her about that room? She understood why so many families decided to take up permanent residence at the Bancroft. Like Vern, those residents had access to all of Seattle's attractions, including world-class medical care, and the hotel had a wonderful homey feel. It would be much the same if they'd lived in town on their own, but without the need to keep up their own place. For an elderly person, living at the Bancroft was a viable option to an assisted living facility. She'd have loved to have her father there, if he'd been independent enough.

Vern had been one of several permanent residents who had chosen to spend his retirement years at the Bancroft. Again, regret came to Felicity. Would she have treated the old man any differently had she known who he was? She'd never know the answer to that, but at least she was proud of the time they'd shared together. He'd given her a piece of his legacy, because of their friendship. She would do everything in her power to help preserve what Vern had obviously loved.

Edward, as the manager, might be able to add more detail about the Bancroft's history before she took everything over to her lawyers' office. She'd ask them to prepare and submit her formal application to the Seattle Historic Preservation Program. Everything had to be perfect. She couldn't afford to make any mistakes.

With luck, perhaps they could finish applying before the end of the week. Time was certainly of the essence, if she were going to keep the hotel and everyone in it safe from Blake Bancroft.

An hour later, with a sense of accomplishment, Felicity packed up her application and the information she'd found. Before she returned to the hotel, she had a stop to make. If she hurried, she could see her father before she had to start work at the restaurant.

◆ ◆ ◆

"Welcome to the Bancroft. Your home away from home," the bellhop said as he placed Blake's bags in the bedroom of the suite.

Home.

Blake tipped the bellhop for carrying his bags, then shut the door as an ache settled deep within him. How long had it been since he'd had a home? There had been times over the past fourteen years when he'd missed his home with a ferocity that had been sheer torture.

His lips twisted in a mockery of a smile. After his parents had died, he'd had a family and a home for all of two weeks before his uncle had sent him away. He and his uncle were too much alike and had never been able to reconcile that fact. Now it was too late. And as a punishment for being alive when his father was not, his uncle had given a stranger the one thing Blake had always wanted—something his uncle knew he wanted—the Bancroft. It was the only place that had ever felt like a home to him while his parents were alive.

He was hiding behind the renovations, he knew, but they'd get him what he wanted for Bancroft Industries as well as for himself. He might not have had any allies as a little kid at boarding school, but now he had a team of expensive professionals to help him take down anyone who stood in his way.

Feeling in control once more, Blake reached for his cell phone. He placed a call to Marcus Grady, the head of his legal team in San Francisco. While he waited for Marcus's secretary to put the lawyer on the phone, Blake paced the sitting area of his suite. The bright and airy décor did nothing to calm the tension inside him.

"Blake," Marcus greeted. "Jesus, it's only been three days since Vernon died. Give a guy a break. I don't have much on your mysterious Felicity Wright yet."

"What do you have?"

"Nothing that says she's a gold digger. She's twenty-nine years old, the only daughter of a merchant marine. Her parents were in a car wreck thirteen years ago. Her mother died. Her father is alive, but I can find nothing more on him other than that his mail goes to a PO box in Seattle. Felicity's not active in politics. She's never been arrested. She comes up clean."

Blake thought about the information, then discarded it. There was nothing there he could use to win the hotel if their battle went to court. "Is that all?"

Marcus sighed. "I'm still digging. I have a call in to a friend from her college years. Maybe we'll find something there." Marcus was silent a moment. "Blake, your uncle's will is fairly tight. We don't have much of a case. I want to prepare you for that sooner rather than later."

"There has to be something. Everyone has something. Dig deeper."

"She might be what she appears—a decent person," Marcus replied.

"Who conned my uncle out of a multimillion-dollar hotel."

"Or else he gave it to her for a reason," Marcus added. "You don't know. Perhaps your best bet is to let her have it. Walk away. It's what your uncle wanted. You don't have to fight every fight just to say you won. You're not the underdog anymore."

Blake stopped pacing and gripped his cell phone harder. Only Marcus could get away with saying something like that to him. "You've known me a long time, but you're treading a razor's edge. Don't push me."

Marcus sighed. "All right. I'll call you when I have something to report."

"Tomorrow." Blake hung up. He could feel a familiar frustration welling up inside. He moved restlessly toward the big picture window that looked out over the Seattle skyline toward the waterfront. He'd thought it would be easier to swoop in and take back what was his. He'd also thought it would be easier to stay remote as he manipulated events to his satisfaction. He'd only been near Felicity for a few minutes in the lobby of his hotel, and he'd found himself thinking and saying things he normally wouldn't.

Blake's grip tightened on the curtains beside him as he remembered the sensation of Felicity's body pressed against his for only a brief moment. A faint tremor had moved through her at his touch. He remembered her heat, her not-quite-hidden attraction. In just minutes, the woman had managed to pry open a crack in his defenses.

He was hardening at the memory. With a groan of frustration, Blake turned away from the view. He had a job to do, and that was to take back the Bancroft Hotel. Pretty, pert Felicity Wright would not stand in his way.

◆ ◆ ◆

Felicity entered Saint Francis House, the assisted living facility where her father lived, and took the elevator to his room on the third floor.

After a soft knock on the door that she knew he wouldn't answer, she let herself in.

As usual, her father sat in his chair by the window, looking over the city's busy streets below. Her father had always loved to watch people—the way they moved from one place to another. Before the accident, and when he wasn't working on the ferries that shuttled people and cars from one part of Puget Sound to another, he'd been a time-lapse photographer. He'd set up his camera in various places around the city and capture the movement of the people and cars along its streets. "A day in the life," he used to call it.

As she pulled up a chair beside him, she wished he still used that camera to see the world. But maybe he did the same kind of thing as he watched the day pass from morning to night in front of his window. She didn't know what he thought about or even if anything registered anymore. He hadn't said a word since the accident. But his silence didn't stop her from talking.

"Hey you." She leaned over and kissed her father on the cheek. He was warm and smooth and smelled like talcum powder, just as he did every day following his hospitalization from the injury. "You look good," she said, taking his hand in hers and giving it a squeeze. He never squeezed back.

Daily she told him all the details of her often too-ordinary life. She'd talked to him for the last three years about Vern and his antics at the restaurant. In many ways, the shadows that haunted Vern's eyes reminded her of her father. Although Vern could talk and respond to those around him, she knew that look of loneliness and regret. She'd never figured out what Vern's regrets were, but they were definitely there.

Felicity shook off the thought and returned her attention to the man beside her. "I got some great news today, Dad. You know that experimental therapy Dr. Mackie wanted to try? Well, you're going to start your first treatment soon. Your procedure is scheduled in two days. The doctor wants to keep you in the hospital for a couple of days afterward for observation. And don't worry about the money. My savings will cover it. We're going to be fine." *For a while at least.* She wouldn't wait until everything was settled with Blake. She and her father had waited too long for this procedure already. This was one gamble she was willing to take.

The Northstar procedure was having considerable success, Dr. Mackie had told her when she'd called him on her nine-block walk between the hotel and Saint Francis House.

"The idea behind the treatment is that the doctor will shut down the right side of your brain using transcranial magnetic stimulation—he called it TMS—especially in the areas involved in speech, allowing the weakened side of your brain to form new connections that might restore your speech."

Her father continued to stare out the window, expressionless as always.

Felicity continued, "You'll have speech therapy every day for the next week. And either you'll make some progress, or we'll determine if a second treatment is advisable."

Again, he showed no sign of having heard a thing she said.

Despite his unresponsiveness, Felicity couldn't hold back a smile. Just the thought of actually doing something proactive for a change instead of waiting to see if he ever recovered filled her with a renewed sense of hope. Dr. Mackie had given her all the usual warnings about getting her hopes up, but she couldn't help it. Her father hadn't said a thing to her in thirteen years. She didn't even need words for the treatment to be a success. She simply wanted to look into her father's eyes and see something other than the emptiness brought on by the brain trauma he'd suffered years ago.

"Now, on to other news," she said, settling in beside her father. She told him everything that had happened to her that day—about Vern's funeral, about him giving her the hotel and restaurant in his will, about meeting Blake, and about moving into the Bancroft Hotel so she could save money to pay for the new treatment.

She'd never been able to talk to her father about the intimate details of her life before the accident. She'd been too young to really see him as anything other than a parent. The accident had changed their roles. Felicity had always believed their newfound relationship, even though it was terribly one-sided, had been a blessing that had come out of their shared tragedy. But on the tails of that sense of peace came a piercing stab of guilt, acrid and sour. It didn't seem fair that she'd been allowed to walk away from that accident when her mother and father had paid so dearly.

She'd been grappling with the unfairness of life ever since. And instantly her thoughts moved back to Blake. Was it fair that she'd been given something that should have been his legacy? Did she truly deserve the gift Vern had given her?

She wished in that moment that her father could talk and give her advice, the way a father usually did when his daughter was in crisis. Instead, she touched his chin with affection. "See you later, alligator," she said the way her father always had in the past before leaving her. In a softer voice she echoed her response, "After a while, crocodile."

She'd get no advice from him today, but now there was hope that maybe she would in the future.

◆ ◆ ◆

Felicity walked back along Terry Avenue toward the hotel when she saw Mary Beth wave at her from the opposite side of the street. Felicity watched as Mary Beth crossed the street. The young woman was small and quite fragile looking, though Felicity knew that wasn't the case. Mary Beth was tough. She'd had to be in order to survive the last few years. "What are you doing here?" Felicity asked at her approach.

"Where's Amelia?" It wasn't yet time for work, and Felicity knew her friend liked to spend as much time as possible with her baby.

"With my brother. Until I had Amelia, I didn't know how lucky I was to have him living at home with me. I needed a break today. We had another tough night."

"Teething again?"

"Amelia decided to get her front bottom teeth at the same time, but they finally broke through. There's hope for sleep tonight." Mary Beth did look tired, but even so, she was dressed like she'd had all day to pull her outfit together. Her leggings, pink silk tunic top, and metallic-colored Roman-inspired sandals were stylish yet cool enough for the warm Seattle day. And, despite the fact that she'd had a baby less than six months ago, Mary Beth always managed to look her best—a lesson from her former life as a Seattle socialite that had not vanished along with her family's fortune.

Side by side they started walking toward the hotel. "Why come to the hotel early for work when you have help at home? I'm sure there are a million other things you'd rather be doing."

Mary Beth slid a guilty look Felicity's way. "Besides needing to change into my kitchen clothes? All right, if you want the truth, I heard the news, and I just had to hear it from you myself." She stopped walking, forcing Felicity to do the same. "Did Vern really leave you the hotel and restaurant in his will?"

"News travels fast," Felicity said with a chuckle. "Who told you?"

"Hans texted me."

"It's true," Felicity admitted, pulling Mary Beth over into the entrance of the alley behind the Bancroft Hotel so they could talk more privately.

"Oh my God," Mary Beth whispered. "This is the best news ever. It's about time something good happened in your life."

Memories of Felicity's past tiptoed into her mind. She saw the shoddy trailer park in the south end of Puget Sound she'd once called home. She saw her father, sitting in his chair, the same chair he sat in every day, all day, staring out the window as though waiting for her mother to return.

Luck had not smiled upon them then. Her father had been placed in a run-down nursing facility. It was all they could afford. And, because she was sixteen and had no other relatives to rely on, she'd been placed in foster care for a short time until she could legally declare herself an emancipated minor and return to the trailer, taking her father back home with her.

"I still can't quite believe it's true." Felicity shook off the memories and looked past Mary Beth, to the seventh-floor windowsill where five pigeons perched together, cooing softly to one another as they did every day. Nothing had changed in their lives, even though the very foundation of hers had shifted.

"You signed papers, right?" Mary Beth asked.

Felicity nodded, bringing her gaze back to her friend. "Several of them."

Mary Beth grinned. "Then it has to be true."

Instead of joy, fear rushed through Felicity in a chilling wave. "Vern's nephew is here to challenge me for ownership."

Mary Beth's smile vanished. "That doesn't matter, does it?"

"I wish I knew for certain. Vern might have wanted me to inherit the Bancroft, but Blake doesn't look like someone who will back down easily." Felicity clenched her hands together, not only at the thought of losing something that had suddenly become vital to her life, but also at the fact that she once again had to pretend she was indestructible.

She'd tried so hard to keep her fears at bay in the days and months after the accident, when it was determined her father would never be able to work again. His pension was all they'd had to keep their small family out of poverty, and it had just barely covered their expenses. Felicity had learned how to make the money stretch from month to month, and it was then she'd taught herself how to cook, not because of a burning desire, but out of necessity.

During those years, Felicity had created a special world for herself and her father. The fear of losing even the run-down trailer or the ability to pay the bills threatened to destroy her daily, while she focused on finishing high school. But the fantasy of keeping everything as it was in case her father miraculously improved had given her something to cling to in the darkness—a reason to keep believing, to keep up the pretense that no one and nothing could harm her.

"Blake Bancroft might finally be the one who breaks me."

"No," Mary Beth said, emphatically. "He will not. I won't let him. You've worked so hard for me, for so many people. You're a good person, Felicity. Vern knew that. With his gift he obviously wanted to see the goodness you give to others flow back to you."

Mary Beth was referring to Felicity's Hungry Hearts program, through which she brought the homeless into her kitchen during the off hours and taught them not only how to cook but gave them the skills and the references they needed to search for employment in the food service industry. Mary Beth was a recent graduate of her program, and Felicity had hired her to work with her in the Dolce Vita. Mary Beth had a talent for baking that rivaled many professionally trained bakers.

"Good things don't usually happen to me, and when they do it makes me a little nervous," Felicity admitted.

Mary Beth's brow knitted in a thoughtful frown. "Weren't you the one who lectured me at length about accepting what was put before me and being grateful? Or was that lecture for your students' benefit and not your own?"

The words brought a fleeting grin to Felicity's face. "I am grateful, believe me, especially for your friendship." Of all her friends, Mary Beth knew what it was like to be on top of the world one moment and to have it crash around you the next. Mary Beth's parents had lost everything in the stock market crash of 2008. Their family had tried to hang on to their wealthy lifestyle for a few years, but they'd all drifted apart. Her parents had moved to Mexico. Her brother had entered the military. She'd moved in with her boyfriend until he'd thrown her out when she'd told him she was pregnant.

A homeless and hungry Mary Beth had shown up one day at Felicity's Hungry Hearts program. They'd been the best of friends ever since.

Mary Beth grinned. "Good. Now, let's put that gratitude to work and cook up something wonderful."

Felicity nodded as she hooked her arm through Mary Beth's and headed back onto the sidewalk and toward the hotel and the kitchen of the Dolce Vita.

Cooking might help her forget how much she should dislike the man who'd invaded her life this morning. But instead of anger and possible resentment, warmth crept through her veins and stole up her cheeks as she remembered Blake's handsome face and the way his smile had softened his features when he'd looked at her. She forced the thought away. What was it Mary Beth had said?

Something wonderful.

Yes, they'd create something wonderful. There hadn't been much of that in her life so far, but Felicity liked the way that sounded.

CHAPTER THREE

"Are you sure you're up to this challenge?" Reid Fairfax asked from across his desk in his downtown Seattle office.

Destiny Carrow sat in the chair opposite the editor-in-chief of the *Seattle Gazette*, Seattle's only newspaper, and smiled. "Of course, that's why I'm here. That's why I wrote that horrible review of Felicity's restaurant." That's why she'd turned her back on her onetime friend. Success came with a price, and for Destiny that price was friendship. "What do you want me to do now?"

Reid sat back in his chair, contemplating her. The man was different than she'd expected. He looked older than the pictures she'd seen online while researching him. His short, kinky dark hair was threaded with gray. His tall, deep-chested frame carried a few more pounds, but the slightly cynical expression in his eyes was exactly the same as every picture she'd ever seen. He was a hard man, and most likely a cruel man, but she needed what he offered her—the job she'd been coveting for the last three years on the news desk. With his help, she could finally make the transition from food writer to reporter, first on a local level, then national. It was her dream, and nothing, not even friendship, would stand in her way to achieve that goal.

"All right, let's get to new business. The Bancrofts are our target now."

"Why? What do you want me to do?"

"I want to ruin what's left of them."

Destiny frowned. "I thought Felicity was the target."

He smiled. "She's the distraction. She was to the old man, and she will be for me. It took me a while to find the old man, hiding away here in Seattle under a false name, but I eventually did."

"Why do you want to ruin them?"

Reid's smile became set in place. "Vernon Bancroft's father and my grandfather were business partners. That's how Vernon got the money he needed to open those hotels." Reid's eyes became glazed as though remembering a time long ago. "My grandfather was the CFO of the company at the time Vernon took his father's place. My grandfather made the mistake once of borrowing money from the accounts he oversaw, and Vernon removed him from the board, dissolved their partnership, and tossed him out of the company."

"Sounds like embezzling," Destiny said with the hint of a laugh.

Reid glared at her. "He borrowed the money. He would have paid it back, but Vernon never gave him the opportunity."

"That was a long time ago."

Reid shook his head slowly. "Vernon's actions have affected my family for years. My grandfather drank himself to death. My father followed the same path after years of trying to sue Bancroft Industries into giving him a piece of what should have been his legacy."

Destiny curled her fingers in her lap, fighting the urge to grab a notepad and a pencil and start scribbling down notes. The angry look in Reid's eyes told her that wouldn't be wise. She'd simply have to remember and research after she was done here. "So what does any of this have to do with Blake Bancroft?"

"Blake's the only remaining Bancroft. Since part of Bancroft Industries should belong to me, and he's the CEO, he's the target," Reid said.

"You want some sort of financial compensation for something that happened years ago?" Destiny asked, suddenly uncomfortable with the role she'd accepted. She had no wish to end her career before it even began. Blake Bancroft had power and influence that Reid Fairfax did not.

"I want to tarnish the Bancroft name the way Vernon tarnished the Fairfax name. You know the saying 'Never argue with someone who buys ink by the barrel.'" Reid's gaze suddenly became clear, and he focused in on her.

"Blake Bancroft is no fool. How do you expect me to take him down?"

"We can't strip him of his power or his money, but we can humiliate him. Bancroft needs investors just as much as anyone. And no one wants to back a loser. Do that, and I'll promote you to the news desk of the *Seattle Gazette*."

Destiny studied his eyes a moment, searching for sincerity in what he'd offered. It was all she wanted—a job as a reporter. Seeing nothing but the truth, she nodded. "All right. I'll approach Blake. I'll let him think I'm trying to do an exposé on Felicity instead. Then, I'll start digging into his past. Everyone has secrets. I'll use his to our advantage."

Determined to do anything she had to in order to get that job, Destiny said goodbye to Reid, then headed for the door. She'd already turned her back on friendship. What more would it take?

◆ ◆ ◆

While her crew finished closing down the kitchen, Felicity headed out to check on things in the bar. After eleven, only Michael and Casper would remain on duty to serve a limited menu to the late-night patrons of the bar. However, she always liked to see how busy they were before heading home. The thought brought a smile. Tonight, her journey home would only involve a trip to the second floor. Living in the hotel had its perks.

The cozy leather wingback chairs were filled with Seattleites and visitors just as in days past. She'd learned today that this very room once hosted the Vanderbilts and the Guggenheims upon opening over 105 years ago. The lounge's signature drinks still welcomed authors, musicians, and artists. At the highly polished mahogany bar, Ryan, her bartender, garnished a Haute Toddy with a cinnamon stick and a lemon twist before setting it on Valerie's tray to be delivered to one of their guests.

At her approach, Ryan smiled. "Sit yourself down for a minute."

Felicity slipped into one of the tall wooden chairs at the busy bar and took off her chef's cap. She smoothed her fingers over her hair, tidying any loose strands back toward her usual ponytail. "Things are hopping tonight."

He reached behind him for a tall flute and a bottle of champagne. "Nothing we can't handle." He filled the flute with bubbly liquid and set it before her.

"What's this?"

"A small celebration of your exciting news," Ryan said with a wide smile. "Not every day a girl inherits a fortune."

Felicity contemplated the bubbles erupting inside her glass. She ached to talk to someone who would understand the fear and the joy that whispered through her since the reading of Vern's will. She was tempted to pour out her troubles to the man who had proven more than once what a good listener he was. Instead, she only allowed her fear to take form as a thought: *It's not mine yet.* She lifted her glass in a salute. "Cheers." She took a sip.

"Enjoy, and let me know if I can do anything to help," he said before moving away to serve another customer.

At this point, she wasn't sure she could do anything other than trust that she could make Blake see why she so desperately wanted to keep what Vern had given her. She continued to stare down into her glass as the sound of soft, soulful rhythm of Brazilian jazz tried to soothe her.

"Is this seat taken?"

At the sound of Blake's voice, her heart gave a wild leap. She twisted around to see him.

He stood a few feet behind her, tall and straight. He'd changed out of his suit and into faded blue Levi's and an expensive-looking gray sweater. If it were possible, he looked even more handsome than he had this morning, despite the loss of his three-thousand-dollar suit.

Great. She'd hoped to look her best the next time they met, not garbed in the most unattractive uniform possible. Her chef's coat and black pants had always been comforting to her before this moment. "It's a public place. I can't stop you from sitting wherever you choose," she said, trying to recover her balance and ignore the tug of his eyes and voice.

Taking her discouraging words as an invitation, he slid into the seat beside her. "Celebrating?" he asked with a nod at her glass.

She shrugged. "A gift from Ryan," she said a little breathlessly as she raised her champagne flute and took a sip.

Blake signaled for Ryan. The bartender answered Blake's summons instantly. "What'll it be?"

"The same," he said, motioning to Felicity's glass.

Ryan turned and filled another flute with champagne. When he returned, he set Blake's glass before him, then set the bottle between them. "Let me know if you need anything else," he said before moving away.

She was uncertain why the interaction upset her, but it did. Blake expected service, and people jumped to do his bidding. Well, she wouldn't be one of those people no matter what his warm, intimate look did to her insides. He could have cocktails all by himself, or with whomever would have him. She had things to do before their day tomorrow.

Felicity moved to stand, but Blake tipped his glass to hers. His eyes glinted with humor and, instead of standing, she found herself settling back into her chair.

"To the next two days together," he toasted as he leaned forward.

Their gazes held. The moment spilled out, lengthened in an odd way that made her heartbeat speed up. "Yes, and may the best *person* win." She'd almost said "man," before she'd caught herself. She didn't need to give him any more of an edge, even verbally, than he already had.

Felicity brought her glass up to his with a clink of sound and took a long sip of her champagne as Blake continued to study her. "The first time Dom Pérignon tasted champagne, he said, 'Come quickly, I am tasting stars.' It aptly describes champagne, don't you think?"

He took a sip from his own glass, then set it down. His lips turned up in a lazy, devastating smile. "You have very delicate fingers."

With slightly shaking fingers, Felicity set down her glass and folded her hands together on the top of the bar. She had delicate fingers? Was he flirting with her? Unsettled by the words, and slightly suspicious of his motives, Felicity stood as the hammering of her heart began again.

"Since you're down here, want a tour of the kitchen? We'll be spending lots of time there tomorrow."

"With pleasure."

The husky sincerity of his deep voice snatched her breath away.

He drained his glass, set it on the bar, then reached for his wallet.

Felicity stalled his hand before he could remove a bill. "This one's on me." Her fingers grazed his skin. At the whisper of a touch, she could feel the tension thrumming through him, felt an answering response within herself.

He smiled, his gaze warm and sensual, as he moved toward her. "Lead the way."

A quiet moment ticked past as her heartbeat returned to normal. What was it about him that always made her feel a little off-kilter? They walked side by side down the hallway and through the swinging door separating the dining area from the kitchen. "The kitchen was moved to its current location in 1966. The equipment has been modernized, of course. It's competitive now."

Pride swelled as she looked over the spotless workspace. Shiny stainless steel prep stations lined the white tiled walls of the kitchen. The back wall was lined with a row of convection ovens. And in the center of the spotless kitchen was an island outfitted with several cooking stations.

At their entrance, her employees stopped working and turned in their direction. Suspicion darkened their faces. Felicity pasted on a cheerful smile, trying to dispel the sudden tension. Along with her news of inheriting the hotel and restaurant, she was certain they'd also shared who Blake Bancroft was. "Let me introduce you to some of my staff." She motioned to her right. "This is Michael," she said, nodding to the older of the two men who wiped down the prep stations. "He has four kids all under the age of six. And this is Casper. He supports his mother and his two sisters."

She turned toward the back wall and motioned toward Mary Beth. She stacked long baking sheets on a rack beside the huge ovens. "This is Mary Beth. She supports a six-month-old daughter and a brother who lost both his legs fighting in Afghanistan." Felicity turned back to Blake. "There are ten others who work in this kitchen and in the restaurant—people with hopes and dreams and dependents." She left the last word hanging.

To his credit, Blake left her side and went to greet each of them with a handshake and one of his devastating smiles. "Sounds like you have a very dedicated team working for you. It doesn't matter who the boss is. Good people will always be able to find good jobs."

"They're dedicated to the Bancroft Hotel and to each other. They love what they do and, because of it, they go that extra mile," Felicity replied.

Across the room, Mary Beth yawned. "Sorry," she apologized. "I feel like I've gone several extra miles today. My late night is catching up with me."

"Go home. I can finish up here."

A hopeful looked settled over Mary Beth's face. "I could really use some sleep."

"Go. All of you," Felicity said, looking at her two other remaining employees. "I've got this."

Casper and Michael took her up on her offer immediately. They both had responsibilities to return to, she understood that. After a hug from Mary Beth and a goodnight from the men, Felicity realized she and Blake were now very much alone.

"How can I help," Blake asked, his tone low, almost a caress, stroking not her skin but her very nerves.

"I can finish—"

"I used to be pretty decent at mopping the floors," he interrupted as he pushed up his sleeves.

The words surprised her. She didn't figure him for the mopping type.

Her expression must have given her thoughts away, because with a chuckle he said, "I wasn't born the CEO of Bancroft Industries." He shrugged. "I had a summer job once at one of our smaller properties near Lake Crescent on the Olympic Peninsula."

"It's kind of hard to be fired from a job where your family owns the place. I hardly see that as a reference."

His smile broadened. "Afraid to test my skills?" His voice lowered, his tone provocative, challenging.

He was displaying an easy charm that made it hard to say no, and Felicity relented. She moved to where they kept the ever-ready mop and bucket and rolled it over to him. "Okay, this I have to see."

With a practiced motion, he lifted the mop, wrung it out, then got to work. "You won't be sorry."

While he worked, she focused on wiping down the counters. She had to direct her energies elsewhere or else she'd be captured by the movement of the corded muscles in his arms and his chest as he pushed the mop from side to side across the tile floor. "Did you grow up around here?" she asked, breaking the silence that had fallen over the kitchen. Or had his family flown him in to work at the popular summer vacation spot in the Olympic National Park?

"I was born in Seattle. I lived here with my parents until they died in a boating accident. Uncle Vernon took me in after that."

At the strained tone of his voice, a shiver worked its way down her spine. They shared a common background. They'd both been orphaned, or as good as in her case. Their eyes met. In his eyes she saw not only a bold and incisive man, but a kind and gentle one as well. She was quite certain in that moment that this was the real Blake Bancroft, not the callous billionaire who was determined to take the Bancroft Hotel away from her.

But did it matter who he truly was? Warm and friendly or cold and calculating, he wanted what she had and would most likely do anything in his power to get it. "Vern raised you?"

He moved to the corner of the room, then dipped the mop in the bucket again and squeezed it out before moving it across the tiled floor in a methodical, steady pattern. "I was eighteen when they died, so I only lived with Uncle Vernon for two weeks until he sent me off to boarding school for my senior year and then to college."

She gazed at him thoughtfully. Again, she didn't miss the similarity. They'd each been abandoned by the adults in their lives and forced to be on their own early in life. Even so, they'd come from entirely different backgrounds. He grew up in a mansion, most likely attended the finest schools and socialized with the best of society, and, even after his parents' deaths, he'd been educated at Harvard, then Stanford, she'd learned from her Google search earlier in the day.

She, on the other hand, had lived in a run-down trailer park on the wrong side of the tracks. Her education had been in cooking schools through scholarship programs. Felicity stiffened. Was she trying to justify why she deserved what Vern had left her more than Blake did? The thought made her feel a little sick. She wasn't usually a selfish person, and she didn't like the thought that she was becoming just that now. With a silent groan, Felicity turned away and busied herself checking to make sure everything was stored in its proper place in the kitchen and all the appliances were turned off for the night.

Her mind drifted back to the handwritten note Vern had left her with his will. "Take care of the Bancroft, Felicity. You'll know what to do."

She shook her head dazedly. Vern couldn't have been more wrong, because she had absolutely no idea what to do about the hotel, about Blake, about her crazy mixed-up feelings for him. One minute she was suspicious of him, the next she was intrigued.

Felicity wished desperately in that moment that she weren't so exhausted. She had to think calmly and clearly about all of this. She wasn't willing to just give over her interest in the hotel and restaurant just because Blake's past wasn't as perfect as she'd imagined it to be. Blake was still a stranger; his motives were obscure, and her own future was important.

She shifted her gaze to where Blake mopped on the opposite side of the kitchen. Watching him work, she wondered about the man who had suddenly entered her life and made her question things about herself she hadn't had the time to think about in years.

Perhaps Blake's idea to spend a day in each other's worlds was exactly how they needed to solve the situation Vern had left them in. A whole day together could reveal a lot about each of them to the other. It was time to peel back the exterior and get a glimpse at his true depths.

CHAPTER FOUR

Felicity waited in the courtyard the following morning surrounded by darkness. The lighted portico allowed her to see through the glass doors into the lobby, so she'd know when Blake arrived. Until then, to calm her nerves she needed the gust of cool wind that touched her cheeks.

Her gaze lifted to the front of the hotel, to the patterned brick-work and rich, detailed facades of terra-cotta. Despite the beauty of the hotel's Italianate style, a sense of loss moved through her. She missed Vern. She wished she'd known who he was before he died. The world had lost more than just an old man. It had lost a legend in the hotel industry. Blake was the continuation of that legacy. Not for the first time did she wonder if she was fighting a battle she ought not win.

"Morning." A voice came from the doorway.

She turned to see Blake dressed in jeans and a t-shirt, with a leather coat folded over his arm. As he moved toward her, he put the coat on. Felicity couldn't tear her gaze away. He looked just as at ease in a t-shirt as he did in a dress shirt. She swallowed against the sudden tightness in her throat.

"I suppose I should apologize for being late," he said, taking her silence for displeasure.

She almost smiled at this new, more human, side of her nemesis. "I suppose you should."

"I'm sorry for keeping you waiting," he said, his tone sincere. "Shall we go?"

She could tell he was restless. Was he the typical Type-A CEO, or had he had a similar revelation to the one she'd had last night—that they shared a lot of the same pain and success? "Then let's get started." She turned to walk up the four stairs leading to the street.

He joined her but stopped at the street. "Where's the car?"

"We're walking." She kept moving along Terry Avenue.

"Ten blocks?" He hurried to catch up with her.

She shrugged. "It's all downhill."

"Until we make our way back."

Felicity tossed him an innocent smile as she kept her brisk pace. She needed the physical exertion to keep her mind on the goal of the day ahead and off of the man who was far too intriguing for her sanity. "If you'd rather stay at the hotel . . ."

"Lead on." He matched his stride to hers. "Anything you can do, I can do, too." At the crosswalk, he placed a hand on the small of her back, as though escorting her across the street. His touch was warm and inappropriately familiar.

She thought she saw the faintest glimmer of humor appear in his expression as they reached the other side of the street, and she wished she'd outpaced his touch—even though part of her responded to the idea that there was a measure of protection in the gesture.

Felicity could feel a flush come to her cheeks. At least she could blame her coloring on the coolness of the morning air and the briskness of their walking.

"This is nice," he said, breaking the silence that had fallen between them. "I usually spend my days going from the car to one meeting after another. It's rare that I get to enjoy the outdoors."

The city was just starting to wake. The streets were largely clear of traffic, and the sound of gulls searching for their morning meal among the fishermen could be heard over their footfalls on the concrete sidewalks. Still, the city wasn't really the outdoors, at least not to most Seattleites. "Why did you move from Seattle to San Francisco?"

"I did my graduate studies at Stanford. And when I took over the company from Uncle Vernon, I decided to move the company head-quarters there. What better state than California, with the strictest environmental regulations in the country, to establish a socially respon-sible green company. At least I'm used to the hills," he said with a smile.

"In your car," she replied, unable to keep the judgment from her voice. "I thought you said you were some kind of expert in living green?"

"Building green. And if you're worried about me keeping up with you, don't be. I'm in pretty good shape."

She could see that. His arms, before he'd pulled on his coat, had been strong and muscular. But it was more than his physical looks that had her on edge. It was Blake's energy. Vitality simmered within him. He'd challenged her from the moment they'd met—physically and mentally. She was certain he'd continue to do so until they parted ways.

Felicity turned her attention to the lavender and pink and scarlet sky. The clouds were thin in the early morning light. They would burn off soon, leaving a backdrop of jagged mountains and dazzling blue wrapped around the city skyline. The smell of salt water grew stronger with every step downhill. It had been a long time since she had walked with anyone down to the waterfront. Felicity had to admit Blake's pres-ence at her side was oddly companionable, despite her wish that it wasn't.

"You don't talk much," Blake observed after ten minutes of silence.

"I didn't know sparkling conversation was a part of our sharing the day together." She closed her eyes briefly, trying to stop the pull she felt toward him. She couldn't allow herself to have any feelings about a man who should be her enemy, even if he was the handsomest man who'd ever mopped her kitchen floor. She opened her eyes, and, despite her intentions not to, she looked at him.

He made a face. "Am I that hard to converse with?"

"Okay," she relented. Giving in to her need to hear his rich, compelling voice, she searched for something safe to talk about. "How did you sleep last night?" Oh heavens, she sounded like his mother. "I'm sure it's difficult sleeping in a strange bed." That was better. At least now she sounded like a concerned hotel owner.

"The bed was very comfortable. I sleep in strange beds all the time." Felicity looked at him quizzically.

"It's not what you're thinking. I travel a lot."

If she was thinking anything, it was that it must be sad not to have a place to call his own. She didn't have much in the way of personal property or possessions, but she had people in her life who loved her. When she was with them, she knew she had everything she needed. Did anyone love Blake? Or was his relationship, or lack thereof, with Vern, an indication of how he managed his life? "That must make you miss your home," she said, looking off into the distance.

"I live in San Francisco most of the year, but in and out of hotel rooms." He shrugged. "It's one of the prices I pay for being in the hotel industry."

Felicity frowned. "I wouldn't like that. I enjoy coming home to my own space."

"How long have you lived in Seattle?" he asked.

"My whole life."

"Have you ever wanted to travel and experience other things?" The animation had returned to his face.

She gazed into his mesmerizing blue eyes. "Right now that's just not possible. My work is here. Everything I know and love is here." Before he could ask her to expand on why it would be impossible to travel, she looked away and quickened her pace. She could feel Blake's gaze on her still, but he didn't pursue the subject. They both fell silent once more.

Felicity didn't speak again until they reached the waterfront and a breathtaking view of water, sky, and mountains lay before them. "This way." She pointed to the pier in front of them with several small fishing boats tied up nearby. The smell of the creosote-treated wooden pier mixed with the salty tang of the water to create a scent that was manifest in Seattle. She headed toward the edge of the pier where a group of men had their morning catch displayed on beds of ice.

"You buy your fish directly from the fishermen?" Blake asked, keeping pace with her as she weaved in and out of the crowd of fishermen and other chefs all hovering around the makeshift fish market. "I'm impressed."

"It's important to me to support the local economy." She strode over to Jimmy Coon's display. "Morning, Jimmy. What've you got for me today?"

"Only the best for you." He gave her a toothy grin. He'd caught king salmon and true cod. "Want your usual order?"

Felicity picked up one of the salmon, checked the eyes, and gently squeezed the firm flesh before she brought the fish to her nose. "Perfect as always." She nodded.

"I'll have it delivered," he said, and she moved past his display and farther down the line to Cal Jeffries, one of the younger fishermen on the docks.

"You don't tote the seafood up the hills, back to the hotel?" Blake asked with a bemused grin.

"They deliver everything directly to my kitchen. No sense hauling around twenty pounds of fish with us, because after we are done here, we head to the market." Felicity glanced over Cal's bins of oysters, clams, and scallops as the shells glistened in the growing sunlight.

"Morning, Felicity," Cal said. "It was a good harvest today. Can I offer you a taste?" He held out an oyster on the half shell to her. "It's as fresh as they come."

Felicity turned to Blake who stood right beside her. "Want to be my taster?"

He hesitated a moment, before he reached for the shell, brought the small oyster to his lips, and let it slide into his mouth, his gaze never leaving hers.

Felicity's heart beat faster. She was unable to look away from his blue eyes. Her skin was warming as the blood ran faster in her veins.

She could smell a hint of wood and something deeper, muskier, in his cologne.

His pulse drummed in his temple as he slowly chewed, then swallowed. "I've never had oysters for breakfast, but this is perfect." His gaze remained steady, drawing her closer. There was something starkly primitive about the two of them standing there, saying nothing and everything all at once.

He inhaled deeply, and she felt the warmth of his breath on her throat as he exhaled. Felicity's heart raced, and she willed herself to look away.

Blake was her rival. She had to remember that. She took a step back, breaking the moment. "Give me five pounds of each, Cal."

"No problem, Felicity," Cal replied. "See you tomorrow."

Felicity nodded and turned away, grateful she could draw a steady breath once more. "Are you ready for Pike Place Market?"

"Lead the way," Blake replied.

Felicity headed along the waterfront. She loved walking along the pier, listening to the creak of the pilings as they shifted with each push of the tide. Salty air caressed her cheeks, tugged at her bangs and the short strands of her hair that framed her face. They walked in companionable silence until they reached Pike Street. For a moment she paused beside the bench she'd first come to as a young girl, sending her hopes and dreams out across the sparkling emerald water of the Puget Sound. She came to that bench often when she searched for answers about her life.

"Is anything wrong?" Blake asked at her side.

She shook her head, clearing the long-ago memories. "I like to come here to think."

"What are you thinking about now?" he asked with a touch of concern she hadn't expected.

She blew out a breath. "How is this going to work, Blake? How are we going to decide at the end of these two days who should get the hotel and restaurant? One of us has to be altruistic here. There are millions of dollars on the line. That kind of money might be easy for you to come by, but it's more than I could ever expect to earn in my lifetime."

"If it's only about the money, we can make that decision right now. I'll pay you one million dollars to release your claim on the Bancroft to me."

A hysterical giggle bubbled up in her throat. She could buy a new restaurant with that kind of money. But what about the rest of her family—her dedicated employees? "It's not just about the money. It's about people. Lots and lots of people. Everyone who works at the Bancroft and the Dolce Vita, everyone who uses the services provided by both, all the people we engage as vendors, even the fishermen we just met. All of them will be affected by the hotel being out of business while you renovate. My God, Blake, people like your uncle *live* in that hotel. Where will they go?"

"There are other hotels."

The sound of a gull squawking overhead seemed thunderous. "None of them is the Bancroft."

Blake's eyes narrowed. "You talk about the hotel like it's irreplaceable."

"It is to me and so many others," she said in a thick voice, her heart aching, because he refused to understand.

"So that's a no to my offer?"

She looked out at the water, searching desperately for some sort of easy answer, finding nothing, she returned her gaze to his. "I need some time to think about what's the right thing to do."

"Do you always do the right thing?"

She forced her chin up a notch and squared her shoulders. "I'll do whatever I have to in order to protect my workers. They are my family. Their lives matter to me as much as my own."

"Very well, then let's keep going. This is your day. Show me why you care so much about the people the hotel supports."

She nodded, grateful to have something else to think about besides the man at her side. "I can do that. Come with me." He followed her across the roadway to the sprawling hillside staircase. At the base, Felicity paused, preparing herself for the climb up the ten-story hill.

Blake stopped beside her, looking up. "Are you trying to intimidate me?"

"Is it working?" she asked.

"I'll tell you after we reach the top."

Side by side, they ascended the wide, concrete stairway already in use by early-rising visitors and locals. As they made their way to the market stalls above, Felicity took advantage of Blake's attention. "Pike Place Market has been open since 1907. That same year the Bancroft opened its doors. The market is recognized as a historic site. It would be wonderful if the Bancroft had the same protection."

Any humor in Blake's face vanished. "I'm not opposed to preserving history, Felicity."

She was about to say more when her cell phone chimed from where it was tucked into her coat pocket. "I have to take this," she said, after looking at the screen and recognizing her father's assisted living facility's number. "Hello," she greeted as they continued to climb.

"Felicity, this is Marguerite." It was the nurse who usually worked with her father, but her voice sounded odd.

"What is it? What's wrong?"

"Your father wouldn't eat his dinner last night, and he won't eat his breakfast this morning. You asked us to call you when he won't eat what the kitchen here serves. He's too thin, and it's a constant worry. We all know he'll eat anything you bring him."

Felicity stopped climbing. She looked at Blake, then silently sighed. Her father had to come first. "I'm on my way. I'll be there as soon as possible." Felicity hung up and turned to Blake. "I'm sorry. I have to go."

"One of your employees?" he asked with a frown.

She shook her head. "It's my father. He needs me."

"Anything I can do to help?"

"No." She ran her hand through her hair. Her father not eating two meals was no emergency, but it usually indicated something else was going on with him. "I don't know." Felicity looked up and down the stairway, trying to determine which direction would be faster to get to the street and a taxi. "It's not urgent, but the sooner I get there, the sooner we can get back to our day."

Strong fingers wrapped around hers as Blake pulled her forward, up the staircase. "This way will be faster." He said nothing more as he reached for his own cell phone. Felicity's heartbeat thudded in her ears. She heard only terse words from Blake's side of the conversation. He hung up quickly and gave her an encouraging look.

They reached the top of the stairway in no time, and Blake led her through the early-morning crowd with an expertise that told Felicity he'd been to the market before. They reached the front of the market near Rachel, the famous bronze pig, just as a large black car pulled up. "In here," Blake said, reaching for the car door and holding it open for Felicity to enter.

She climbed into the backseat. Blake slid in beside her. "Where to?"

As much as she wanted to get to her father right away, she was uncertain about revealing that part of her life to the man beside her. He was still an unknown. "Take me to the Bancroft Hotel," she said. "I can make my way to my father from there."

Blake informed his driver, then sat back.

"How did you do this?" Felicity asked when her breathing settled to a more normal rate.

"My driver is always on call."

"And he just happened to be in the area?"

Blake looked straight ahead, his expression serious. "Peter knows where I am at all times."

Felicity sank back against the plush leather interior, grateful for the transportation, but also a little unsettled by this obvious wealth. "I don't even own a car, and you have a driver," she breathed.

She sat stiffly in her seat as they quickly made their way up the hills, toward the hotel. She would gather something from the kitchen to tempt her dad with, then be on her way to Saint Francis House.

When the driver pulled up into the drive of the Bancroft Hotel, Felicity opened the door before the driver could assist her. "Thank you," she said to Peter. To Blake she said, "I appreciate your help."

"Would you like me to come with you?" he asked, his hand poised on the door handle, ready to follow her.

"I've got things covered from here. Perhaps I can call you when I'm done?" she asked.

Blake reached for his wallet then withdrew a business card. He held it out to her. "The bottom number is my cell, but if you call any of the numbers, someone will know how to get hold of me."

She accepted the card, then shut the door, and tucking the card into her pocket, she hurried inside. She knew exactly what to bring her father to get him to eat.

CHAPTER FIVE

Blake's gaze stayed on Felicity a moment before she stepped away from the car and turned to go in to the hotel's lobby. She looked so forlorn. His hand clenched on the leather seat beside him as he fought the urge to go after her. Her features had been heavy with worry as she stood there, her platinum blonde hair fluttering in the soft August breeze.

"You have to admire her resilience," Peter said from the front seat. "She's been through a lot in the last couple of days."

He had to agree, given the emotional highs and lows she must have experienced since his uncle had died. And still she'd displayed a determination that surprised even him. In spite of his offer to buy the hotel for more money than she would get if they went to court, she persevered. And in spite of his annoyance over that fact, he found himself reluctantly admiring her courage.

Good God, if he continued in this vein, in another minute he'd be feeling sorry for her having to deal with *him*.

"Peter, take me to Mount Pleasant Cemetery. I need to see my uncle's grave." It was one of the few places open at the early morning hour and somewhere he'd intended to go since he'd flown in yesterday.

"You think he left you any answers there?" Peter asked.

Blake leaned back against the seat as the car set in motion. "No. I'll probably never know why he did what he did."

Peter's eyes appeared in the rearview mirror. "Why he left the hotel to Felicity? Or why he sent you away all those years ago?"

"Either."

"Then let's hope for your peace of mind that you find those answers somewhere," Peter said as he headed toward the North Queen Anne area of town.

"I prepared myself for the worst years ago. The old man can't surprise me much anymore."

"He surprised you by leaving the hotel to Felicity."

Blake released a pent-up breath. "That he did."

"Would you like to go for a run around Greenlake after the cemetery? Your usual hour?" Peter asked.

"Sounds perfect," Blake agreed.

Peter knew his habits, knew him so well, having been his driver, butler, and confidant for the past ten years. It was rare for Blake to let someone past his guard, but then again Peter was more brother to him than employee. Blake started at the thought. Was that what Felicity felt toward her workers? His little chef had called them her family.

His little chef.

How easily possessiveness crept into his thoughts when they concerned Felicity. He'd been with her for barely an hour this morning and already she was winning him over to her side. "Christ," he muttered through clenched teeth. "Better make that run an hour and a half. I think I'll need more distance to put my mind at ease."

Peter's shrewd gaze fixed on Blake's face. "She's getting to you, is she?"

Blake expelled his breath in a long, irritated sigh. "In more ways than one."

◆ ◆ ◆

Felicity stepped off the elevator and made her way to her father's room. She looked down at the bundle in her hands. She'd brought a ramekin filled with still warm and gooey macaroni and cheese. It was her father's favorite meal, the one that brought a tiny shimmer of vitality into his eyes as he took a bite. Perhaps it would work its magic now. She pushed the door open.

Silence greeted her. Taking a deep breath, she closed the door and headed toward the silent man in the chair by the window. The room was lit by the sunlight coming through the window. It would be another warm August day, but inside her father's room it would remain the usual seventy degrees. At her father's side, she reached out and brushed an errant lock of gray hair away from his face. "Hi, Dad."

She sat down in the empty chair beside him and searched his features. There was nothing there. No response. No recognition. Nothing. So she did what she always did and launched into a one-sided conversation about her day so far. As she talked, she unwrapped the food she'd brought, and, using a fork from the undisturbed tray the kitchen had provided this morning, she offered it to him. He took the fork and ate.

She waited breathlessly for him to smile at her, though she knew the latter was wishful thinking. But he eagerly finished every bite of the macaroni and cheese. At the action, tears welled in her eyes and spilled onto her cheeks. If she'd ever needed an affirmation that the treatment she'd scheduled for tomorrow was the right thing to do, she had her answer now. "You're still in there, aren't you, Dad?"

When he'd finished his food, she slipped her arm gently around him, pressing her head against his. She had no idea how long she held him, breathing in the scent of his soap, until she was roused at last by a knock on the door. "Come in—"

The door opened and Marguerite entered the room. "Sorry to disturb you. I just wanted to check and see if you had any success."

Felicity pulled away from her father and stood. "Yes, just like always. He'll eat my macaroni and cheese."

"I'm so glad." The elderly nurse smiled. "Sometimes I think he just holds out, so you'll come down here and sit with him again."

That would mean he'd have to know she was with him in the first place. Holding on to the hope that he really did notice her presence, Felicity kissed her father goodbye, then left her father in Marguerite's care.

When she was back at the Bancroft, Felicity reached for the business card Blake had given her earlier today. She stared down at the bold letters and numbers printed on the stark-white card. She pulled her cell phone from her pocket and dialed.

A ring sounded three times on the other end before an unfamiliar voice picked up. "How may I help you, Miss Felicity?"

Felicity startled. "Who am I speaking with?"

"This is Peter, Mr. Bancroft's driver."

"Yes, of course. Hello, Peter," Felicity said. "Is Mr. Bancroft available?"

"He's detained at the moment."

A feeling of deflation settled in her stomach. "Oh. Well, just tell him I called."

"Is it urgent?" he asked.

"No. Just let him know I need to speak with him when he's available. I'll be in room six twenty-nine at the hotel."

"I'll let him know."

"Okay, Peter, thanks." She ended the call. She stood and slipped her phone back into the pocket of her chef's pants before leaving her room. A quick glance at her watch told her she had a couple of hours yet before she needed to get started prepping for lunch at the restaurant. In the meanwhile, it was time to do the one thing she'd been putting off for a week. It was time to box up Vern's things and hand them over to Blake.

◆ ◆ ◆

Felicity stood outside of Vern's room, the electronic key in one hand, a big, empty box in the other. Four other big boxes waited by the door for her to fill. The hotel room's door looked like any other, but behind it there would be memories of Vern, things about his life she didn't know, and perhaps didn't want to know. As owner of the hotel, it was her responsibility to see that his things were returned to his family.

Grief rippled through her as she stared at the plain white door. She couldn't make herself move. She just stood there, seeing Vern as he'd been just last week, sitting in the dining room chatting with her over end-of-the-meal decaffeinated coffee with two Splendas, one cream. She knew he liked sweets even though he was diabetic, hated mushrooms, and begrudgingly added powdered fiber to his morning coffee. She knew a lot about his dietary habits and needs, but almost nothing about the man himself.

Behind the door were possible answers about why he kept his true identity a secret or why he hadn't shared the fact that his heart was growing weaker. If she'd been able to get him the medical help he'd needed, perhaps . . .

She took a deep breath and blew it out. She'd been killing herself with what-ifs for the past week. It was time to move past that pain. She tilted her chin up, knowing there was no further point in putting this off, in pretending she didn't need to do this, and opened the door. A swath of sunlight from the window filtered out into the hallway, and she followed the light inside.

Housekeeping had taken care of cleaning the room, but it was up to her to see to Vern's personal possessions. She moved about the living room, collecting stacks of paper here and there, placing them gently in the box. Inside one of the drawers in the living room, she found three pictures of a man, a woman, and a child who looked remarkably like Blake. Were these pictures of his childhood? Carefully, she added them to the box of things to be sorted through later and continued gathering Vern's belongings.

At the desk, she stopped when she saw a framed picture of herself and Vern that had been taken a month ago when she'd thrown him a party to celebrate his eighty-third birthday after hours in the Dolce Vita. At Felicity's request, all the restaurant and hotel staff had come.

The cardboard box slid from her fingers and hit the floor with a thud. Tears came to her eyes as she picked up the frame and traced the cool surface of the glass. Both of them were smiling, and there was no worry in their eyes in that moment. "Oh, Vern . . ."

"You really did care about him, didn't you?" Blake's voice sounded behind her.

She turned to face him, the picture still in her hands, and nodded. "I'm sorry. I was going to wait for you to do this . . . but I've put it off too long already. Do you want to help me now?"

"What do we need to do?" he asked, a look of understanding in his eyes. "Maybe we'll both find some answers about my uncle . . . and your friend."

◆　◆　◆

Despite the fact he felt weighed down and heavy, the words slipped out easily and without blame. That was new for him when it came to his uncle and Felicity. Maybe his run this morning had calmed him more than usual, or maybe he was starting to accept she'd had a place in his uncle's life more so than he ever had. The picture Felicity clutched to her chest was proof of that. His uncle didn't look manipulative or angry in the moment with her. The thought both cheered and depressed him as he looked about the room.

Felicity moved toward him, stopping by his side. "Do you want to work on the bedroom together, or would you prefer to do it yourself?" she asked, gently touching his arm.

He looked down at her delicate fingers on his arm and the cold inside him dissipated. "I'd welcome your help."

They worked silently, side by side, going through Vern's clothing and boxing it up. Most everything his uncle had left behind would go to charity, only a few personal items, such as the papers she'd gathered, his watch, and the picture of him and Felicity had been put aside.

"There isn't much here to indicate Vern had a family," Felicity commented.

Disappointment shot through Blake, not at her comment but at the fact they hadn't found anything to indicate why his uncle had regarded him with such disdain Blake's whole life.

"There was nothing to indicate his wealth either, except for a few financial statements near the bedside," Blake added as he removed the last of the sweaters from the chest of drawers. He moved them to the box nearby when a small, leather-bound book fell to the floor.

Blake's fingers were steady but not his heartbeat as he picked up the book. He flipped the book open to find a black and white picture of two young men.

"Do you recognize the photograph?" Felicity asked.

"I don't know who the man on the right is, but the one on the left is most likely my grandfather."

He set the picture aside and looked at the pages of the book. The first page was blank. He flipped to the second and frowned.

"What does it say?" Felicity asked.

"It's an unfinished note of some kind addressed to me. It reads *Blake, I*—then stops." He couldn't keep the pain inside him as he spoke. "Why was everything between my uncle and me unfinished? Was he leaving me an explanation? A warning?" He slipped the picture back inside the book and snapped it closed.

Blake rammed his fingers through his hair. For years, he'd wondered what was so horrible about himself that made people push him away. His teachers had. His parents had. His uncle had.

"Maybe Vern was starting to rethink some of the things he'd done over the years. At dinner each night, he was starting to talk about some of his regrets in life."

"Did he ever mention me?"

She hesitated, then finally said, "No."

Blake clenched the book in his hands. "I don't know why I expected anything more."

"I'm sorry."

He frowned at the sympathy in her eyes. A lump of constricting sorrow tightened his chest. He shrugged the sensation away and set the book alongside the watch and the picture. "I stopped needing my uncle's approval a long time ago."

Blake went back to emptying the dresser. He closed up the last box and set it outside the door. He looked over the few possessions his uncle had left behind, feeling suddenly that his own life had very little worth as well. He might be obscenely wealthy, but what did he have to show for anything? He had no family left, and no one special in his life. He had plenty of employees, but none who would particularly miss him when he was gone. His only legacy, much like his uncle's, would be in the hotels he left behind.

Not liking where his thoughts had led him, Blake stiffened. "Since we are done here, I've got something I must do."

Felicity picked up the watch. "Do you want to take this with you, or should I send it somewhere?"

"Donate all of it," he said, keeping his tone bland.

She frowned down at the watch. "I don't know much about antiques, but I'm certain this is valuable."

He turned and headed toward the door. "As a matter of fact, it's completely worthless. Do whatever you want with all of it."

Without looking back, Blake headed for the elevator, ready to leave all remnants of his uncle's life and advice behind him.

◆ ◆ ◆

On his way back to his own room, Blake grabbed his cell phone and placed a call to Marcus, in an effort to fight the ache inside him that made him long for things he knew he could never have. Things that could only hurt him more. And he'd been hurt enough for one lifetime—by both his uncle and his parents.

He opened the door to his room and stepped inside, waiting for Marcus to pick up. Work was what he needed to focus on to get his equilibrium back.

"Blake," Marcus greeted him, obviously recognizing the number. "Can't you ever go on vacation and just relax?"

"This isn't a vacation, and you know it," Blake replied. "You promised me an update on the Heritage Hotel." He'd been in negotiations with a small hotel property in the Bay area that was built in the 1900s. The location was ideal. The hotel itself would be almost as expensive to repair and bring up to the standards set by Bancroft Industries as it would be to tear it down and build something new.

"Jamison wants you to agree to restoration, not a teardown," Marcus said.

"I'll agree to nothing except the purchase price."

Blake could hear Marcus's frown, even though he couldn't see it on the other end of the call. "Can't you bend just a little this time?"

"For seventy million dollars, I should be able to do whatever I want with the place."

"He's seeking historical protection."

Blake groaned. Why did the owners of the older buildings always grasp at that straw? Felicity was no exception. Historical protection could not protect a building from destruction if the owner wanted it torn down. "All right. Raise the offer to seventy-two million. I want that building, Marcus."

"Done. I'll let you know what he says."

Blake hung up feeling even more unsettled than when he'd left his uncle's room. He clenched his jaw, wanting desperately to control this one area of his life. He might not be able to force others to abide by his wishes, but he could make it pretty damn hard for them to say no.

◆ ◆ ◆

Later that evening, Felicity told herself she still wasn't waiting for Blake to come find her. It was only because she couldn't sleep that she returned to the kitchen long after everyone else had gone home. When she couldn't sleep, she did what she always did; she made her way back to the Dolce Vita to cook.

With a rolling pin, Felicity pressed the *sfogliatelle* dough into a thin layer on her marble cutting board. The dough would be gathered like a jelly roll, cut into chunks, then formed into a flaky, layered pouch. She would eventually stuff each pouch with creamy ricotta filling.

Setting down the rolling pin, she started to gather the dough when a sound came from the corridor outside the kitchen. She froze, and held her breath as the footsteps came closer and the kitchen door swung open. A thrill moved through her when Blake appeared, dressed in the same jeans and t-shirt from earlier today.

"Hey," he greeted. He stood there, neither coming forward nor retreating, but she could feel a tension in him that echoed in her.

"Can't sleep?"

"Too wound up from the day." He leaned against the doorjamb. His t-shirt molded to his chest, and the material of his jeans clung to his muscular thighs and hips with blatant delineation.

A tingle of appreciation moved through Felicity, and she hurriedly lifted her gaze back to his face. "Are you hungry?"

He watched her from the doorway. "I'm sorry I disappeared on you earlier."

She dropped her gaze to the dough in her hands, pressing the delicate pastry with more force than was necessary. "You don't owe me any explanation." Felicity swallowed to ease the tightness in her throat. "Want some *sfogliatelle*?"

At her invitation, he came forward, stopping inches from her. Her nerves flicked as his woodsy scent teased her. Despite his claim to sleeplessness, he seemed more at ease than he had earlier today. "What is it?" he asked.

She moistened her lips. "It's an Italian pastry—flaky with a hint of sweet." She reached past him to select one of the pastries she'd finished that were cooling on a rack. She brought the treat to his lips and offered him a bite, and then fully realized what she was doing. Blake wasn't one of her kitchen staff who would think nothing of the gesture.

His lips parted. Her chest constricted. She pulled in a deep breath and slid the tip of the pastry into his mouth.

Blake took a bite. He closed his eyes, chewed, and let out a soft moan. "It's amazing. It might be the best pastry I've ever had." She'd had plenty of time to perfect her cooking techniques over the years, working at any number of restaurants late into the evening while she attended classes during the day.

He opened his eyes and took the *sfogliatelle* from her fingers. Instead of offering her a bite, he scooped up a dollop of the still warm orange-flavored ricotta filing. He held his finger out to her. "Your turn. Enjoy some of your own cooking."

Felicity hesitated for a moment before she parted her lips and closed them around his finger. The scent of him and the taste of sweet cream overwhelmed her senses. She found herself staring, unable to look away from those deep blue eyes. She could feel her heart beating harder, her skin warming as the blood ran faster in her veins.

He popped the remainder of the pastry into his mouth and chewed, perhaps not knowing he gave her time to get her wildly vacillating emotions under control.

"Where did you learn to cook like that?" he asked.

"I spent six years in cooking schools locally and in California. It was from the Culinary Institute of America at Greystone that I received my degree. After that, I received a national scholarship that allowed me to spend a year in Italy working and studying. I worked for a variety of restaurants, but found my true calling in Naples. The food, the people, the countryside—they all spoke to me."

"Why did you return home, if you were so happy there?" he asked, his tone sincere.

She shrugged. "I had obligations." She looked away, not wanting to elaborate and uncertain if she would see compassion or suspicion in his eyes. "I brought the best recipes home with me. I've tried to re-create much of what I learned in Italy here at the Dolce Vita."

"No wonder Uncle Vernon ate here every night."

Felicity tensed, preparing for a round of insults about her relationship with his uncle.

Instead, Blake hooked his finger underneath her chin and lifted her head until her eyes met his. "That was a compliment." Something slid sideways, and suddenly his smile was charming, and his touch sizzled.

Felicity drew a ragged breath. "What are we doing, Blake? I have no idea what to expect from you. One moment we're getting along, the next we're adversaries."

A bemused look crept over his features as his thumb moved down to her throat. "You are such a surprise. This would be so much easier, if you were like all my other competitors."

"I'm not like your other rivals?"

His gaze locked with hers. "No, you're not."

Her knees went weak, and she could feel heat rise to her cheeks. She should step back, away from his touch, but she couldn't.

He cradled her head, leaned in, and met her lips in a slow, gentle kiss that was nothing like Felicity expected. She'd braced herself for an assault, something more in line with Blake's business practices. But his tenderness surprised her; it was a tenderness that melted her reservations. He might be her enemy, but she wanted this, she deserved this: a stolen moment in his arms.

Felicity leaned into the kiss, demanding more.

And he gave her exactly what she wanted. His hand traveled down her spine, stopping at the small of her back. He cradled her waist, and pulled her even tighter against him. His tongue traced along the seam of her lips, urging them to part, but when they did he didn't plunge inside. Instead, his assault was just as devastatingly tender, which did more to fire her own desire than a steamy kiss might have.

Time suspended until, with a groan, he pulled back. But he didn't release her. He continued to cradle her in his arms as though he liked the feel of her against him.

This was pure insanity. And yet Felicity couldn't step out of his arms. Some strange force kept her there. "That wasn't supposed to happen."

"Wasn't supposed to, but it did." His voice was raw, another surprise.

She gazed up at him. "What do you want with me, Blake? I'm confused. Do you want the hotel or something else?" She couldn't say the words . . . couldn't ask him if he wanted her. His kiss said he did. But why?

"I want the hotel. Make no mistake about that." He kissed the top of her head, the gesture both charming and sweet despite his words. "But, if we are honest with each other, we both want so much more."

She went still. "What?"

"We might battle over the hotel, but clearly we are compatible in other areas."

She frowned. "What are you saying?"

"That we could be very good together."

A treacherous warmth slowly crept across her skin. She fought the weakness with all her might. She'd been down this road once before with James. She wouldn't allow herself that kind of weakness again. "You want a physical relationship with me?"

"Yes, Felicity. Sex."

A part of her urged a "yes" in return, but another part spoke. "That would be dangerous and foolish."

"Dangerous or not, I want you. We're both adults. We can separate business from pleasure."

Maybe he could. Felicity forced herself to step back, out of his embrace. "Not until the Bancroft is settled between us."

He reached for her, but she took another step back.

"It could be settled now, if you'd only accept my offer."

She shook her head, partially to clear the leaden effect of his words and partly because of her own foolishness. "Are you trying to seduce the hotel out from under me? Is that what this is?"

"No." He met her gaze. Something reflected in his eyes for a heartbeat, before it was replaced with desire. "For some reason, I can't get you out of my mind. I think you feel the same way."

Felicity shook her head, trying to be convincing. She had experience in the realm of relationships, but she was certain even that experience had not prepared her for what Blake would demand of her.

"Come here, Felicity. Why can't we indulge in what we both want?"

Despite doubts and more rational thoughts, an electrical shock went through her at the raw possibility. She found herself taking an involuntary step toward him, before she stopped herself. No, she couldn't give in.

"Think about it. No ties. No promises. Just passion."

She drew a deep breath and exhaled slowly. "My first impression was right."

A frown furrowed his brow. "About what?"

"You're dangerous."

"That can be a good thing," he told her with a twinkle in his eyes.

He seemed certain he could separate their business from the pleasure. She wasn't sure about her ability to do the same. When she committed to something, it was with her whole heart and soul. "No." She moved farther away, hoping the distance would help her think more clearly. "We need to go back to our original agreement."

His brow rose fractionally. "Which was?"

"You spend the day with me in my world, then I spend the day with you in yours. The only thing that happens between us is the hotel."

He returned her steady regard. "Are you asking for another day with me, because of the day's interruptions?"

"It seems only fair."

He hesitated, staring at her as though committing her features to memory. "I say we need to amend our original agreement."

"How?"

A half smile hovered on the edges of his lips. "If we spend the day together again tomorrow, you'll have had two days to convince me that the hotel belongs to you. I want equal time."

"A day and a half," Felicity countered.

He leaned forward, his face just to the side of hers. His nearness making her heart beat all the faster. "I want two full days, and that doesn't include travel time," he whispered in her ear.

Her breasts tightened. Flight time to San Francisco could be easily accomplished while still giving them plenty of time to see his "world."

He lifted his hand to her chin again. His gaze held hers as he searched her face for something. "Two full days. Those are my terms."

Before she could move, he lowered his lips to hers again.

Felicity moaned at the contact. This kiss was different than the last one. This kiss was demanding, inviting, blatantly sexual.

And it made her burn.

"You are so very tempting," he whispered as he drew back. "Do we have a deal?"

Her body on fire, she nodded, though she wasn't certain if she had agreed to the two days, the sex, or both.

"Back to the waterfront in the morning, then?" he conceded.

She shook her head. "My sous-chef can take care of the fish and the market. Besides, it was obvious from the way you moved through Pike Place Market that you'd already been there many times. I wouldn't be showing you anything new."

"I've never seen the market through your eyes," he said with a grin, the one that made her heart speed up and her knees go weak once more. She gripped the prep table beside her for support.

She couldn't argue that the man affected her physically. The chemistry between them was undeniable. But just because there was chemistry didn't mean she had to act on it. She'd felt attraction before. Not lately. She'd been far too busy these last three years to even think about men in that respect. "I have something else planned. Meet me here in the kitchen at ten o'clock in the morning."

There was a long hesitation, until he finally nodded. "All right," he agreed, "as long as you promise to be cooperative with me when it's my turn."

Too late, she saw he'd cornered her. Who knew the extent of cooperation? Still, she inclined her head. "I promise."

He reached over and snagged another *sfogliatelle* from the counter beside him and tossed her a self-satisfied smile as he headed for the door. "Until tomorrow then." The words were spoken with a silken sensuality that warmed her to her core.

Felicity watched as the door flap closed behind him. Who was she kidding? How was she going to keep him at arm's length if whenever they were together she went up in flames at just a hint of a smile?

She released a groan and tipped her head back to stare at the ceiling. She was in so much trouble, more than she'd ever dreamed possible.

Blake was her rival for the Bancroft, and yet all she could think about was the offer he'd made. He wanted her. It was sex, pure and simple. No strings. No attachments.

A physical relationship between business adversaries? Was such a thing even possible?

"Oh, Vern," Felicity sighed. "Did you know what you were doing when you left me this gift?" She wouldn't put it past that cunning old man.

CHAPTER SIX

Hospital waiting rooms were never Felicity's favorite place to hang out. She clenched her ice-cold hands together, as though coupled they might generate some warmth. Leaning back in the stiff chair, hope tightened her chest until she could hardly breathe. The experimental procedure had to work. It had to bring her father back to her. She'd placed so many of her hopes and dreams on this procedure for so long.

After what felt like hours later, a man in blue surgical scrubs pushed into the waiting area. His mask hung loosely around his neck and a cloth skullcap, featuring every Marvel action hero, covered most of his dark brown hair.

He approached Felicity with a smile. "Felicity Wright?"

She nodded, not trusting her voice as she pleaded silently for success. Blood roared in her ears, muffling the words. She took a long, shaking breath and balled her fingers into fists.

"His brain activity has increased. Early signs look favorable despite the many years of damage."

A sense of euphoria threaded through all the questions racing through her mind, making her feel as though she had wings. "He'll be okay?" she asked as tears of joy scalded her eyes.

"It will take time, and lots of therapy, but it appears the procedure worked," the doctor said softly. "We'll need to keep him here for three days to monitor his progress."

Felicity took her first easy breath since she'd brought her father in early this morning. They finally had the money to cover not only the procedure, but his stay in the hospital as well, thanks to Vern and his gift. If she got nothing else from being the owner of the hotel, even a temporary one, this was enough. Vern had given both her and her father a possible cure.

Felicity smiled at the doctor. "Can I see him?"

"Of course," he replied. "Follow me."

◆ ◆ ◆

At his bedside, Felicity leaned over her father and kissed his cheek. "Hi, Dad."

He stared at the ceiling above him—the silver depths of his eyes showing no recognition at all. "You've had a busy day so far," she said, reaching out and stroking his hair. She kept hoping against hope that he would hear her, blink his eyes, twitch a finger, something. But there was nothing except the droning beep of the heart monitor and the quiet strain of her own breathing.

Felicity settled into the chair beside the bed and took his hand. All the busy talk she usually pressed on him died in her throat. She was very glad he'd gone back to eating, so the procedure could go ahead. There were no immediate results. And still she'd been so hopeful that it would bring the man her father had been back to her.

Closing her eyes, she saw her father at her sophomore year father-daughter dance. He'd been so handsome in his dress merchant marine uniform with its shiny brass buttons and white hat. He'd come home that day with a surprise for her—a long, cream-colored dress purchased just for her. She'd felt like a fairy princess that night, dancing with him in the high school gymnasium under cutout paper stars. "You'll be my princess forever," he'd said, filling her heart with joy.

A week later, her mother was dead. After her father had recovered from his physical injuries, he could move about, but usually ended up sitting in a chair by the window every day, watching the world go by, saying nothing at all. His brain had been damaged, the doctors had said. He might recover someday, but only with the help of an expensive treatment that she'd been saving for over the past ten years of working in restaurants.

That day had finally come, thanks to Vern. And they would get the results they wanted eventually.

Felicity smiled and opened her eyes. "Don't worry, Dad. You just rest and let your brain do the rest. When you're ready, I know you'll come back to me."

◆ ◆ ◆

Two hours later, Felicity was back at the hotel, back to her normal routine. Her burdens suddenly felt lighter, as though nothing could take away her happiness today—not even Blake's absence could put a dent in her mood. Today was a great day.

"Here's the last of it," the driver of the delivery truck from the food bank said as he handed the overly large box down to Felicity from the flatbed of the vehicle.

"Looks like lots of celery was donated this week," Felicity replied, glancing at the slightly withered vegetables in the box. What could she teach her students to make with celery?

"Thanks for your help." The food bank driver nodded his appreciation before he jumped down and headed to the cab of his truck.

Felicity handed the box to TJ, one of the homeless men enrolled in her Hungry Hearts cooking program. He took the food into the kitchen through the back door. She followed, glancing at her watch one more time. It was already past ten, and Blake had yet to show himself.

Had her rejection of his offer last night been the end of his negotiations for the hotel? She'd made it pretty clear all she wanted out of their arrangement was the hotel and the restaurant. Blake was a billionaire. They were from two totally different worlds. Sex, or any kind of a personal relationship with the man, was out of the question.

In the kitchen, Felicity gathered her students around the prep table holding all the boxes that had been brought from the food bank. She'd worked with the food bank for the last year, teaching how to prepare healthy, protein-rich, and tasty meals with what was donated that day. She looked over the contents in the boxes. Finally an idea formed. "Today I'm going to show you how to make braised celery with onion, pancetta, white beans, and tomatoes. Grab a partner, and go to your stations."

"TJ and Monica, would you give two heads of celery to everyone?" As she did every week, Felicity had set up several hot plates around the kitchen for the teams to use. Local businesses had donated not only the hot plates, but the pans and utensils her group used. The community was behind her and her unusual program. "When you get your celery, wash it thoroughly, then cut off the leafy tops. You can use those later to flavor stock. Remove the stalks from their base, and use the peelers to pare away most of the strings. When you're done with that, cut the celery into pieces about three inches long."

They all got to work. They knew the drill. This current group had been in session for seven months now, and it kept growing. She'd started with six students, but now she hosted between thirty and thirty-five students every Thursday morning. If the classes grew much larger, she'd have to add another day to her program. Felicity circulated around the room, answering questions and demonstrating how to use the peeler to take off the strings.

The primary purpose of the class was to teach the participants how to feed themselves and others. A secondary purpose was to teach them professional kitchen skills they could use to find entry-level positions in the restaurant industry. Soon, she'd be able to recommend several of her students for work in local kitchens. She'd hired Mary Beth, Michael, and Casper from the class herself. They'd all proven themselves to be exemplary students and now employees.

"May I help?"

Felicity looked up to see Blake standing not far from her.

He was dressed in a lightweight blue sweater that intensified the color of his eyes. "I'd like to help, if I may."

"You know how to cook?" Felicity asked, suddenly acutely conscious of the way his sweater hugged his chest and flat stomach. She swallowed, reminding herself that Blake was not on the menu today, or any day.

"Toast, only, but I follow directions very well." His voice had lowered, his tone provocative, challenging, demanding. A tone that, despite her vow to resist him, sent a jolt of desire through her veins.

She pointed to her left. "Toby needs a partner," she said, grateful her voice did not betray her.

Blake headed toward the young black man who worked alone. He offered Toby his hand, greeting him as he would a business partner. The newly homeless young man took his outstretched hand with some hesitance. "Nice to meet you," he said.

With an effort, Felicity returned her attention to the rest of the class. "Next, each of you will need an onion and four tomatoes from the boxes. Slice the onion as thin as you can. Remember the proper way to hold a knife. No fingers on the top of the blade."

As Felicity gripped a knife from the prep station beside her to demonstrate how to hold the handle, her gaze sidled back to Blake. Why was she so acutely aware of him? She didn't even have to look at him to see him in her mind's eye. He was bent over the onion, demonstrating to Toby how to handle the blade. As he moved his arm up and down, she could see the muscles of his washboard-flat abs ripple beneath his thin sweater.

"He's not bad," Mary Beth said from behind Felicity's shoulder.

Felicity turned around. "What?"

"I see the way you're watching him," she said with a mischievous grin. "I envy you."

"There is no reason to envy me," Felicity said, and even though she tried to look elsewhere, her gaze shifted back to Blake. Her senses should have been filled with the savory scents of celery and onions, yet the only fragrance that came to her was Blake's woodsy scent. Felicity held back a groan.

"You're crazy if you don't appreciate what he has to offer."

Felicity didn't answer as she watched Blake scoop up the onions and place them in a saucepan. He handed Toby a wooden spoon, encouraging the young man to participate in the cooking. Even as Toby stirred, Blake's gaze rested on her. She looked into his eyes, into the unwavering, unshakable blue, and felt her world slowly reel.

Mary Beth's eyes cut between Felicity and Blake. "The temperature in this kitchen is getting hotter by the moment. That man couldn't care one lick about the onions in his pan."

Felicity pulled her attention from Blake and set the knife back on the prep table. "I don't want to talk about him."

"You'd rather do things that don't require talking?" Mary Beth raised her brows suggestively.

Felicity rolled her eyes. "Can we please get back to cooking?"

"Sure," Mary Beth agreed, looking back toward where Blake stood, "but that won't stop him from looking at you."

She *wouldn't* look at him again. There was no sense in torturing herself. She would ignore him and keep on teaching her students. He was here to get to know them, and hopefully feel compassion for them. If he cared about what she did with the hotel and restaurant, perhaps he wouldn't try to take it away from her.

"While you finish slicing the onion, I'll come around with the pancetta and a can of white beans," Felicity said, pleased she sounded somewhat normal despite the warmth flooding her traitorous body. "If you don't have access to pancetta, you can always substitute bacon, sausage, even chicken or tofu. Just use some sort of protein. Protein keeps you from being hungry longer than just vegetables or carbs."

She made it around to three of the groups, delivering the necessary supplies before she slowly, helplessly, looked across the room at Blake.

He was staring at her.

She forgot to breathe.

Even from across the room, his gaze felt like a flame licking at her skin. She raised her chin, fought to concentrate on what she was doing. She struggled not to close her eyes and let her other senses stretch toward him, wrap themselves around him.

"What do we do with the tomatoes?" asked Rick, a young man in his thirties with a shaved head. Where his hair would have been, a coiled snake was tattooed on his skin, giving him a street-tough look when he was anything but.

Rick's question gave her something to focus on. She drew a deep breath. "When the onions are sautéed a golden brown, add the pancetta and beans. While you wait for those to brown, go ahead and dice the tomatoes. You'll add them last, and cook them until they're warm."

It wasn't working. Her heart rate sped up as his gaze caressed her face, her throat, then lower still. She could feel her nipples harden and the center of her womanhood tingle with an urgency she'd never experienced before.

"Felicity," Mary Beth said from behind her, placing a hand on her shoulder and giving her a push forward. "Put the man out of his misery, and allow yourself some fun for a change."

The words were enough to break whatever enchantment Blake had cast over her since entering the room. Felicity lifted her chin. She could resist him. She was capable of anything she set her mind to.

Grasping the thought, Felicity proceeded with the lesson, and succeeded in her task simply by not looking at Blake. She looked anywhere but at him. When the cooking was complete and the food plated, she escorted her students to the dining room, so they could enjoy their meal together.

Before she could circulate among her students, Blake stopped her with a hand on her arm. "Interesting use of your time and the hotel's resources."

"My time is mine." She drew a tight breath. Her gaze slid to his. Her nerves stretched in telltale anticipation—anticipation that would never be fulfilled. "And, come to think of it, the hotel is mine, too. Everything but the pancetta was donated."

He arched a brow. "I meant no offense. I happen to think the program is a brilliant idea. Yours?"

She nodded, relieved they wouldn't battle over her use of hotel resources. She firmed her lips. *Her* hotel resources.

"You're an intriguing woman, Felicity Wright," he said in a low voice. "Far more intriguing than I gave you credit for."

Her heart accelerated at the soft touch of his hand on her arm. She swallowed. "Thank you, I think."

He must have known the effect he was having on her, because he slid his fingers along her sleeve to her shoulder until they came to settle at the base of her neck. He moved his fingers leisurely back and forth. "What else do you have planned for me today?"

Despite the thick fabric of her chef's coat, her skin warmed at his touch, and her blood ran faster in her veins. "We'll start with a tour of the hotel, then I want to introduce you to our housekeeping department, service staff, and our security team. When we're finished there, you'll shadow me while I prepare for the dinner rush. After that, we'll relax with cocktails for two in the rooftop garden."

He offered her a mischievous smile. "I'm all yours."

She felt more than heard his words, as if they were a caress stroking down her body, warming her from the inside out. She knew he was waiting for her to reply, no doubt with something equally as playful and sexy. But she couldn't find the words. She could barely find her brain, let alone assemble sufficient wit to compose a sentence, especially not with his woodsy scent invading her senses, and certainly not when he was touching her.

Felicity forced herself to straighten, to step away from his touch. With an effort, she drew a deep breath, regaining some semblance of mental and physical distance. "Let's start right now with the tour of the hotel." She walked away from Blake, heading toward Mary Beth. With her previous experience, the young woman often helped her finish up the class when Felicity's other restaurant duties took her away. "Can you take over?"

Mary Beth's eyes twinkled as her gaze shifted between Blake and Felicity. She took in Felicity's heightened color and smiled. "Of course."

Felicity turned to face Blake.

His blue eyes held hers. A moment passed, then he held out his hand. "Shall we?" His voice had lowered, his tone provocative, challenging, demanding.

She took his hand, felt a sizzle along her nerves. "It's time for that tour."

He smiled intently. "I'll follow you anywhere you want to go."

And Felicity knew she'd unwittingly accepted more than just his hand. The sensation of his hand in hers sent a jolt of electricity through her. She swallowed hard as she guided him out of the kitchen and down the long hallway into the lobby.

He arched a brow at her, as though he, too, felt the soft searing in his blood, but he remained silent.

She should be thinking about the hotel, about her employees, about anything other than the man at her side. A glance sideways at his lean, perfect body tempted her in a way she'd never been tempted before. Not that she'd had much time in her life to be tempted. She'd spent most of her teens and early twenties working as many jobs as she could, saving for the procedure her father had had this morning. Maybe that's why Blake's appeal was so strong now.

They spent the next hour with Edward's wife, Marie, who paraded them through the various rooms on each floor. She proudly touted the skills of her staff as she introduced each maid to Blake.

They spent another two hours with the service staff overseen by Edward, watching the bellhops and porters, concierge and reception staff engage with the guests, providing a level of service that most hotels didn't even strive for these days.

And while most of the time was spent in conversation with staff or patrons, Blake never lost an opportunity to stand close and brush his fingers across her arms, her back, or along the curve of her hip. The air between them all but crackled as they made their way through the hotel.

That afternoon, a couple was using the rooftop garden as the site of their wedding ceremony. She and Blake stood in the back, observing, while the couple exchanged their vows. Felicity hoped Blake could see through her efforts today that the Bancroft was so much more than just a place to sleep or eat. It played an important role in the community as an employer, a safe place for residents, a job training and education center, a place where shared lives began.

After the wedding concluded, she took Blake back down to the lobby and asked the question burning through her thoughts. "Have I convinced you of anything yet?"

"You've convinced me that you work very hard and that your employees are extremely loyal to you, even though you just took over the hotel."

Raising a hand, she brushed back a flyaway strand of hair from her temple and noted his eyes followed her hand. "They know me from the restaurant. I'm a familiar face."

"Unlike me."

Once again they were close, and once again that excruciating awareness arced between them. "Yes," she said. "You're an unknown, and they're wary of how you'll change their lives."

He reached up and gently touched the back of one finger to her cheek. "Change is inevitable."

"Most people don't like change. It scares them."

He held her gaze. "Are you scared, Felicity?"

"Of you? Yes. No . . . I don't know anymore," she said in a rush.

His eyes flared and a look of satisfaction crept across his features.

She stepped back, away from his touch. "There is something more I want you to see—a part of history that is preserved right here at the Bancroft. Come with me," she said, taking his hand.

She led him through the bar area and toward the back stairs that were almost forgotten and rarely used. Four steps down, she released his hand so she could unlatch the door. When the door opened, the scent of stagnant air greeted them. Felicity moved down the darkened stairway, reaching for the old-fashioned light switch at the bottom of the stairs on the left side of the wall. A sizzle of sound preceded the soft flood of yellow-gold light that followed.

"What is this place?" Blake asked beside her. "I've been in this hotel many times as a child, and I never knew this place existed."

"It's the old wine cellar. Probably not somewhere your parents thought to take you," she said, stepping into the room. "This cellar was built for the original hotel back in the early 1900s." Edward had helped her track it down. She stepped aside and allowed Blake to enter the room.

With interest, his gaze traveled across the arched red brick that made up the ceiling before dropping to the flagstone floor and the piles of wooden crates stuffed into every corner. "That's an odd way to store wine," he commented with a frown.

"It's not wine. Go ahead, take a look," Felicity encouraged. He took several steps away from her and bent to inspect one of the wooden crates. Felicity watched in the filtered light as he lifted up a flat wooden shoe with a jute strap, a parasol, and a china doll.

He twisted toward her. "These are someone's possessions."

Felicity nodded. "They belong to the Japanese families who lived in the Bancroft. Following the attacks on Pearl Harbor, when all residents of Japanese descent were forced to leave their homes, businesses, and communities and enter internment camps for incarceration, they left everything they had behind. These crates contain their belongings as well as the memory of their hopes and dreams."

He set the china doll back on the top of the crate where he'd retrieved it. "These things belong in a museum."

Felicity shook her head. "They belong to the two families who lived here during that time. I researched the guest register from that time period and found two family names: Fujimoto and Nishimura. It would be wonderful to find their descendants and return their possessions. But in the meantime, their history is preserved right here, undisturbed."

Unfurling himself, he stood and came toward her, taking her hands in his. "You have a soft heart, don't you?"

"I—" She startled at the feel of his hands. They closed around hers as though he truly cared and wanted to offer her his support. She couldn't remember the last time someone touched her that way. She'd been the strong one in her shrunken family, for others at the hotel, for the community for so long, that she'd all but forgotten what it was like to take comfort from someone else. There was really no need for him to hold her hands. That he did scorched her all the way to her caged heart.

"I understand your need to preserve their memory, and your need to preserve the history of the Bancroft Hotel. I really do . . ."

She swallowed, then stiffened. She could hear the "but" coming. She pulled her hands from his. Was she foolish to think she could influence him by revealing the suffering of others? "Why can't you make an example of green living out of one of your other hotels?"

"The Bancroft is the first hotel my family purchased. It's the flagship hotel. The one we need to make an example for the rest of the chain."

Irritated, she met his gaze. "Why not use the second hotel your family purchased? The Bayside Hotel in San Francisco is very similar to the Bancroft. Besides, you actually own that one."

Instead of the anger she expected at her statement, his features lightened. "You've been doing research on me and my family?"

Dear God, the man was handsome when he wasn't trying to manipulate her. "I'll do anything I have to do to keep this hotel."

"Anything?"

She frowned. "Don't push me, Blake. I'm quite serious. This hotel and the people who work here mean everything in the world to me. I promise you, if pushed, I'll go to great lengths, even if that includes enduring personal hardship, to keep the Bancroft and her employees safe."

He locked gazes with her. "It might come to that," he said, his tone no longer amused.

She stared at him, trying to get a reading on his mood and feelings, but the man was a brick wall. "I'm ready." She turned her back to him and moved back up the stairs. "In the meanwhile, you are still obligated to spend the rest of the day with me. Prepare yourself for a long afternoon and evening in the kitchen. It's time to prep for lunch, then dinner."

CHAPTER SEVEN

Felicity looked about the dining room of the Dolce Vita as her employees gathered with her at the big table in the back. She smiled, feeling at peace despite the fact Blake was seated next to her. His arm brushed against hers as he reached for his water glass. Once again awareness arced and all but crackled between them.

Mary Beth sat on Felicity's left and leaned toward her, keeping her voice low. "How did the morning with Blake go?" She put a hand out for the large serving platter of gnocchi from Michael as the staff enjoyed their evening meal before they opened for the dinner crowd.

"I feel like I'm losing this battle before it's even started," Felicity said quietly, looking around the table at all those who made up her eclectic family.

Mary Beth passed the plate to Felicity. "Did you hear from the Seattle Historic Preservation Program?"

Felicity served herself, then, avoiding Blake's gaze, passed the plate to him. Their fingers touched and her pulse quickened despite her attempt to keep her response under control. "Nothing yet."

Mary Beth frowned. "Then what's wrong, because something is?"

A knot centered in Felicity's stomach as she slid her gaze to the man on the other side of her. He talked with Maria, one of the younger waitresses who sat across from him. The pretty girl smiled, her face animated as she hung on Blake's every word. "Am I wasting my time trying to convince him of anything? While I drag him around the hotel and introduce him to the staff, a part of me feels like he's just going through the motions, waiting for an opportunity to show me how little I know about hotel management. It's frustrating."

"I'm sure it is." Mary Beth smiled. "You're new to all this. But you're a quick learner."

Felicity frowned. "What are you smiling about? This isn't funny."

"You could always seduce the hotel out from under him."

"Are you forgetting I already own the hotel?"

"Maybe he just needs encouragement to back off."

"Or he's stalling while he goes behind my back and prepares a whopping lawsuit."

Mary Beth's smile faded. "Can I give you some advice?"

Felicity nodded.

"Sometimes you have to trust people to do the right thing, or you can make yourself miserable while you look for demons that aren't there."

The words were like tiny nicks from a razor blade, and she flinched at each one. "We've both had enough demons in our lives."

Felicity turned in Blake's direction once more. This would be so much easier, if he were the monster she wanted him to be, but he wasn't. "All right. I've tried worrying. Maybe it's time to try a little trust."

Neither of them said anything more. There was nothing else to do but to accept Mary Beth's practical advice and see where it led.

At the thought, Felicity focused her attention on her sous-chef, who stood to explain the specials for the evening, while the others continued to dish up their plates. She found comfort in the routine. The staff would each take a turn describing the newest dishes, until everyone, from the dishwashers to the headwaiter, could explain each and every new wine and food item.

"Our antipasto specialty tonight is *fiori di zucchini* or fried zucchini flowers. The sweet, subtle taste pairs nicely with a glass of

Prosecco," Hans explained, gesturing with his hands in his usual flamboyant style.

All through the meal, Felicity was conscious of Blake at her side. After she'd shown him the wine cellar, there'd been a subtle change in his behavior toward her. She couldn't quite put her finger on what the change was, but something was different. There was still the sexual awareness between them, but something else as well.

Acceptance? Contentment? Need? Could she label the golden warmth that flowed through her when he was near? Was it wise to allow herself to feel that way? She frowned at the reality of her situation. Wisdom wasn't her top consideration every time a look, a touch, or a smile turned her from a rational human being into a mass of quivering need.

She should be furious with herself for letting him have this effect on her, and yet, if she were honest with herself, she was enjoying letting her guard down, just a little. Indulging herself couldn't hurt as long as she didn't act upon her feelings.

"What are y'all doing?" a feminine voice asked from behind Felicity. There was a beat of silence before the speaker's identity registered in Felicity's mind. She turned to look behind her at the same moment as Blake.

Destiny Carrow offered one of her chocolate-wouldn't-melt-in-her-mouth smiles. Sweet and bitter at the same time. "I hope I'm not interrupting."

Felicity noticed Blake's eyes flare with interest as he took in Destiny's formfitting black dress, black tights, and black boots. Only a silver chain about her neck and her bright red hair gave the woman any color. But color never seemed to be an issue with Destiny. Her words, both spoken and written, seemed to draw people to her.

Felicity shifted in her chair, stood, and faced her onetime friend. She tried to pull up the advice Vern had given her when Destiny's scathing review had hit a few days before he died. He'd told her not to let Destiny inside her head. Doing that was more difficult than she'd imagined it would be, especially when Destiny's gaze drifted to Blake and her interest flared. "This is a private event, Destiny. Didn't you read the sign?" Felicity asked, her tone sharper than she'd intended.

Edward stood. A frown marred his usually cheerful face. "I'll see her out."

"Are you mad at me, Felicity?" The pleasure on Destiny's face slowly faded. "You took my review of your restaurant wrong, didn't you?" she asked in a low voice. "It was meant as encouragement."

Felicity struggled to form a calm reply. She would not reduce herself to Destiny's level. Even so, Felicity pinned her former friend with an angry gaze. "You have a right to your opinion. I'm glad my patrons feel otherwise."

Destiny frowned. "If the review didn't hurt your business at all, then what are you so upset about?"

"Why are you here?" Felicity asked, not wanting to continue the current line of their conversation.

Destiny pursed her lips and her eyes feasted openly on Blake. "I heard a rumor that I wanted to check out. Something about a handsome stranger coming to the Bancroft Hotel."

Felicity held her breath as she, too, looked at the man beside her. A faint stubble covered his angular jaw, and even though he had ditched his expensive suit for the chef's coat she'd given him to use while they'd been in the kitchen, the garment did nothing to hide his muscular chest. He was disarmingly seductive. So much so that it made her mouth dry and her palms damp just to look at him. "We have visitors to the Bancroft all the time. It is a hotel, you know."

"Ah, but this visitor is different." Destiny tapped a well-manicured finger on her lips in a theatrical way. "The rumor on the streets is that Blake Bancroft is in town, and that he wants something that was given to you." A cold, hard edge crept into her voice.

The soft sound of voices interrupted Felicity's thoughts as her employees broke the silence that had descended over the room. "You know about the restaurant?" she asked, surprised that word had leaked outside the hotel so quickly and directly to Destiny's ears.

"And the hotel." Destiny's eyes sought Felicity's, daring her to deny the rumor.

"It's true, but none of that concerns you."

"That's where you're wrong. The public has a right to know about what's happening at the Bancroft, especially with a nasty family fight brewing."

Felicity ignored the barb. "You're a food critic. Why would you want to do a story on what's between Blake and me?" Felicity asked with a frown.

Destiny's dark eyes sparkled. "I'm a reporter who works as a food critic. This story is going to launch my career as a serious journalist."

Blake stood and handed Destiny his card. "If you want information about the hotel, Bancroft Industries' public relations team would be happy to talk to you."

Destiny took his card and slipped it into her purse. "A quote from you would make the story that much stronger."

That's all she needed, for Blake to have the press on his side of this issue. Felicity tamped down her anger. Giving vent to her emotions would only make things worse. "Please leave, Destiny. The restaurant isn't open to the public yet. If you want to investigate, you'll have to do it during our hours of operation."

Destiny smiled, then turned to Blake. "Want to go find somewhere we can talk? You look like you could use a drink." She raised a brow, waiting for a response.

Felicity tried not to react, pasting a bland expression on her face. Inside, she was reeling.

"This isn't the time or place for an interview. As I said, you are welcome to talk to my PR team."

Destiny removed a pen from her purse. She reached for Blake's hand, turned it palm up, then wrote her number on his skin. "I'd rather hear from you," she said with a sly smile. "Call me."

"That's it," Edward erupted. "If you won't leave on your own, I'll escort you out." He stepped between Felicity and Destiny, towering over the petite redhead.

Destiny took two steps back, but her chin came up and her eyes narrowed. "This isn't over, Felicity," she said as she turned and walked out of the dining area. Edward followed. Felicity supposed it was to make certain the food critic left the hotel.

At Destiny's exit, the weight of disappointment settled in Felicity's stomach, and she found it hard to breathe.

"What is going on between you two?" Mary Beth asked in the silence that stretched over the room.

In her heart of hearts, Felicity mourned the loss of Destiny's friendship. She looked around the table at the concerned faces of her staff and forced a small smile to her lips. "Casper, I think it was your turn to describe tonight's specials."

Casper stood. A compassionate look crossed his features before he launched into his recitation.

Felicity heard not one word. Absently she traced the handle of her fork with her finger. What was it with this week? She'd received the best news of her life when Vern had given her the Bancroft Hotel, and yet everything seemed to be conspiring against her ability to enjoy his gift.

"Friend or enemy?" Blake asked as he slipped an arm across the back of her chair and leaned in, keeping his words between the two of them.

Blake's fingers on her shoulder were warm and consoling, and she liked the feel of him pressed against her side. "Hard to say these days," Felicity replied.

"Every successful business person has frenemies, you know. The onetime friends who seem to turn on you when you start to achieve success. I take it she gave you a bad review?"

Was he trying to make her feel better? "The worst."

"Don't let her get to you."

Felicity stared down at the hand resting against her shoulder, the one bearing Destiny's phone number. "She can hurt me, if you give her that interview."

Blake gave her a lopsided smile. "I haven't called her yet. Besides, I promised this day to you. And thanks to our time together, I now know how to peel and cook celery. We've had a tour of the hotel. You've used me as free labor in your kitchen. What's next?"

She appreciated his lighthearted tone and his attempt to make her feel better. "This evening, you're going to help me dress each dish before it leaves the kitchen."

With his other hand, he reached up and tucked a strand of hair behind her ear. "I usually like undressing things better."

Felicity felt her cheeks warm. "Wait until you see people eat what you prepared. There's no feeling like it."

His brow arched. "This I do have to see to believe."

"By the end of the night, you will." Felicity drew a slow, even breath, relieved that Destiny hadn't stolen what Felicity had worked all day to achieve. She'd prove to Blake that the Bancroft was more than just a place to stay for a night or two or a place to dine. The Bancroft was a vital part of the community and a second family for everyone who worked within its walls.

At least that was what she hoped to prove before the night was through.

CHAPTER EIGHT

Blake leaned against the counter while he watched Felicity work in the Dolce Vita's kitchen. She inspected each dish before placing it in the warming window for the wait staff to pick up and deliver to the patrons of the restaurant. He'd learned during the last two hours that working in a kitchen was as physical as it was choreographed.

"It's like meshing a ballet with professional basketball," Felicity had told him when they'd started working this evening.

She'd been right. He hadn't worked this hard in a long time. He was exhausted after only two hours. How did Felicity do this every night? He pushed away from the counter and went to join her. She dressed a long, narrow plate with five ravioli. "What kind of ravioli is this again?" he asked, surprised that he really did want to know. He'd dined in many of the finest restaurants around the world, and yet the way Felicity blended flavors and textures in the dishes she served fascinated him.

"Butternut squash with cashews in a passion fruit vinaigrette and a coconut emulsion." She handed him a sprig of fresh sage. "Tear off the leaves and sprinkle them across the plate."

He did as she'd asked, but he couldn't stop wondering about the woman beside him. "Why did you decide to be a chef?"

"Being a chef?" Her laugh held a brittle tone. "It's a life that chooses you; you don't choose it."

Blake paused. It was the kind of answer he usually gave—the kind that politely revealed nothing. Which made him hunger to know more. "How much longer will the dinner rush last?" he asked as he stretched the small of his back.

"Tired already?" she asked with an arch of her brow.

"I'd be lying if I said no."

She grinned and took the plate from his hands and set it in the pass-through window. "Hans?" she called to her sous-chef. "Will you take over?"

The younger chef nodded and set down the spoon he used to stir a large pot of marinara sauce. As Felicity stepped aside, he took her place, inspecting the dishes that were ready to be served.

Blake followed Felicity from the kitchen. "Your sous-chef is very obedient. All your employees are, really."

"Sometimes," she said absently. Then with a frown she added, "I don't manipulate them if that's what you mean." Her posture became defensive.

He raised his hands in a gesture of submission. "It was an observation, not a comment on anything."

She nodded, accepting his explanation, then said no more, dismissing the subject. "Come with me, I want to show you the other side of working in the kitchen."

They headed into the dining room. She stopped just out of sight of the patrons. "Watch them. This is the payoff for all our hard work." She smiled as her gaze moved over the crowd. Every chair in the restaurant was filled and several more people waited in the bar area for tables to open. He looked from table to table, watching as diners sampled their food. He saw the plate of ravioli he had just garnished as it was delivered to a young woman in her early thirties. She thanked the waitress, then eagerly picked up her fork and took a bite of the handmade pasta, and groaned her pleasure. Enjoyment slid through him like a warm, magical elixir. And something inside him unraveled.

Felicity was right. It was almost better watching them eat than eating the food himself. "What's next?" Blake asked.

"I thought we could talk," she said with a soft smile.

At the soft curving of her lips, a warmth flowed through him. A feeling of connection, camaraderie clung between them, something new and fragile. He was loathe to let it go, but they couldn't stand there in the dining room forever. "Talking it is. Here?"

She shook her head. "If we stay here, we'll be interrupted by either the employees or the guests. How does the rooftop garden sound?"

"Great."

Her face lit up and she smiled. "I'd like to get out of these clothes and wash off the scent of garlic, if you don't mind."

"Are you asking for help with the task?"

"No." She chuckled, the sound both nervous and surprised. "Meet me there in twenty minutes. That is, if you still need more convincing about why the hotel should remain in my care."

"I'm not ready to surrender yet, if that's what you're asking."

Her smile faded along with the intimacy of the prior moments. "Make yourself comfortable here in the lobby, or you can make your way upstairs. I'll join you as soon as possible, and I'll do everything in my power to change your mind."

In the next heartbeat she was gone. *Make yourself comfortable?* He hadn't been comfortable since the first moment they'd met. Something about Felicity's determination set him on edge, and brought out a strange protective instinct in him that he hadn't felt for ages. Usually he only felt need when it came to women, but with her, he felt something more, something softer, tender.

Blake frowned and dismissed the thought, donning the mantle he'd shaped over the years. He had a job to do, and such thoughts would not help him achieve his goal. He was too close to getting what he wanted to let emotions get in his way.

◆ ◆ ◆

Felicity raced to her room and unlocked the door. She had to shower and find something appropriate to wear. She had to change Blake's mind about the hotel.

Eager to return to Blake, Felicity headed for the bathroom and turned on the shower, letting it warm up while she took off her usual chef's attire. She'd shown Blake what she could about the people who worked at the restaurant and the hotel, and she'd shown him the patrons who used the services she provided. It was time to hit him hard with the last weapon in her arsenal. She reached for a small box beside the bed and set it on the coverlet, hoping what was inside would do the trick.

Then, clipping her hair on top of her head so as not to get it wet, she stepped into the water. She allowed the warm moisture to soak away the scent of garlic as well as her doubts. Minutes later, refreshed and certainly more awake, Felicity shut off the water. She grabbed a towel and, as she dried herself, wondered what might be appropriate to wear.

She wasn't trying to seduce him, yet an alluring dress might help her cause more than a blouse and a conservative pair of pants ever could. On that thought she stepped from the bathroom and headed to her closet. Her choices were few. She had the black sheath dress she wore the day before, a peach-colored sundress, or her dark blue satin wrap dress. Paired with her red heels, the attractive yet subtle blue dress would be perfect for her cause.

Felicity set aside her towel and slipped into her bra and panties, then her dress. After she'd tied it about her, she ran her fingers through her dry hair, settling the platinum-blonde curls loose about her shoulders. She scooped up the box and stepped into the hall, making her way to the hotel's bar for the cocktails she'd asked Ryan, her bartender, to prepare for her.

Minutes later, armed with two peach Bellinis and with the small box tucked under her arm, she stepped out into the warm night air in the rooftop garden. Blake was already there. He had changed into black pants with a perfectly pressed white shirt. He turned at her entrance, his face alight with an appreciative smile.

Felicity found herself caught and held by the warmth in his eyes. It would be so easy to go to him, to reach out and touch his lips, gently trace the smile with her finger. Desire flared. She held it in check as she moved toward him and offered him a tall champagne flute.

"What's this?" he asked, accepting the proffered glass.

She put the small box on the table she'd set between two wicker chairs. "A peach Bellini, Bancroft-style."

He took a sip. "Delicious," he said, his tone warm and stirring as he studied her from head to toe. Desire swam in the depths of his blue eyes.

An answering warmth flared to life deep in her core as she took a sip of her own drink and turned her attention to the sun as it slowly sank beneath the horizon, casting threads of orange and red over the Seattle skyline. "There is something wonderful about a sunset," she said more to herself than to further their conversation.

Even though she wasn't looking at him, she could feel Blake slip beside her, resting his hip against the edge of the brick balcony. Felicity continued. "Here in Seattle, the sun seems to hover at the horizon as though waiting for something."

She'd always loved that fact. The sun did just sit there, especially in the summer, waiting, as the horizon turned a darker gray. With every moment that went by, the sky deepened from gray to dark blue and finally to black, until night was upon them. In comparison to the sun, the night had a beauty in its own way—one of mystery and possibility.

It was the possibility that flowed through her now.

Silence settled between them, stretched as the softness of the night descended. The solar lights that dotted the balcony came on, flooding the area in a warm, gold light. She turned away from the balcony edge and returned her glass to the table between the two chairs. She picked up the box and took off the lid. Inside she removed three pictures and handed them to Blake. "I found them in Vern's room before you came to help me."

Warm evening air ruffled his hair as he accepted the old photographs. His smile faded and his voice dropped to a near whisper. "Where did you say you got these?" His fingers trembled ever so slightly as he tried incredibly hard to be invincible. His gaze clung to the picture of himself as a child, posed between his mother and father at the front entrance of the hotel. He flipped to the second picture of himself and his parents a couple of years later, this time on the same balcony he and Felicity occupied now.

His features softened as he looked at the last one—his mother, holding a baby in her arms. Felicity assumed it was Blake, though she didn't know for sure. "I don't have many photographs of my parents. They were put into storage somewhere after the accident. It's been so long no one remembers where they are."

Felicity had read that his parents had died in a boating accident sixteen years ago. Painful longing flitted across his features. She knew the look. It was the same one she'd tried so hard to hide throughout her entire childhood. She could see the twist of pain that moved through him. Admiration flared. He'd been orphaned, abandoned by his only family, and left to figure out life on his own. She wasn't certain how he'd done it . . . how he'd taken that pain and fashioned it into something he could live with. He could have used what had happened to him and turned it into anger. Instead, he'd turned his energy toward the environment much like she did toward the homeless.

"My parents and I lived at the Bancroft for a time while our house was being built on Mercer Island."

"From the photos, it looks like those were happy times."

He flipped back to the two of him and his parents. "They were. My parents died shortly after this last picture was taken." His voice was thick, as though holding back his emotions. "I'm the reason they're dead."

"Why would you say that?" she asked.

A faraway look entered his eyes. "I've never told anyone this before."

She said nothing, simply listened.

"My father and I fought on the day before he and my mother died. It was a heated argument about something stupid. I threw a handful of coins at him. It startled him enough that he slipped and hit his head on the floor. My mom suspected he had a concussion, but he wouldn't do a damn thing about it. He drove their boat into the rocks because of that concussion. I've blamed myself for their accident ever since."

An almost aching tenderness unfolded within her. The need to reach out, to thread her fingers with his, rose like a wave in her. She wanted to take him in her arms, without words—to let him know that she cared, sympathized. "None of what happened to your parents was your fault. It was an accident."

"Felicity—" Her name, spoken so gently, hung between them. Slowly he lifted his eyes to hers. "Thank you for that."

"With the perspective of adulthood, you have to see that the accident could have had any number of causes. Your parents wouldn't want you to carry the blame for what happened to them." Her heart thudded against her chest at the look of relief in his eyes. She couldn't say anything more. Instead, she simply brought a hand up to his cheek and rested it there. The world slowed to an aching, exquisite crawl as longing she had tried so hard to ignore spiraled through her.

He pressed into her touch. Moonlight cast him in a cameo of pale light as her breath caught, released, then became a sigh of wonder when he reached up and brushed a lock of her hair behind her ear.

The moment spun out, seemed to lengthen, and a thick, charged silence followed. A cloud drifted past the near-full moon, leaving only the soft, glimmering gold light to wrap around them, closing out the world beyond.

He continued to watch her, neither moving forward, nor retreating. The same desire she had seen in the kitchen earlier today shone in his eyes, yet he waited. Waited for her?

Something had happened between them tonight, something special. They shared a bond that went beyond words, a bond that went straight to her heart. Overhead, the wispy black cloud that covered the moon moved on and mixed the golden hues with blue-white light.

"I'd forgotten what this place meant to me once." He trailed his finger across her cheek, to her chin, down her neck and into the V between her breasts.

Her breasts tightened.

The night whispered about them, and cooling air swirled around their feet. He brought his hands to her waist and pulled her closer. She could feel herself shift upward as his lips descended.

Felicity shivered at the contact. This kiss was different from his last one—feather soft at first. And it made her burn.

He left her lips and trailed a blazing path down her jaw to her neck, his tongue tracing her skin ever so lightly. She wrapped her arms around his shoulders and surrendered her weight to him.

"You're so tempting," he whispered, then traced the curve of her ear with his tongue.

She knew she should pull away, that she should fight the raging need in her. This man had the power to take everything away from her. He was supposed to be her opponent. If she gave in to her own desire, he would have the power to hurt her more. Would that possible hurt be worth the risk? Because all she wanted to do right now was give herself over to the pleasure he created in her and spend the rest of the night exploring every inch of his body with her lips, her hands, and her tongue.

He found her mouth once more. His tongue slipped between her lips to touch hers. At the contact, a jolt of pure electricity shot through her body and landed in her core. Slowly, with a tiny portion of her brain that was still capable of rational thought, she lifted her lips from his but didn't look away.

His midnight eyes were filled with blatant desire, and, for a heartbeat, she was tempted to continue, to see where the night would take them. Her body still on fire, she took a step back.

Blake held on to her hands, but allowed her to put some distance between them. "Tell me something?" she asked.

He arched a brow, but didn't say anything as he kept looking at her as though he wanted to devour her right then and there.

Standing there, bathed in moonlight, with his hair slightly tousled, he looked more dashing than any man had a right to. The air between them was rife with tension, with mutual need. The force of it took her breath and made her both weak and strong at the same time. "Has anything I showed you today made you reconsider your plans for the Bancroft?"

"I would like to say no, but then I'd be lying."

Warmed by his words, she squeezed his hands. "Thank you for your honesty."

He gave her a tight-lipped smile. His eyes were alive with humor and hunger. "There's no reason to lie."

A thousand emotions tore through Felicity. Gratitude, humor, but most of all desire. With a groan, she pulled away and walked over to the balcony's edge, gazing once more across the city. She had to look anywhere but at him, or she knew where the night would end . . . in his bed.

"Tomorrow it's your turn to show me your world." He came to stand beside her, and her heart sped up once more. He didn't even have to touch her for her body to react. "Is there anything special I need to pack?" She turned to face him.

He reached out and caressed her jaw with the back of his hand. "What I want to show you doesn't require any clothes at all," he said with a grin.

She shivered at his touch. "I'm sure public nudity is frowned upon in San Francisco."

"Oh, c'mon," he said, his voice teasing. "We'll set a new fashion trend."

She looked at the sky, imploring divine aid. "Dear God, wherever he takes me tomorrow, please make it be warm if clothing is optional."

He laughed. "All right. Whatever you have I'm sure will be fine. You might want a summer dress, maybe a swimsuit, and definitely something formal."

Felicity's laughter faded. *Something formal?* "When is Peter picking us up for the airport?"

"At noon."

Great. That gave her two hours after the stores opened to find not only a swimsuit, but a formal gown worthy of Blake Bancroft. And she knew just who to ask for help.

To Felicity, clothes were meant to cover her body and provide warmth. In Mary Beth's prior life as a socialite, she had learned how to use clothes to make a statement.

Felicity took in the man before her. Oh, she definitely needed to make a statement if she were going to win the challenge he put before her. On his territory, she would need every advantage.

CHAPTER NINE

Blake flipped up the hood of his windbreaker as he stepped outside the Bancroft Hotel. He was about to get started on a morning run that would help him forget about the woman who occupied far too many of his thoughts these days, when he noticed Destiny leaning against the lamppost on the corner across from the hotel. She was dressed in a gray jogging suit, and, upon seeing him, crossed the street.

"Destiny," he greeted, not even trying to keep his irritation from his voice. She held a white bag and two cups of coffee in her hands. "When you didn't call, I knew I had to take matters into my own hands." She offered him an encouraging smile. "I brought breakfast for two."

Blake frowned. He hadn't called Destiny, because he had no intention of telling her what should remain private between him and Felicity. "I'm going for a run."

"Mind if I join you?"

He arched a brow. "With coffee and donuts?"

"They're spinach feta wraps, and . . . oh, I suppose it really doesn't matter what they are." She looked around her, then moved to the other side of the street again and deposited the food with a young boy walking a dog before returning to Blake's side.

"Isn't he a little young for coffee?"

She shrugged. "He's got to have parents around here somewhere. Let's go."

When Blake realized he wasn't going to get rid of the reporter, he figured he would simply outrun her. He started off down Terry Avenue the way he and Felicity had walked just the other day. A run along the waterfront had seemed like a good idea this morning. Now he wasn't so certain.

"Rough night?"

He'd had a hard time sleeping as his thoughts kept going back to Felicity. "Do I look that bad?"

"I doubt you've looked bad a day in your life, regardless of sleep, or other activities," she said, keeping pace.

"I have no intention of discussing the Bancroft with you," he said as a gull squawked overhead.

"We can talk about whatever you want to talk about."

"What do you want, Destiny?" He settled into his usual rhythm, feeling irritated that she was keeping up with him.

"Was your uncle always manipulative?" Her tone was carefree, but Blake sensed the question was more important to her than she tried to reveal.

"Are you asking for my sake, Felicity's, or yours?" The staccato of their footsteps punctuated each word.

She looked at him briefly, then turned her gaze back to the street before them. "Don't be dramatic. I just want to know why the old man left Felicity the hotel over you. She was company for him, but nothing more. So why would he be that generous with her, unless there's more to the story."

"It's a story I don't know. If you want any information, you'll have to go to Felicity herself."

"She'll never talk to me. Not now."

"Because of whatever feud is between the two of you? She said you used to be friends."

They came to a light at Alaskan Way and were forced to stop. Blake jogged in place while Destiny doubled over, trying to catch her breath. "Sometimes life makes certain choices for you."

The sharpness of Destiny's tone caused him to look at her in surprise. "What do you mean?"

She straightened. "Nothing." The light changed, and she bolted across the street.

The scents of salt and sea and creosote touched his senses as he crossed the street to join her. "Why write a story at all? There's no news there." As they had the other morning, fishermen lined the wharf, trying to sell their morning catch.

"You're wrong. Whatever happened between your uncle and Felicity is newsworthy." Her cheeks were mottled, and she was starting to show fatigue.

"What's newsworthy about an old man dying? And he died of natural causes, so don't even think of going down that path." The sound of their footsteps on the pavement joined the rumble of voices coming from the makeshift market.

"But there's more to this story than your uncle dying unexpectedly. I intend to prove that Felicity knew who Vernon Bancroft was before he died, and that she manipulated him into leaving her this hotel."

"For your own revenge, or for the good of the community?"

"Maybe a little of both. Felicity is living in the past, as far as the Bancroft is concerned. The glories of the old place faded long ago. It's time for the Bancroft to step into the future. That's what you want, isn't it?"

"It's all I want." He was lying to himself. That wasn't all he wanted. His motives weren't as pure as he was trying to convince himself. His corporation wanted one thing from Felicity; his body wanted something more.

"Then let's make that happen together. Let me take you to dinner tonight. We can talk and see where that leads us," she said suggestively.

One part of his mind accepted that what Destiny was doing could be good for him and his cause. The other part, the part in turmoil, wanted to whisk Felicity away and keep her safe from Destiny and anyone else. He shook his head at his own thoughts. He couldn't have it both ways. There was no way for him to have the Bancroft as well as the woman who currently owned the place. And he certainly wasn't interested in talking about himself or his uncle Vern. "We're done here."

"Then I'd watch your back if I were you."

"Is that a threat?" His tone was like ice.

"No. It's a promise."

She stopped running and Blake shot ahead, leaving her and her shallow threats behind. He hadn't made it to his current level in the company without making a few enemies along the way. Destiny's threats didn't scare him. Besides, that's what his security guards were paid to protect him from.

What did disturb him was the fact that he hadn't taken Destiny up on her offer to tarnish Felicity's reputation and ultimately her ability to make the hotel a success.

Why did he hesitate now? This was business after all.

Was what she'd shown him over the past two days actually changing his mind—that the Bancroft was more than just a hotel to many people? Did he have the right to destroy all that, regardless of what he thought about Felicity?

Blake groaned at the thought of her. He couldn't seem to forget the way she smelled or the way she moved. Her lithe body was a symphony of grace, and all too easily he could imagine her in his arms.

His hands flexed unconsciously, as if trying to dispel the sensation of Felicity beneath his touch last night on the balcony. She had been soft and warm and sweeter than anything he'd ever tasted before. What was it about her that intrigued him so? Just the thought of her fingers brushing against his flesh made his blood thicken and his body tense.

He stared off into the distance, trying to regain control of his desire without much success. Not when he knew what lay ahead. They would spend the weekend together in close proximity. If he'd thought her hard to resist in Seattle, she would be temptation itself on their trip. His original goal had been to prove to her that the Bancroft deserved to become a leader in green technology. He would convince her of that, and so much more. A slow smile came to his lips. He could accomplish both tasks in the proper setting.

Felicity had agreed to give him two whole days, but he'd never mentioned exactly where he intended to take her. On that thought, Blake pulled out his cell phone. He had two hours to arrange an alternative plan.

◆ ◆ ◆

When Felicity entered the lobby that morning, she found Mary Beth waiting for her. Felicity barely had time to offer her friend a greeting, before Mary Beth whisked her out of the front entrance and into Blake's unengaged limousine parked in the circular drive.

"I hope you don't mind, but when I saw Peter waiting here this morning, I asked him if he would escort us around town," Mary Beth said. "I know I should have asked you first, but this seemed so much more expedient. We'll have more time for shopping this way."

"No, I don't mind," Felicity said as Mary Beth ushered her into the backseat. "Where are we going?"

Mary Beth stepped into the limousine, and Peter closed the door. "We'll start at Luly Lang on Fourth Avenue."

As Peter started the car, Mary Beth settled back against the plush leather seats. "Lord, I love this car almost as much as I love spending other people's money."

In the rearview mirror, Felicity could see Peter smile at the two of them before he returned his gaze to the road. It didn't take long to drive down the hills to the shopping core of Seattle's downtown between Fifth and Sixth Avenues. Peter pulled the limousine to the curb and came around to open the door.

Mary Beth stepped out. "Come on, let's get started. We don't have much time."

Felicity hesitated at the entrance of the high-end boutique. "I think we are shopping in the wrong end of town for me. I can't afford—"

"Felicity, you helped me once. Please let me help you now. This is important. In order to play in Blake's world, you have to look like you belong there. Besides," Mary Beth said as she linked Felicity's arm with hers and pulled her toward the entrance, "as owner of the Bancroft Hotel, you have a certain image to uphold."

Felicity hesitated a moment more as Mary Beth's words sank in. Finally, she allowed Mary Beth to drag her along into the high-end designer store. Mary Beth was right. For the next two days, she would need to elevate herself to Blake's level, and she'd never felt more dull and inadequate as she did when she was in Blake's vibrant presence. "Only a few things . . ." Felicity conceded.

Mary Beth nodded as she moved about the store. "You follow food blogs, but I follow couture. I still remember the days when this used to be my life."

When it came to fashion, Mary Beth did know what she was doing; she proved it every day by dressing better than anyone else Felicity knew. And she did it all on a limited budget.

"Why can't we shop at the stores you usually go to?" Felicity asked, still hesitant about spending more money than was absolutely necessary.

"Because you need the best—not an imitation of the best—to take on a man like Blake."

Reluctantly, Felicity nodded.

Mary Beth responded with a confident smile as she turned back to the garments near her fingertips. "You need warm colors. Or black.

You'd look stunning in black. I'm thinking a fitted bodice and a flowing skirt. Let's play up your assets."

"My what?" Felicity laughed.

Mary Beth frowned at her. "Do you own a mirror? In the right clothes we'll show off your small waist and curves." She shook her head. "I don't know how you do it. You're the only chef I know who doesn't look like she's a world-class chef around the waist."

"Get serious, Mary Beth. I'm like everyone else."

A supercilious look crossed Mary Beth's face. "You really have no idea just how beautiful you are, do you?"

"I'm an ugly duckling."

"No. You're a swan." Mary Beth's eyes filled with humor. "Wait and see. When I'm done with you, you won't be able to deny it."

◆ ◆ ◆

Felicity stood in front of a giant bay of mirrors with her arms up, while Mary Beth and one of the saleswomen fitted her with dress after dress. Even though she was a little dismayed about the amount of money they were spending, Felicity forced herself to relax and remember Mary Beth's advice about fitting into Blake's world. When they'd finished at Luly Lang, Mary Beth led her to more of the stores along Seattle's retail core.

An hour and a half later, they were back in the limousine. Felicity leaned back against the plush leather interior with a sigh of relief. Four stores, three dresses, two tops, and a swimsuit later, she was more tired than if she'd cooked in her kitchen for two days straight. "I'm glad we found the dresses we did."

"I think you should wear the mocha-colored dress for whatever formal event Blake has planned. It's wonderful with your skin."

"Yeah, it shows so much of it," Felicity said dryly.

"That will be to your advantage, my dear."

"Peter, take us to 1910 Post Alley."

Felicity startled. "We're not going back to the hotel? I need to meet Blake at noon."

Mary Beth raised a brow. "You have time for this. Besides, he's not going anywhere without his driver."

For the next twenty minutes, she and Mary Beth sat in a charming teahouse in Seattle's Pike Place Market enjoying a cup of chamomile tea served in Sèvres china cups of almost transparent delicacy. The floor-to-ceiling windows allowed them to watch visitors to the Market while they sat back and relaxed for a few brief moments. Mary Beth had been right once again. The cup of tea was the perfect end to their shopping trip.

"Are you ready for what Blake has in store for you over the next few days?" Mary Beth asked.

Felicity nodded. "I've taken care of everything my father might need while I'm gone. When the hospital releases him, he'll return to the assisted living facility. He'll have a private nurse for the next couple of weeks. She'll see to his therapy and make sure he's okay while I'm gone."

"Sounds like you're ready to take Blake on."

Felicity grimaced. "I don't think anyone could ever be ready to do battle with that man." She sighed. "Even with a private nurse, I'm still nervous about leaving my father. I'll be worried about him the whole time."

"I'll look in on him for you."

Felicity gave her friend an appreciative smile. "I hate adding an extra burden—"

"It's no burden," she interrupted. "My brother is more than happy to help out with the baby. Amelia really likes her uncle, too. I feel so lucky to have turned my life around."

"It wasn't luck that did that. It was your hard work."

"Do you have a game plan for dealing with Blake on his turf, other than dressing the part?" Mary Beth asked over a sip of her tea.

A game plan. "I'm not sure I have any plan at all other than to try to persuade him that the Bancroft should stay as it is."

Mary Beth nodded. "You'll be fine. Especially now. You're different since meeting Blake."

"How so?" Felicity set down her cup.

Mary Beth wrinkled her nose. "I'm not sure exactly. But I'd say you're not so easy to intimidate."

Felicity laughed. "I don't know about that. I was *very* intimidated by the salespeople at Luly Lang and Neiman Marcus."

Mary Beth chuckled. "They're paid to be intimidating. Regardless of them, you're definitely more in control since you've met Blake."

"There is so much more at stake, that's why."

"That's not a bad thing, Felicity." Mary Beth shrugged. "Who knows, perhaps you'll come back from San Francisco and be a force to be reckoned with. Blake won't stand a chance against you."

In that moment, Felicity hoped Mary Beth was right for a third time that day. Blake was a powerful opponent. She would have to be just as determined and just as strong if she were going to keep what she so desperately wanted.

CHAPTER TEN

After his run, Blake returned to the hotel and placed a call to Marcus. "Any news from Jamison about the offer on the Heritage Hotel?"

"The old guy wants to speak with you in person," Marcus replied in his usual efficient tone.

Blake frowned impatiently. "That won't work. I'm heading out of town. Can we speak over the phone?"

"He's a traditionalist. He likes to do his business face to face."

Blake glanced at his watch. He still had an hour before he had to meet Felicity. "Then set us up for a Skype call. I want to get this taken care of, and soon."

"Why the hurry? That's not like you."

"I just want it all settled. Take care of it. That's what I pay you to do," Blake said.

There was silence on the other end of the line for a moment. "Can you give me ten minutes to set up the call?" Marcus asked.

That would give him time for a shower. "Meet you online in ten." Blake hung up and headed for the shower. Ten minutes later he greeted Donald Jamison across the computer screen. "Good morning, Mr. Jamison. I appreciate you meeting me on such short notice."

The older man set his lips stubbornly. "You and I both know that I don't have a choice about selling my property to you, but I wanted to talk to you in person about tearing down the hotel." His voice quavered, and, for the first time, Blake hesitated when it came to pushing one of his adversaries into a corner.

He had the advantage. The old man was desperate. Two days ago, Blake would have forged ahead without a moment's thought. "Why are you so resistant to me tearing the place down?"

"The truth?" he asked, his features suddenly drawn.

"Yes," Blake replied.

Jamison met his gaze. "My Jenny died here. If you tear the place down, then you also take away my last memories of her."

Blake reacted to the words with guilt and an unusual surge of compassion. The memory of the pictures Felicity had shown him last night played across his mind. His lips twisted into a bittersweet smile. "I do understand." He paused for a moment, thinking, then sighed. "Would you be open to an alternative offer?"

"And what might that be?"

"Seventy-two million. You stay as a resident of the hotel to oversee its management and restoration."

Jamison's tired gray eyes brightened with surprise and perhaps even tears. "You're not going to tear it down?"

"You make a compelling argument." Blake released a sigh. "No, I won't tear it down." How could he do so with a clear conscience? "I'll have Marcus draft the agreement if we have a deal."

Jamison nodded. "Forgive me for saying this, but I'm surprised. Men like you usually don't back down. What made you change your mind?"

"All I can say is that I'm seeing our arrangement through new eyes," Blake replied.

"I am grateful for that."

After settling a few other necessary details, they signed off. Blake sat back in his chair still a little baffled at his unusual behavior. It was the first time he'd ever negotiated a deal that had absolutely nothing to do with monetary value. It was so unlike him, and he didn't want to contemplate why.

◆ ◆ ◆

An hour later, Blake and Felicity were seated in the plush lounge area on his private jet, preparing for departure from Boeing Field.

Felicity's eyes were wide as she settled into the soft leather seat and buckled her seat belt. "You own your own plane?"

"What gave it away—the Bancroft Industries logo on the side?" He rarely saw his world through the eyes of anyone other than business associates with a similar lifestyle.

A curious mix of excitement and tension radiated from her. "This isn't a plane; it's a flying mansion."

He shrugged as the plane taxied down the runway. "I like to work while I travel. The plane gives me an office, a bedroom, a dining area, a bar, and a bathroom complete with a shower." Blake covered Felicity's hand with his. For a moment he thought she would pull away. Then, slowly, her hand turned and held tight to his. He mustn't read anything into it. She seemed particularly tense since walking onto the plane. He couldn't blame her. She'd just left her entire support team behind. The woman was open and vulnerable. An inexplicable irritation moved through him at the thought. Would he use her malleability to his advantage? Such tactics wouldn't have stopped him before. But with her, his usual business dealings felt wrong.

"Do you fly much?" he asked, giving her hand a squeeze, whether trying to comfort himself or her, he wasn't certain.

"Not since Italy, and rarely before then. You might have noticed I have a hard time relinquishing control. I like things a certain way."

He raised a brow as the jet became airborne. "You have OCD?"

"No, I have CDO, or at least that's what it should be if the letters were arranged alphabetically," she said, her tone serious, but her body relaxed.

Blake studied her a moment until he noticed the corner of her mouth quirk. He responded with a smile. "Very funny."

She shrugged, her gaze going to the window as they gained altitude. "I do hate being out of my element. Please promise me there will be no surprises."

He couldn't promise her that. That's what this trip was all about—unsettling her, putting her off balance, winning her over to his way of thinking about the hotel. "We had an agreement. You had two days, now I get mine. I intend to show you how a hotel can be socially responsible and environmentally friendly without sacrificing service."

Her gaze shot back to his. "That's how I run the restaurant," she said, her tone defensive.

"You do a terrific job there. It's much harder to accomplish with a hotel unless you do some major revisions."

"It's not the remodeling that disturbs me. It's the effect it will have on my employees' lives. They need their jobs to survive."

An almost desperate passion simmered in her voice whenever she brought up that point about her employees. Was there some sort of hardship in her life he had yet to be aware of? As he mulled over the thought, he abstractedly squeezed her hand once more. "Don't worry about anything for the next two days. Just give yourself over to seeing things through different eyes. Will you promise me that?"

He saw a moment's hesitation before she nodded and leaned her head back against the soft leather seat. "I'm sorry. I'm not trying to be testy. I'm not used to shopping for clothing first thing in the morning."

"Only fish? They are so much less demanding of your energy."

His quip brought a smile to her face. "Fish, I understand. Fancy clothing is a world unknown to me. It's exhausting." She sighed. "I don't know how you do it."

"I hire people to do it for me." At that moment, his attendant appeared beside them, offering two Waterford flutes filled with champagne. "Thank you, Kayoko," Blake said with a smile at the small Japanese flight attendant who'd been handling all his travel needs for the past five years.

Felicity took a glass and stared down at the bubbling liquid. "If I drink this, I'll probably fall asleep."

Blake took a sip of his champagne, hoping Felicity would do the same. "We have a bedroom you may use, if you would like to take a nap."

After a sip of her champagne, she set the glass down and sent Blake an apologetic glance. "A two-hour nap sounds fabulous. Would you mind?"

"Not at all." He released her hand. "Kayoko will show you to the bedroom. Make yourself comfortable. I have plenty of work to do while you sleep." It was the truth. He'd ignored the business for the past few days he'd been in Felicity's company—something he couldn't ever remember doing since he'd taken over the company from his uncle. "Sleep well. If you need me, I'll be right here."

"I won't need you." She straightened and moved briskly down the hallway after Kayoko.

He tried not to let the comment hurt him as she disappeared into the lavish bedroom where he usually slept on long flights. He imagined Felicity lying on the cool, linen sheets, her hair splayed about her head, her body warm and willing. His groin tightened, and he groaned against the deep-seated ache that burned through him.

How would he ever get any work done, knowing she slept only a few feet away? With an effort, he reached for his laptop and turned it on. When Kayoko returned, she scooped up his champagne glass and set a Scotch down in its place. He released a sigh. "It shows that much, huh?"

Her eyes filled with understanding. "She seems different than the women we usually travel with," the flight attendant said with a sweet smile.

The fact that Felicity was in his bed by herself set her apart. Kayoko was right. Something was different, but the difference was with him, not Felicity. Bit by bit, she was breaking down the barriers he'd erected around himself. He'd distanced himself from feeling anything but ambition since his parents had drowned. He preferred to live that way—in a safe cocoon free from turmoil.

It was so strange that Felicity had succeeded where others had failed. It annoyed him and fascinated him at the same time.

If he didn't know any better, he'd think his uncle Vernon had left the hotel to her so they could meet, have a reason to interact. But that was something a loving uncle might have done for a beloved nephew. And Blake knew Vernon was not that, nor was he.

Blake could feel his blood pounding through his veins as he stared down at his glass of whiskey. He brought the glass to his lips and tossed back the contents in a single swallow.

Kayoko raised a brow, but silently turned and retrieved the bottle, pouring him another splash of the amber liquid.

"It's going to be a long flight," he said. "You might want to leave the bottle here."

She set down the bottle, then left him to himself. He logged on his computer and pulled up the spreadsheets his accountant had sent him. The numbers helped him put Felicity from his thoughts.

He had work to do.

◆ ◆ ◆

Felicity moaned as she felt a warm, strong hand sliding over her bare stomach to her hip. Instinctively, she turned in to the caress, her body instantly on fire with need.

Blake rolled her over on to her back and captured her lips with his. Her senses swam at the contact, and a hot shiver went through her. As he continued his assault on her lips, his fingers dipped below the coverlet and moved lazily up her thigh.

Felicity groaned and was tempted to open her eyes, but the dream was too close to her own longings to want to banish it yet. Instead, she breathed in his familiar woodsy scent as she tasted the heat of his mouth.

His kiss was fierce and hot, yet strangely tender as his hands worked between her thighs. He ruffled the curls at the apex of her womanhood before he dipped his fingers inside the folds. His thumb rotated gently.

She clenched her teeth as a hot, convulsive shudder tore through her.

He didn't release her; instead, his thumb flicked slowly back and forth. Every muscle in her body clenched as she fought for control, fought to stave off the tension that coiled tighter and tighter with each movement of his fingers. She could no longer think coherently as she reached for the source of her pleasure.

She wanted him inside her.

Her heart pounding so hard she couldn't get her breath, she clutched his shoulders and drew him down beside her. She bit her lip expectantly as he stretched along her body and settled between her thighs. He moved closer, his rigid manhood pressing against her core. Just when he was about to slide inside, a hard bump jarred her awake. The world around her slowed, and she felt herself slide forward on the sheets covering her legs.

Dazed, she glanced around the unfamiliar room. It took her a full minute to realize she was alone in Blake's bedroom aboard his private jet. The plane had landed in San Francisco, and she'd been asleep the entire time.

Had it all been a dream? Her heart pounded in her chest as she drew a shaky breath. Suddenly she was conscious of the cool sheets beneath her and the silence that surrounded her. The feel of his hands on her body had seemed so real. Tension still lingered, demanding release—a release that wouldn't come anytime soon.

As her heart settled into a more normal rhythm, she got up and moved on unsteady legs toward the door. *Heaven help her.* If her dream had been any indication, the next few days in Blake's presence would tempt her as never before. Steeling herself for what was ahead, she moved into the living area.

Blake turned toward her, his gaze as heated as her cheeks. A slow smile spread across his face as he devoured her with his eyes. Could he see the rapid rise and fall of her breasts that forced her taut nipples against the silk of her blouse, or sense the desire that pulsed in her veins unquenched? No man had ever given her such a look. And she'd never responded to a man the way she did to Blake.

He stood. "I trust you're feeling less tired."

She glanced restlessly around the lounge. Less tired. More worked up than ever. "Yes, thank you," she said past the dryness in her throat. "Have we arrived?"

"I was waiting on you to deplane. The others have gone on ahead of us with our bags to prepare."

Felicity glanced out the windows. Palm trees swayed gently beneath a sudden, gentle breeze. A brilliant orange-red sunset lingered past them, hovering on the horizon. *Sunset?* "How long was I asleep?"

"Six hours."

She looked at him bewildered. "How can that be? We just landed?"

"Yes."

She moved toward the door of the plane and stopped at the ramp. Stretched beyond the stairs were emerald-green mountains that looked as though they were covered in velvet that plunged toward a white sand beach. The sun hovered just above the horizon, casting a golden glow across the tropical paradise. The sweet scent of jasmine and orchids hung in the air, seducing her with its headiness as warmth caressed her skin.

She twisted back to Blake. "Where are we?"

He came toward her. "Hawai'i. Kauai, if you'd like me to be specific."

"But we were going to San Francisco," she said, her voice rising.

He slid his hand beneath her arm, guiding her toward the air stairs. "No, you assumed we were going to San Francisco, and I let you believe that."

She pulled her arm out of his grasp. "You tricked me."

He stopped on the stairs beside her. "You agreed to go with me anywhere I chose to take you that could demonstrate what I wanted to show you about environmental protections and sustainable living."

She wanted to argue, but she remembered agreeing to those very terms. She'd never imagined he would take her here. With a quick glance at the man beside her, the reality of her situation hit her. She'd be in Hawai'i for two days while Blake tried to convince her that the Bancroft Hotel was better off under his management.

How was she going to fight him when he wasn't playing fair? Felicity took a deep breath and fought the urge to strangle him. "Hawai'i?" she groaned.

He smiled wickedly. "This is where I can best make my point about sustainability. What better place to protect than paradise?"

She pushed her hair away from her face, feeling somewhat defeated already and they hadn't even stepped onto Hawaiian soil. She was in so much trouble from herself, from Blake, from the tropical paradise they were about to enter.

Sighing, she crooked her arm out from her side. "All right, let's get this over with."

Beside her, Blake flashed a dazzling smile. "Paradise awaits us," he said as though he'd read her mind.

Felicity pasted on her best smile and headed to the bottom of the ramp where Kayoko waited with two leis made from purple orchids.

The flight attendant slipped one of the traditional flower greetings around Felicity's neck, then Blake's. "Welcome to Hawai'i." She motioned off to her left. "Peter has your car ready to take you to the hotel."

Blake escorted her to the car and allowed her to slip into the backseat. In a fluid movement, he slid in beside her and gave her a devilish smile that made his blue eyes come alive with humor and hunger.

A thousand emotions tore through Felicity—excitement, fear, desire, doubt, but most of all happiness. She had no responsibilities for two whole days. Mary Beth would step in for her father if something came up. Edward would look after the hotel. And Hans would take care of the restaurant. It had been three years since she'd had any time off from the restaurant or her obligations to her father—three years since she'd had a moment to relax.

"Where are we going?" she asked as they headed off the tarmac and away from the airfield.

"Bancroft Industries owns several hotels on this island. We are going to a modest hotel called the Mano Kea just off Poipu Beach. It's one of my favorite places to stay on Kauai, and it's the greenest of the Bancroft properties."

And so it begins, Felicity thought as she stared out the window, watching the long white beach on one side of the car, and the jutting velvet mountains on the other. Despite the fact that they were so close to the ocean, the air smelled as though it were laden with honey instead of the salt so prominent in the air along the waterfront in Seattle.

It didn't take long before they turned off the main road to stop in a circular drive. Peter came around to open the door for them. Blake stepped out, then offered Felicity his hand. She slid across the seat to emerge from the car and stilled. The modest hotel was not a hotel at all; it was a palace.

The white-stone palace towered three stories high. Arches and colonnades graced the front of the building. Behind the building-long balcony were windows, covered in intricately carved filigree wood shutters. Three golden domes, reflecting the bright orange of the setting sun, dominated the center and east and west wings. Two fourteen-foot brass-bound doors, stamped with scenes from Hawai'i's Polynesian past, led into the palace. A small courtyard with a graceful waterfall fronted the entrance.

"It's beautiful," Felicity exclaimed as she followed Blake inside, only to have her words snatched away by the tropical beauty that awaited her inside. A paradise stretched before her, with palm trees and bright-colored flowers surrounding a waterfall that filled the lobby with its soothing sound. "It is real?"

"It's manmade, but operates much like the fountains of old with no motors or pumps. We collect the water in a reservoir in the hills, then send it downward through a series of aqueducts. Gravity does the rest."

"Impressive."

"I'd hoped you'd feel that way." Blake's eyes crinkled as he chuckled. "This hotel is a LEED Gold–certified building. It not only protects the environment, but also serves as a refuge for several endangered species."

Blake moved through the lobby like a man in charge of his troops. In what seemed like only moments, he had two porters and two maids depositing their suitcases in an overly large suite on the third floor, with one bedroom on the right side of the room and another on the left. Before she could object, the maids had her suitcase unpacked in the room on the right.

With a charming smile on his face, Blake showered his employees with generous tips, until finally they closed the doors of the sitting room, leaving the two of them alone.

"I hope you don't mind that I booked us into the VIP suite together. The hotel is always full. I had to move two clients to a different hotel and pay for their entire vacation so we could have this suite."

"That was very generous of you." Felicity remained where she stood.

"It's business."

Only this wasn't business as usual, at least not for her. Two days in paradise with Blake, sleeping across the sitting room from him? How was she going to survive, unless she focused on the one thing that was guaranteed to take her mind off anything . . . cooking.

"I thought we could clean up and have dinner on the veranda."

"Dinner," she said a little desperately. "That's a great idea. I'd like to see the kitchen here. If I'm going to find out how this hotel differs from the Bancroft, then I'd like to start somewhere I understand."

Blake hesitated only a moment before he nodded. "By all means. Right this way."

As she moved past him, he placed a hand on the small of her back, as though it were necessary to guide her from the suite, down the stairs and out the door to a separate building not far from the main building. His touch ignited the simmering desire that had coiled inside her since leaving Seattle, and she felt her control slipping.

Blake escorted her across a stone walkway illuminated with tiki torches and toward an arched doorway. "The kitchen has its own building, since it was added after the hotel was originally built in the early 1900s. The goal was to keep things as close to the original building as possible."

"Is that what you would do to the Bancroft? Keep as much of the original building as possible?" she asked even though it sounded like she was admitting defeat, which she definitely wasn't.

He shrugged. "I won't know for certain until we start the inspection."

Her lips thinned into a grim, determined line. She needed to believe she would succeed in her efforts to keep the Bancroft.

Blake guided her along the pathway until she could hear the low rumble of male voices in the kitchen, accompanied by the clinking of plates and silverware. They stepped through the doorway to the tantalizing aromas of spices and savory meat. Her stomach rumbled in appreciation as she walked into the stainless steel kitchen. Four men worked at the grill and stove, and two women bustled around the kitchen dressed in blue and white floral dresses with flowers tucked into their hair near their left ears.

"Haku," Blake greeted one of the men behind the grill.

The Hawaiian smiled easily and, after wiping his hands on the white towel tucked into the belt of his apron, came to greet them. "Mr. Bancroft, so good to see you."

"I apologize for interrupting you during dinner," Blake said as he shook the chef's hand, then clapped him on the shoulder.

"No worries. *Aloha.* I don't usually find you in the kitchen," Haku said as his gaze focused on Felicity's face.

"I'd like to introduce you to a friend of mine, Felicity Wright. She's a superb chef at the Bancroft Hotel in Seattle."

Blake's compliment caught her off guard as the cook grasped her hand in both of his and gave it an enthusiastic shake. "Haku Kepoo. It's a pleasure to meet you. Come, let me show you how we do things around here—Hawaiian style." He pulled her back toward the grill, leaving Blake standing alone.

She wanted the distraction, she reminded herself as she walked away listening to Haku talk about what they were preparing for the evening's menu. Yet watching Blake's expression fade as she left him behind brought a heavy sensation to her chest. A pain that made no sense to her, but it was there, acknowledging everything she tried so hard to deny.

She liked Blake Bancroft. Perhaps a little too much.

CHAPTER ELEVEN

Blake left the kitchen and Felicity in the hands of the friendly chef and went directly to the suite. He palmed his cell phone and placed a long-overdue call to Marcus.

"It's eleven at night, Blake. I already finalized the deal with Jamison."

"This isn't about the Heritage Hotel."

"Then what's it about? I was sleeping," Marcus said, less than pleased to hear from him.

"What do you have on Felicity?"

Marcus groaned. "We couldn't have talked about this yesterday?"

Blake frowned into the phone. "I've been"—distracted, enchanted, consumed with lust—"busy."

"Where are you?" Marcus asked with a yawn.

"Hawai'i."

There was a pause, a ruffle of crisp linens, then Marcus said, "You took her to Hawai'i?"

Blake shifted uncomfortably. "It was a last-minute decision."

"You don't make those kinds of decisions," Marcus said, his tone serious. "That's twice in one week. You must really like this girl."

Blake did, and he wanted more.

The realization surprised him. He wanted to know her. When they'd first met, he'd thought of her only as another business adversary. Yet the more time he spent with her, the more he became aware she was a woman of intense passions. She was generous to a fault, faithful to her friends, and had deep bonds with her employees. She was one of them, yet she was also forced to stand apart. Alone. Every day that he spent with her he saw some new facet that intrigued him and drew him to uncover more.

She was coming too close, and that both exhilarated and scared him.

"What did you find out about her?" Blake asked, forcing his thoughts back to the conversation.

"I found her father."

"Where?"

"In a hospital in Seattle. He had a procedure done on Friday to help him regain his speech."

Blake gripped the phone more firmly. "He doesn't talk?"

"He hasn't said a word in years."

"Did the procedure work?" Blake asked with a frown.

"Hard to tell at this point."

Blake let that news slide over him before he asked, "Why doesn't he talk? What's wrong with him?"

"The whole family was in a car accident years ago. Her mother was killed, and her father injured."

"A brain injury?"

"I haven't found anything definite, but I'd assume so."

"Anything else?" Blake asked, his thoughts going in a million directions.

"She spent a year abroad. Had very little contact over there with anyone except her employers. There was one employer she had a short affair—"

"Dig deeper into the father." Blake cut his lawyer off. "I want to know more. Details about the accident. Her father's medical history. His prognosis." Her father was her weakness. He could use that to his advantage.

Marcus sighed. "I do have other legal matters to oversee for your company."

"That's why I pay you an exorbitant salary."

"That does take some of the sting out of working with you," Marcus said more cheerfully. "I'll be in touch."

Blake hung up the phone, his thoughts zinging in a million directions.

He strode across the suite to the door. He finally had a tiny insight into what drove Felicity, and with that knowledge, he knew he held the card that could win the battle between them.

Feeling more enthusiastic than he had in a long while, Blake hurried down the hallway and, taking the steps to the outside two at a time, went back to the kitchen in search of Felicity.

◆ ◆ ◆

"Felicity?"

Blake's voice, so rich and welcoming, curled around her as he walked toward her in the glow of the tiki lights that surrounded the patio outside the kitchen. She'd set one of the unused staff tables with linens, silverware, and goblets from the kitchen, showcasing two plates of Hawaiian BBQ short ribs that Haku had prepared.

If the fall-off-the-bone ribs were an indicator, the Hawaiian chef was an expert when it came to meat. He'd slow cooked the ribs in a variety of sauces for the past six hours. When she'd taken a small taste in the kitchen, the meat had melted in her mouth and sent her taste buds soaring.

She motioned to Blake to sit down. "Haku showed me how he makes his Hawaiian barbecue."

Blake sat in the chair opposite her. "He must really like you. He's never shared that recipe with me. He says it's what will keep him employed, and he's right. People come from all over the island to eat here." Blake studied her from over the rim of his water glass.

"I can understand why." Something hot and dry curled in Felicity's throat. His eyes were like pools of promise, beckoning, calling to her to trust him.

She couldn't. He had the power to break her. With trembling fingertips, she reached for her food. They ate in silence, listening to the breeze as it rustled through the palms overhead. All around them, slow-moving shadows danced in the pale light of the torches. A rounded moon hung high in the sky, a circle of the purest gold, a moon that seemed as much a fairy tale as the rest of the day had been.

When he had finished eating, Blake sat back in his chair and studied her once more.

"Why are you and Destiny so at odds?"

The words came unexpectedly, jarring Felicity to sit up straighter. "What made you think of Destiny at a time like this?" They were sitting in paradise, isolated, alone, and his thoughts had gone there?

He shrugged, but the intensity of his look was anything but casual. "She came to see me before we left. She seems very intent on ruining you. Why?"

Felicity's stomach lurched at the thought of Destiny and Blake together. Felicity knew the reporter would stop at nothing to get what she wanted. "We used to be friends, but something changed between us two weeks ago. I've gone over and over that time in my mind. I can't figure out what might have happened. She's been attacking me ever since; first with a terrible review of the Dolce Vita, then by trying to partner with you." Her eyes went wide. "You're not going to, are you?"

He frowned. "I don't want to take you down, Felicity, nor would my family appreciate the negative attention on our hotels. I just want what should've been mine in the first place."

Not for the first time did she have a pang of guilt over that very fact. The Bancroft should be his, but Vern must have had his reasons. If only she knew what those reasons were, this would be so much easier. "Damn you, Vern," she said, then was startled when she realized she'd said it aloud.

"He was a cunning old fox, wasn't he?"

"He was only ever very sweet to me, never manipulative."

Blake's eyes narrowed. "My uncle was sweet? Impossible. And he was always manipulative with me."

Felicity groaned. "I feel as though I'm missing something. Some deeper meaning in that message he left me along with the will. *Take care of the Bancroft, Felicity. You'll know what to do.* Well, I don't. I have absolutely no idea. And there's that unfinished note for you. I wish I could figure out what it all meant." Felicity stood, no longer able to contain herself to the chair, pacing restlessly across the terrace.

Blake pushed his chair away from the table, watching her as she moved back and forth. After a moment's hesitation, he said, "I was never able to predict what my uncle would do."

"What is there to be gained from us being at odds with each other?"

Blake snorted. "I didn't know him well enough to even guess at a reason."

She kept pacing back and forth as the minutes ticked past.

He sighed. "You know pacing isn't going to solve our problem."

"Yes, I know. But I can't get my mind off why Vern did this. I mean," she went on, one arm sweeping wide as she turned, "why did he go to such lengths to see that you and I would battle it out over the hotel? Why not just leave me the restaurant and you the hotel?"

He rose and caught her in his arms as she passed near and pulled her against him.

Her entire body responded with a wave of heat that sent her pulse racing. She braced herself against the sensation.

"I might be persuaded to accept that, Felicity." His deep voice saying her name in the darkness made her senses jolt almost as much as the odd way he was looking at her. She forced herself to return his steady gaze. As they stared at each other, the breeze evaporated, leaving in its place an oppressive, warm silence. The only sound was the soft mingling of their breath in the motionless air. Felicity kept her flash of temper in check. That didn't solve the problem of keeping her people employed. "Until I understand why Vern did what he did, or until you can convince me otherwise, the Bancroft remains in my care."

A headache banged to life behind Felicity's eyes. She stepped back out of Blake's arms and moved to the railing. She leaned against the barrier, grateful the night breeze had picked up once more. Tipping her head back, she allowed the breeze to caress her face. She closed her eyes, reveling in the sensation when she felt Blake's gaze on her body like a tangible presence. Almost a touch. Slowly she turned toward him. Their eyes met, held. The warmth in his look sent a shiver skittering along her flesh. The silk of her blouse seemed somehow thinner, the night colder than it had a moment ago.

"Why do you have to fight me for the hotel? You have so many already, and I only have the one," Felicity asked with a tired sigh.

He leaned back on his heels and studied her. "Life isn't about fairness."

Her head throbbed and her temper snapped. "Don't tell me what life is about. While you've been living in posh hotel rooms with enough money to do as you please, even fly to Hawai'i on a whim, I've been living a real life with bills and responsibilities and lots and lots of worries."

She latched on to her anger. Anger she understood far better than longing or desire. Anger had always spurred her forward in her life, challenging her to push beyond her abilities, to become more. Anger had helped her pick up the pieces of her life after her mother died and the father she'd always known had failed to come back to her.

Like a fire starting with a single flame, her anger took hold and built into a raging inferno. "You can't tell me you've ever known what it was like to go hungry, or to shiver in the darkness because the power had been shut off. Or that you'd been so lonely that you wondered if another person in the entire world even cared if you were still alive."

She turned back to look at him, and he trapped her with his gaze. "You're right. I'll never know those things, and I hope to God other children in this world will never have to know that kind of pain."

She blinked, her tirade momentarily derailed.

He moved slowly toward her, holding her gaze, and gently took her arm. "What do you expect me to do? I can't fix all the problems of the world. Even I don't have enough money for that."

"I'm sorry," she said, her angry suddenly spent. "That was uncalled for."

"Don't be. You have a right to your beliefs, as I do mine. That's why I put my efforts into the environment. At least there's a tangible quality to the difference I'm making. I can test the air quality and know it's improved on some level for every person on the planet."

She frowned, letting him turn her and guide her back toward their table. "Helping one child out of poverty can make just as significant a change." Her voice vibrated with emotion.

Silence wrapped around them. The world shrunk to just the two of them, standing face to face in a tropical paradise.

"Let's not fight about the hotel tonight," he said, breaking the silence as his hand came out, stretched toward her.

She stared at the flat, pale circle of his palm. Unbidden, a wave of longing washed over her. How good would it feel to place her hand in his, to let his fingers thread through her own, to feel like she wasn't always so alone?

◆ ◆ ◆

Felicity looked up at him from under her long eyelashes. Blake's heart hammered at the vulnerability he saw in her eyes. A vulnerability that touched him on a level he didn't want to think about. He wanted to wipe away the pain he saw in her eyes, wipe away her horrible memories. And along with that need to protect her came an even stronger urge to hold her to him, to revel in her scent, her softness, her warmth.

He hadn't felt like this in so long. No, he corrected himself, he'd never felt this way about a woman before. This wasn't just lust, like he'd tried to convince himself when they were in Seattle. He felt a bond with her. It was like they were two parts that made up a whole. Which was ridiculous. It had to be. He didn't believe in such things, did he? At least he hadn't before he'd met her.

She made him want to believe. Made him long for things he'd forced out of his life so many years ago to keep moving forward. What would it be like to wake up next to someone he actually cared about in the morning, to feel her warmth cocooned next to him, his hand on her flesh, hers in his hair?

He hadn't allowed himself to think of such things while he climbed his way to the top of his uncle's empire—an empire that had started with his grandfather. Because Vernon hadn't married or had children, the Bancroft legacy would have passed to his much-younger brother, Blake's father, had he lived. And Blake was there now, at the top. He could conquer just about anyone and anything . . . except Felicity. Was that what drew him to her? The fact that she was a challenge he had yet to master? Or was there something more?

Something was different between them tonight—something had changed since their time in Seattle. The sadness in her eyes had seemed to ease since they'd arrived on the island. Was it the distance from all her responsibilities that had finally allowed that to ease? Or did it have anything to do with him? He studied her as his heartbeat thrummed in his chest, the beat slowing then speeding up.

Beneath the silvery glow of the moon, her beauty struck him anew. He'd thought her somewhat plain upon their first meeting. How wrong he'd been. A breeze swept across the terrace and ruffled through her loose hair. Strands fluttered across her face. She eased the renegade strands away from her nose and mouth and tucked them behind her ear.

The innocent motion captured his focus. He took a moment to savor the look of her right now—carefree and beautiful. A gift he wanted most desperately to unwrap, to indulge himself in over and over again.

He'd offered her himself, and she had refused. She wanted more than just a sexual partner. What was it she craved? *Love?* Did that emotion even exist? Closing his eyes against the unfounded agony in his heart, he stepped back, away from her and the odd pull she held over him this evening.

He shook off the unwelcome thoughts. "Come on. Let's clear the table and return the dishes to the kitchen, then I'll walk you back to the suite."

After they returned to the suite, Blake led Felicity into the lush bedroom with a king-size bed covered in a green tropical print. He shifted his gaze away from the bed and back to Felicity who stood before him as still as a statue.

To his surprise, she lifted her hand and ran her fingers down his jaw. The warmth of her touch sent chills through him. He knew in that moment that she wanted him to kiss her, and he knew what it cost him to hold himself back.

He simply reached up and ran the pad of his thumb over her lips. She barely bit back a moan. He shifted closer. She smelled so good, like a single rose in a bouquet of exotic flowers.

The air between them was rife with tension, with mutual desire and need. The force of it stole his breath and sent his heart thudding in his chest. And just when he thought he wasn't strong enough to walk away, he pulled back.

He wanted her with a need that defied reason, and yet, he knew that if they were ever to be together in that way, she had to be the one to initiate it. If she wanted to kiss him, she would have to bring her lips to his.

"Good night, Felicity," he said as he turned toward the door. It was the first time he'd ever denied himself something he wanted.

Outside the room, he closed the door, then leaned back against the wood, fighting the raging need inside him. It was raw and vicious, and it made him ache for things he had so rarely had in his life.

He had to put her out of his thoughts, or he would never be able to sleep.

But even as he stood there, the loneliness of his life settled around him. What was he fighting Felicity for—supreme dominance in his field? Or were there other things worth fighting for—like people, relationships, love?

With a groan he pushed away from the door. There was that word again. *Love.* A useless word that made people do stupid things.

He had a hotel to win away from her. That's what he needed to focus on. She was the only thing standing between him and success.

CHAPTER TWELVE

Blake got up early, and while Felicity slept, he headed for a meeting with the managers of his hotels on the island. He'd sent word to them last night to meet him in the boardroom of the Mano Kea Hotel. He was the first to arrive and helped himself to a cup of coffee Haku had supplied, along with a light breakfast of exotic fruits and macadamia nut scones. He was about to reach for a scone when a ruckus sounded at the door. He turned to see, not his managers, but a member of his security team.

"Pardon the intrusion, sir," Patrick, one of his security guards said. Patrick shoved a young man with a shaved head and dark, assessing eyes into a chair near the doorway. He kept one hand clamped on the man's shoulder while he held a camera with a large telescopic lens out to Blake. "I thought you'd like to know I found this young man trying to climb the side of the building near the balcony of your suite. This camera was around his neck."

Blake accepted the camera, flicked it on, then reviewed the digital photographs on the memory card. Images of Felicity and himself since their arrival in Hawai'i played across the screen. "You've been following us. Why?"

The young man eyed him rebelliously. "It's a free country."

"And the rules of this great country you speak of still apply. I can charge you with trespassing on private property, attempting to break and enter, not to mention stalking." Blake returned his hard stare. "And unfortunately for you, the police chief of the island is a friend of mine."

His features hardened. "You don't scare me."

"Oh, you'll be scared when I'm done with you, if you don't start talking," Blake said in an ominous tone.

The photographer glared at him. "You rich guys are all the same. You think you can buy anything you want with money."

"There's more to me than money," Blake said, pushing back his sleeves to reveal his muscular forearms. He knew it was a scare tactic, but it had worked for him at boarding school several times when threatened. "Now start talking."

Sudden fear replaced the rebelliousness in the photographer's eyes. "I was just doing what I was told."

"Which was?" Blake questioned.

"To take pictures of you and your lady friend in . . ." he hesitated.

Patrick tightened his grip on the young man's shoulder. "Go on."

"In compromising situations," he said in a pain-filled rush.

"Who's paying you?" Blake asked.

"I don't know her name."

"Describe her," Blake demanded, turning the camera over and removing the memory card.

"Twenty-something. Red hair. Nice looking."

Destiny. Was she still trying to find a way to discredit Felicity? Blake removed, then palmed the memory card and handed the camera back to the young man. "Patrick here is going to escort you to the airport. You're going to get on the next plane out and never come back here again. Do you hear me?"

He clutched the camera to his chest and nodded.

"And when you make your way back to Destiny, please give her a message from me."

"What's that?"

Blake tossed the memory card to the floor then stomped on it, shattering the plastic into a hundred pieces. He scooped up a few of the chunks and sprinkled them into the young man's hand. "Tell her my answer is still no."

When Blake turned away, Patrick lifted the man to his feet and ushered him out the door.

Blake had no time for reflection or anything else as his five managers he'd invited to meet with him entered the room. Refocusing his thoughts, he greeted them individually and asked them to help themselves to breakfast, so they could start the meeting. While he truly was looking forward to hearing their updates on each of the hotels, he was far more interested in the woman whose image had been displayed on the camera's small screen.

Damn you, Destiny, Blake lamented once more, before giving himself over to the business at hand.

◆ ◆ ◆

Felicity had woken up at the sound of the door to their suite closing. She slipped out of bed, then smiled. It was still early enough that perhaps if she headed down to the hotel's kitchen, she could ask Haku if she could prepare a surprise light breakfast for her and Blake. On the way to the kitchen, she heard Blake's voice and followed the sound to a boardroom at the back of the hotel. She peered into the room to see Blake and two other men talking.

She knew she should announce herself, but as the conversation between them became more heated, she back away from the door, then stood there, unable to move away. She listened to Blake and a man she learned was his security guard. The younger man must be a photographer who'd been caught trying to take photos of her and Blake. When Destiny's name was mentioned as the instigator of the plans, anger sizzled along Felicity's nerves. How dare Destiny attempt to exploit her relationship with Blake?

What relationship? There was nothing between them but a few innocent kisses. And despite Blake's obvious displeasure over the photographer's actions, she didn't know his true motives. He might have been acting merely out of protectiveness. For men like him, protectiveness toward women was ingrained. Wasn't it?

If Blake sent this photographer away, like he claimed he would, would that solve the problem? Or would there be others trying to capture a private moment between the two of them that could be used against her? She'd have to be careful during what remained of their time in Hawai'i. She couldn't afford the gross publicity such pictures would bring as she struggled to establish her foothold as owner of the Bancroft Hotel.

The hallway suddenly filled with noise and activity as three men and two women headed for the room just as Blake's security guard and the young photographer stepped out. Felicity kept moving toward the kitchen, but not before she heard Blake greet the five new arrivals in a cheerful voice. From his greeting, she could only assume they were employees.

His words of praise toward them brought a smile to her lips. Blake might pretend he was a hard-edged businessman, but in the last few days she'd seen the rounded corners beneath.

She didn't know much about him. But underneath his businessman exterior, she could tell that he had a genuinely good heart. That fact intrigued her more than it should, captivated her at times. And when she looked at him, as she had only moments ago, her heart beat a little faster and the strangest sensations settled deep in her core.

◆ ◆ ◆

An hour later, Blake returned to their suite. They shared the crab cake eggs Benedict with bacon and hollandaise sauce she'd gone to the kitchen to create for them, before they started their first day of his part of their arrangement. After a twenty-minute drive, they pulled up in front of a dazzling white building that stretched across a white sand beach. Infinity pools of cerulean blue flowed from one level to the next until they reached the shoreline, making the hotel appear as though it was an extension of the sea itself. Thoughts of Atlantis came to mind as Blake escorted her from the car and into the lobby.

"The Leilani Hotel is the pride and joy of Bancroft Industries. It has the lowest greenhouse-gas emissions of any hotel in the world. It was built three years ago with sustainability in mind. We call her our green pearl."

"Why did we not stay here?" she asked the obvious question.

"Because I wanted more privacy," he said, then frowned, his thoughts no doubt going back to the photographer from this morning. "Come on." He offered her his hand. She slipped her fingers into his and allowed him to lead her into the hotel.

The lobby was all white stone that was carved into rounded angles with multiple stairways leading to the reception area. In the center of the lobby was an oval-shaped pool of the deepest blue. Palm trees and exotic tropical flowers limned the water's edge, swaying softly as if moved by some interior breeze. From high above her, white, foamy water tumbled downward, splashing noisily in the pool's glassy surface, sending ripples of waves from edge to edge.

"The Leilani relies on solar and geothermal energy to power all the buildings and to heat the pools. While she was being built, we were able to recycle ninety-three percent of the construction waste generated. Outside you might have noticed a colossal blue pipe."

She shook her head. Her focus had been on the endless display of pools. "What does the pipe do?"

"The apparatus pumps seawater that cools the hotel," Blake explained. "One of the biggest energy savers for us is our cooling system. The hotel pumps salt water up through deep wells and then circulates it through two three-hundred-sixty-ton chillers that provide air conditioning throughout the buildings. Once warmed, that seawater is released through the waterfall, then channeled back into the sea through the pools you saw out front. The mechanism saves us an estimated thirty-six thousand dollars in electrical cost each year. It also reduces the carbon dioxide released annually by more than three hundred twenty-eight thousand pounds."

Her head spinning with not only the technology used, but the savings, she allowed Blake to lead her up an open stairway. He placed his hand at the small of her back, guiding her along. His touch was warm and comforting as he continued his tour of the exquisite hotel.

"We use only one-hundred-percent recycled paper products and soy-based inks, but last year we diverted about one hundred and fifteen tons of recyclable waste—that's the equivalent of nearly three humpback whales—that would have ended up in the garbage. That was about nineteen percent of the solid waste generated by the hotel. The recyclable plastics and paper materials are all separated and shipped back to the mainland for processing."

Felicity stared in awe at the beauty of the place. Images of luxury bombarded her as they walked through the meeting areas, ballrooms, dining rooms, and finally into the guest spaces.

"We are part of a recycling program that allows us to donate leftover toiletries to Clean the World, an organization that steams and disinfects the items then ships them to developing countries to fight hygiene-related illnesses. And we are experimenting with bulk containers instead of single-use bottles in some of our hotels."

Breathing a little faster at the extent of the hotel's efforts, Felicity grasped for perhaps one thing he hadn't been able to do anything about. "What about the unused toilet paper?"

He laughed. "We do have an endless supply of toilet paper, but we divert that from the landfill by furnishing the employees' locker rooms and personal homes with hundreds of leftover tubeless rolls."

She stared at Blake in breathless wonder. He really had thought of everything. She followed him through several elaborately decorated rooms. When they'd finished that part of the tour, Felicity could no longer hold back asking what she wished to see most. "Will you take me to the kitchen?"

"I'm surprised you lasted this long before asking," he said with a smile. "This way."

An elevator, backed with glass, descended into the open-style lobby once more. They got out on the first floor and headed down a long hallway that was decorated with tiled murals of island life. "It's a beautiful hotel, Blake," she admitted with a tiny twist in her stomach. If he could renovate the Bancroft Hotel with even a portion of what he'd showed her today, the hotel would not only be more beautiful and energy conscious, but a better steward of the environment. Felicity held back a groan. His attempt to sway her was working.

She drew a tight breath and hoped her sudden distress didn't show on her face as they entered the kitchen. At the sight of the state-of-the-art commercial kitchen, Felicity's knees went a little weak. She reached for the nearby counter, steadying herself while Blake proceeded to discuss the top-of-the-line appliances, stainless steel prep areas, and storage areas.

"Any waste grease from cooking is collected and converted to bio fuel," he explained.

Not giving her much time to recover, he guided her past a wall of refrigerator and freezer units, before they stepped through a doorway leading to a greenhouse with both soil and hydroponic areas. The plants there were laden with ripe fruits and vegetables.

"We are able to grow most of the fresh ingredients for the menu ourselves," he explained as they made their way through the enormous structure.

"What do you do about food waste?" she asked, as she walked past the succulent tomatoes on one side of the aisle and strawberries on the other.

Blake pointed to the enclosed black receptacles at the back of the greenhouse. "Inside those units are thousands of worms composting organic waste. When they're done, we have nutrient-rich fertilizer that we can then incorporate back into the growing process." He moved her toward a different aisle on the side of the building. "Over here, we have receptacles that collect wet food waste that gets boiled up and packaged to send to pig farmers. They come every day and collect the food so it's not sitting around. It's free food, and it keeps a bunch of waste from going to the landfill. It's a win-win for everyone."

He led her out of the greenhouse, back into the warm, perfume-laden air that did nothing to ease the chill that had settled inside her. "The hotel really is ahead of its time," Felicity conceded, forcing aside a sense of impending doom.

"Sustainability is contingent on the power of creative thinking." Blake smiled at her with an almost unbearable sense of pride as they headed back to the waiting car. "We intend to do much like this with every hotel in our chain within the next ten years."

She stopped beside the Tesla. "Why start that conversion with my hotel? There have to be others that will be easier to convert."

"There are," he agreed. "In fact, I just purchased another hotel in San Francisco. But as I said before, the Bancroft is our flagship hotel. It sets the pace for the entire hotel chain, and for the Bancroft name."

"I'll have to rename the hotel since it will no longer be part of your corporation."

"Only if you win our wager." Blake opened the car door, inviting her inside.

Pain cut through her at the thought of losing the hotel, even if it would be for a very good cause. That cause didn't take into account her employees. She knew what she had to do. The Bancroft was hers, and she would do whatever she had to do to see that it remained that way. Determined to succeed, she slipped into the car. "What else do you have in store for me today?"

He slid in beside her and closed the door. "I thought we could take our lunch beside the pool at our hotel, then catch a little sun before getting ready for the party later tonight. We'll leave the hotel at six o'clock."

"Where are we going?"

"To get away from it all. I find I'm in need of a little more privacy than even the Mano Kea allows."

"In formal dress?"

He nodded and turned his attention to Peter, directing the chauffeur to return them to the hotel.

"That's it? That's all you'll tell me?"

A mischievous grin lit up his face.

CHAPTER THIRTEEN

Felicity met Blake in the sitting area of their suite at six o'clock that evening. She was dressed in a sea of mocha-colored silk and chiffon. Blake's gaze traveled from her coiled hair, across the formfitting bodice gathered to reveal the soft rise of her breasts. His eyes filled with heated appreciation as he continued to devour her with his gaze—down the length of her floating chiffon skirt where it clung to her hips and then on down to her slippered feet. "You're beautiful," he said, his tone guttural.

She could barely respond past the dryness in her throat. Blake was resplendent in a black tuxedo with a black bow tie. The late-afternoon sun came through the window, edging his dark hair with streaks of gold. "Thank you." She finally managed to force the words past her dry lips.

"Come." He offered her his arm and once again guided her through, then out of the hotel. After a quick ride in the Tesla, they exited the car on a helipad. The helicopter's engine started at the sight of Blake and the rotor blade started to turn, sending Felicity's skirt fluttering in all directions. She gasped and tried to grab the edges of the cloth, desperately trying to keep her clothing in place.

Blake appeared at her side. He scooped her into his arms and carried her the short distance to the helicopter, depositing her gently inside before joining her. He slid the door closed. "My apologies. I didn't consider that when I booked our transportation," he shouted above the noise of the rotating blade. He handed her a pair of headphones as he settled into the seat beside her. "Hang on. We'll be there in a few minutes."

Felicity did just that. Her heart pounding in her chest, she clung to the edge of her seat. She'd never been in a helicopter before. The vibrations unsettled her, as did the sensation of lift. They shot straight up before moving forward, heading out toward the ocean, into the setting sun.

Where could they possibly be going, she wondered, until a large vessel came into view. They headed straight for it and the helipad on the top deck. The pilot set the helicopter down lightly, as though he'd performed the action many times before. He quickly killed the engine at a signal from Blake. When the rotor blades had ceased their movement, Blake took the headphones from her and offered her his hand. "Come inside with me," he urged.

Felicity let herself be drawn forward, out of the helicopter, across the deck, and onto the main area of a luxurious yacht. Music drifted to them, punctuating the night. As they walked, Felicity gazed up at the full moon and let the restless breeze settle the nervousness that twisted her stomach into a knot. They were on a yacht in the middle of the Pacific Ocean. This was not anything she could have imagined when she'd accepted Blake's invitation. She had nowhere to hide for the next several hours. She was at his mercy.

He turned toward her and smiled tenderly, as though reading her thoughts.

"Everything will be all right, Felicity. You're safe here."

For some reason, she believed him as she allowed him to pull her inside the main cabin. People turned to watch as they entered the crowded ballroom. In the past she would have felt terribly self-conscious with so many eyes searching her, but not tonight. Wrapped in an incredibly sumptuous gown, with a smoky quartz and diamond necklace at her throat and her hair coiled up in an intricate knot, she felt carefree and calm.

On the far side of the room a four-piece orchestra was playing Vivaldi, but only a few strains could be heard above the conversation and the delicate clink of glasses. White-coated waiters circulated among the guests, offering canapés and Moët et Chandon champagne.

A gleaming wood floor sparkled beneath her feet and crystal chandeliers glittered overhead. An ice sculpture of an open giant clamshell dominated the buffet and was filled to overflowing with succulent shrimp. Beside the ice sculpture sat beluga caviar, lobster, light pastry confections, and a colorful display of tropical fruit.

Blake took two champagne flutes from a waiter's tray and handed one to her. Sipping her champagne, she watched as the guests ebbed and flowed throughout the large room, laughing and dancing and having a good time. She thought she recognized at least three movie stars among the crowd. "Are these people friends of yours?" she asked, studying a man in a white headdress with a robe created from gold and silver thread.

"He's a sheik and a friend of mine. He likes spending time on my boat when he's in town. Over there is the British consul to Hawai'i, and next to him is Reid Fairfax, owner of the *Seattle Gazette*. Let me introduce you around."

"This is your yacht?"

He nodded. "A guy's got to have a few toys."

"Are there any forms of transportation you don't own?"

He lifted his brows, considering, then smiled. "I don't have a rocket, yet."

She returned his smile. "Well, then you better get on that."

"I'll see what I can do." His smile filled with contentment as he slipped his arm around her waist and pulled her forward into the crowd.

For the next hour, they mingled with his guests. She met many people she would never have had access to if it hadn't been for Blake.

He told everyone about her restaurant, and several people made promises to come see her there on their next trip through Seattle. And while she enjoyed speaking with each person she met, she came away from the whole thing feeling a little sad.

Though he'd introduced these people as friends, not one of them asked him anything personal or inquired about his uncle's recent death.

She knew how lonely her own teenage years had been with a father who didn't speak and her need to avoid bringing attention to her situation. Had Blake's past been even worse despite his status? He might have all the money in the world, but was that what really mattered? Was that why he came looking for her? Despite all the people who surrounded him each and every day, he was lonely.

"You look suddenly very intense. Care to share your thoughts?" Blake asked over the sudden rise in excitement in the room.

"I'm just overwhelmed by all this," she said, hoping he didn't ask anything more. He didn't as the noise in the room increased. The crowd parted and Felicity got her first look at the source of the commotion as Rihanna strode forward and took the microphone at the front of the room.

"A friend of yours?" Felicity asked, slightly breathless with surprise.

"As one of her supporters, she does the occasional special event for me." Blake's cocky smile faded as Rihanna's voice filled the room. "Dance with me, Felicity."

A tremor ran through her entire body as he caressed her elbow, encouraging her forward into his arms for a slow dance to the lyrics of "Stay."

Blake's arm slid around her waist, and his left hand closed around her fingers. He moved to the music with effortless ease, taking her with him across the dance floor.

"I've never danced with a woman as enchanting as you," Blake whispered close to her ear.

A thrill moved through her. "You're just saying that so I'll stop stepping on your feet."

"You can step on my feet anytime whenever we are this close and you look this lovely." Felicity's breath caught in her chest at the husky timbre of his voice and the desire in his eyes. For one breathless moment, his smoldering eyes studied her face feature by feature while he slowly pulled her closer against his chest. His head bent and his mouth claimed hers in a kiss of violent tenderness and tormenting desire. The fingers splayed against her back, and Felicity felt all her resistance, all her will begin to crumble and disintegrate.

She kissed him back with her whole heart.

The music faded as Blake dragged his lips from hers. "Felicity, I—"

"May I have the next dance?" the man Blake had introduced as Reid Fairfax said, offering her his hand.

Blake held her a moment longer, as though hesitant to let her go.

"Do I want to—?"

"Dance." Reid lifted her hand from Blake's shoulder and placed it on his own, pulling her out of Blake's arms. An odd expression settled on Blake's face. If she didn't know better, she would have to say he looked almost sad to see her go.

Rihanna's next song was a faster tempo, for which Felicity was grateful as the older man led her across the room to the sound of "Umbrella," blocking her view of Blake.

"It's a very small world, Ms. Wright. We both live in Washington State, yet we're here in Hawai'i at the same time. What are the chances?"

"Well, since we're both friends of Blake's and this is his yacht, I'd say pretty good." Felicity wasn't sure why, but something about the man set her on edge.

His teeth clenched and something beyond desperation lurked behind his eyes for a moment, then vanished as quickly as it had appeared. "Clever."

Felicity wasn't sure the word was a compliment.

Reid smiled. "Nevertheless, I'm glad you could accompany Blake on this adventure. He has so little time for fun."

"Are you his social director now?" she asked, stopping her movements, no longer in the mood to dance.

Reid's laugh boomed out. "You are a funny one, Ms. Wright." He released his grip on her.

The music she'd only moments before enjoyed turned discordant.

Just then, Blake appeared at her side, pinning Reid with a dire look. "Everything okay?" he asked, placing a hand on her back in a protective fashion as he'd done before. His touch was warm, welcome. "I'll take it from here," Blake said, escorting her away.

Felicity cast a glance back over her shoulder as Blake escorted her from the room and didn't miss the self-satisfied smile that pulled up the corners of Reid's mouth. He wanted Blake to come to her rescue. It was almost as if he'd wanted the younger man to feel a hint of jealousy.

The question was, why?

"What is your relationship with Reid Fairfax?" she asked as Blake escorted her through the doorway and down the stairs toward a hallway lined with staterooms.

"We're acquaintances, nothing more. Why do you ask?"

"And yet he's here tonight."

Blake stopped before one of the rooms. Withdrawing a keycard from his suit jacket, he waved it in front of the card reader. A soft click sounded, the door released and he twisted the handle and threw open the door. His fingertips trailed sensuously down her arm. The fire that always seemed to smolder between them flared to life.

"He invited himself." Blake stepped aside and waved her through the doorway.

"Where are we going?"

"My stateroom, because neither of us can keep up the pretense any longer," he said bluntly.

Felicity wanted to deny it, but she couldn't. The unveiled passion in his eyes found an answering response within her.

She stepped into the elaborately appointed room, fully aware as she did that she was accepting what came next. Stalling to allow her heartbeat to settle, she glanced around the sitting area. The cabin was well decorated with a cream-colored plush sofa facing two soft leather chairs. The room was breathtakingly elegant with its gold accents and contrasting red pillows.

In the center of a low cocktail table was an arrangement of orchids. Blake snapped one off and twirled it in his fingers as he moved toward her. "For you." He slid the flower behind her ear. The soft, fruity scent enveloped her.

Her heart fluttered in her chest as he pulled her into his arms and traced his finger across the top of her ear where the orchid petals met her skin. "Do you like exotic flowers?"

"They're pretty. Hard to care for," she said, unable to stop the quaver in her voice. "I prefer roses."

"Good to know," he said as he bent his head and kissed her, skillfully parting her lips and laying claim. She knew why he was kissing her—knew what his purpose was—and even though she suspected he had every intention of seducing her, she didn't in that moment care.

What she cared about was the heat smoldering between them, the fire in her blood reigniting that unfulfilled passion she'd experienced in her dream yesterday. He wanted her, and she wanted him.

That was enough of a reason to set aside her reservations and move against him, demanding his heated attention in return. Tonight, she wanted to forget about the hotel and only think about the way he made her feel, because in his arms she could surrender herself to the flames of her passion.

She hesitated only a heartbeat as her thoughts went back to this morning and the photographer Blake had sent away. But just as quickly as the thought came, it vanished. They were on a yacht in the middle of an ocean. Who would disturb them there?

The tension from a moment ago eased, replaced with the need to kiss Blake back with all the pent-up desire she'd been denying since they'd first met. She parted her lips and surrendered. A groan of pure desire escaped his lips, encouraging her. She taunted and teased, then delighted when he deepened the kiss. The heat rising between them melted her bones, and she surrendered. She knew where they were headed, and it was already impossible to change their course. There was no reason they should. She was tired of fighting the passion that flared so powerfully between them.

His arms tightened around her, crushing her breasts—already peaked and tight and aching—to the hard solid planes of his chest. His hand swept down her back, pressing her to him, then sliding lower, over her hip. He grasped her bottom and angled her hips to his so he could move against her, so he could mold her against the rigid length of his erection, let her feel and anticipate having that hard length inside her, taking her to new heights.

He broke the kiss and stared down at her with those midnight eyes, eyes dark with passion—passion she'd stirred to life, passion that had turned every muscle in his body to hard-edged steel. Carefully he slid the silk from her shoulders and reached for the zipper hidden at the side of her dress.

A whisper of sound punctuated their breathing. With careful fingers, he spread her dress apart and eased it down her waist and over her hips, letting it pool around her feet. He slowly lowered his head and licked her nipple lazily.

A hot shiver moved through her. His tongue was warm and moist. His breath on her skin was like a thousand fingertips caressing her. Her knees felt weak and rubbery as she looked down at his dark head bent over her breast. When his teeth toyed with the hardened bud, a streak of fire seared through her, and she felt the muscles of her stomach clench.

She could feel herself readying for him, feel the lust forcing away the last fragment of reason from her mind. Waves of heat engulfed her, making her long for him in ways she'd never expected. "Blake—" The word was part whisper, part plea.

He straightened, and she took the opportunity to slide her fingers beneath his tuxedo jacket and slip it from his shoulders. It fell to the floor atop her dress. She reached to unbutton his shirt, then tossed it aside, hungrily gliding her hands over his chest.

He lifted her, and she wrapped her legs around his waist as he captured her lips once more. She gloried in a wave of intense pleasure at the feel of his hard, developed abs flexing between her thighs, fueling the fire that Blake had lit within her from the moment they first touched. Still locked together, he carried her across the room and kicked open a door, revealing a pristine white bed. He carried her to the edge and carefully laid her down. A heartbeat later, his pants were gone. He stretched out beside her and slowly, seductively sketched his palms over her naked flesh.

Her skin burned wherever he touched, leaving trails of searing sensation across her breasts, her arms, her waist, her thighs. Wherever his hands went, his lips followed. Heat danced across her flesh. The tension built, higher and higher, until she thought she would burst from sheer pleasure.

She was breathless when he drew back to stare into her face. In his eyes she saw a fire unlike any she had seen before. "You are truly a beautiful woman." His voice was hoarse, raspy.

The way he looked at her made her feel beautiful and so many other tumultuous emotions. She wanted him with the same urgent, scorching passion with which he wanted her. That knowledge made her bold as she splayed her fingers against his rock-hard chest. She brushed his nipples with her fingertips and was rewarded with a strangled gasp from him. Emboldened by her success, she allowed her hands to drift lower down his narrow waist, to the apex of his legs, until her hand curled around his hardened length.

His jaw clenched and his head lolled back as she continued her delicious torture, stroking his silken length with delicate hands. Never before had she allowed herself to be this bold, to take control, to have her partner at her mercy. A thrill coiled through the heat flooding her limbs. It was wildly exciting, the thought that she could bring such a powerful man as Blake to this place of carnal delight.

His hands clenched, and he brought his gaze back to hers. His hooded eyes only partially concealed his smoldering gaze. "I need you, Felicity."

The intensity of his passion tightened her chest. "Yes," she breathed, barely able to force the single word from her dry throat.

He pulled her against him, then rose up on his knees. From the nightstand beside the bed, he withdrew a small silver packet and quickly slipped protection over himself. He moved over her, settling between her thighs. His lips claimed hers again with tormenting sweetness, and her body responded to the intimate sensuality of his demand. She pressed herself against his hardening body, wanting more as the flames of desire consumed her.

He thrust in.

Her body arched under his. She moaned, the sound trapped in their kiss. She reveled in the sensation of him, so rigid and heavy, moving within her. She met him, matched his rhythm, wound her legs about his hips, drawing him deeper. Her heart pounded so hard she couldn't get her breath. Her hands clutched futilely at his shoulders as she thrust upward, taking as much of him as he offered her.

With a low cry of wild satisfaction, she matched his rhythm, delighting as he stroked her hard and fast, then slow and gentle. As soon as she grew accustomed to one rhythm, he changed it, the tension inside her coiling tighter and tighter. His thrusts grew deeper and faster. She hovered on the brink until the tension exploded with a force that sent a fiery release through every muscle in her body.

An instant later, she could feel Blake spasm again and again within her, feel him shatter around her in a glorious release.

Spent, he slumped on her. She could feel his heart racing, pounding against her chest, feel the tempo of his heart echo where they were still joined.

She drew a slow, shallow breath of satisfaction, then raised a hand to his hair and, tentatively, caressed. He nestled against her as a quiet, tender moment ticked past.

His heartbeat gradually slowed; his breathing eased. Finally he stirred, withdrew, and moved off her only to settle against her side, his hot flesh against her own. His hands refused to release her as he played with her exposed breasts, stroking, circling, teasing, as if he was afraid to let the moment end.

Dear God, what had just happened between them, Felicity wondered dazedly. She had never in her life experienced anything like her intense encounter with Blake.

"I lost control," he said, his voice still uneven, the tone a caress.

She hadn't ever dreamed such satisfaction or satiation were possible as a heavy languid sensation pulsed through her blood. "We both lost control." She laughed shakily.

The physical vortex they'd just created had been wild, mind-bending, sense shattering—just as he'd claimed it would be. Clearly the man had delivered on that promise. But he'd led her to that emotional whirlpool not as partners or lovers, but as friends. Intimate friends. Sexual equals.

When he'd made her his offer in her kitchen on the night they'd first met, she'd never thought it would happen. And just for the time being, she wanted to lock down the part of her brain that objected, wanted to force out reason in an effort to keep herself from getting hurt.

She studied Blake's profile. His lips quirked, and she recognized the fleeting smile for what it was—smug, male satisfaction.

"What are you thinking about?" she asked, unable to help herself as she realized she wanted him all over again.

"That you are so unexpected." He turned toward her and slid his hand to her cheek, cupping it gently.

"You are every bit as devastating as I knew you would be." At his broad smile, she turned her face into his hand, kissing his palm.

A groan tore from his chest. He twisted onto his side and trailed his hand from her cheek, down her abdomen, until his fingers settled playfully in the curls protecting her womanhood. "If you don't stop that, I might need to be devastating once more," Blake teased.

She arched her brow. "Is seduction what you planned all along when you brought me to the *Eclipse*?"

He tugged her curls teasingly. "Yes and no. I really did have something to show you on the deck above us."

"What's that?" she asked teasingly.

His fingers delved in her wet heat, and she could feel herself readying for him again. "Indulge me once more, then I promise to show you."

Without another word, Felicity did.

CHAPTER FOURTEEN

Hours later, when all the other guests at the party had either left or gone to their own cabins for the night, Blake listened to the rustle of the water against the hull of the ship. His eyes, however, were on the woman leaning against the railing beside him. He slid his arms around Felicity's slim waist hidden beneath his tuxedo shirt. She'd slipped into his shirt instead of her dress when he'd asked her to come with him to the top deck.

Her blonde hair caressed his naked chest, and the delicate scent of her caused his head to swim and his groin to tighten once more. He in his tuxedo pants and bare feet. She in his shirt and nothing else.

Felicity nestled back against his chest, and her gaze fixed on the distance. "What is it you wanted to show me?"

He drew in her fragrance as he gathered her even closer. The light of the full moon overhead cast a silvered glow across the ocean. "The stars."

"What do the stars have to do with the environment or your efforts to sway my opinion to your side?"

"Nothing at all. I just wanted to show you the stars. I had no ulterior motive."

A soft breeze continued to tousle Felicity's hair as she tipped her head back and searched the inky black sky. Thousands of stars glittered like diamonds overhead. With no other lights around, it was easy to see not only the stars, but the planets, satellites as they rotated about the Earth, and the Milky Way as it stretched across the sky in a swath of orange and gold. "I don't think I've ever seen anything so beautiful," she breathed.

He pulled her closer and kissed her lightly on the top of the head. "I've seen this sight a hundred times. But with you, it's like I'm seeing it all over again."

"Do you stargaze often?"

"I wanted to be an astronomer when I was young. I spent so much time alone, but wherever I went the stars were there, watching over me. I've never told that to anyone ever before," he admitted with a chuckle. "What about you? If you could do anything or be anything, what would that be?"

She pressed her lips together in thought, then said, "If money were no consideration, I'd want to own a kitchen, maybe a whole building that was dedicated to my Hungry Hearts program. Nothing makes me happier."

"Very admirable."

She shrugged. "I'm not so sure it's as noble as all that. I'm the one whose life is changed each time someone new walks into my program."

"You give a part of yourself to each of them, too. I saw that while we worked in your kitchen with your students."

Felicity accepted his compliment, but as she did, he reflected on how he and Felicity approached their passions in very different ways. She worked to change the people of the world while he had focused his efforts on the environment. She took a risk each and every time she reached out to someone in need. He played it safe. Effecting change in the environment never forced him to put himself out there or risk his heart; only his pocketbook was on the line. Disappointment filled him as he returned his gaze to the stars. Even his fascination with the heavens kept the things that intrigued him at a distance.

Why was he so afraid to take a risk, to put himself out there and possibly feel pain? He was a wealthy man, yet he couldn't afford to let anyone into his heart. That uncomfortable knowledge settled around him as he pulled Felicity even closer against his front, drawing her warmth to him, allowing her to once again melt the icy places deep inside.

It felt so good to be near her. So right.

CHAPTER FIFTEEN

After a day spent teaching Felicity the ins and outs of running a hotel the size of Mano Kea, Blake walked Felicity back to their suite. Sitting on the sofa in the sitting area was the large, red box tied with a white bow that he'd asked the hotel manager to deliver to their room.

"What's this?" Felicity asked, moving to the sofa.

"It's for you."

Frowning, she untied the bow and opened the box. Her breath caught as her gaze snapped to his. "A chef's coat, black pants, and red Hawaiian-print skullcap? What's this for?"

"We have a luau at the hotel every Saturday. Haku wanted to know if you would be interested in helping him prepare the dishes this evening."

Gratitude shone in her eyes and an answering warmth curled inside him. "I'd be delighted." She scooped up the garments and headed to her side of the suite to change. She reappeared five minutes later, wearing her chef's outfit and a smile.

For the first time in a long while, joy filled him simply because of her smile. "Ready?" he asked.

"For cooking? Always."

They went to the kitchen, and Haku immediately set Blake to the task of peeling, then slicing several mangos that would be used for garnish, while Felicity helped the Hawaiian chef prepare two different sauces to be used in the feast to come.

After he'd finished preparing the mangos, Blake watched Felicity as she moved around the kitchen, her features soft and at peace. Cooking seemed to center her as nothing else did. For the first time, he wondered about the hardships she'd talked about in her anger the day before yesterday. What horrors had she experienced that had created the woman before him? Suddenly it was imperative he know.

With a frown, he watched her work. He could push Marcus harder, hire detectives to do all the usual things he did to his business associates as well as his enemies. Yet with Felicity, such tactics were starting to seem . . . wrong. He'd never really cared much about his business rivals' feelings before he'd negotiated with Donald Jamison over the Heritage Hotel. Was it Felicity's influence that had made him suddenly hold himself to a higher standard?

He watched her transfixed. He'd never seen a more beguiling woman in his life. Despite her chef's coat, he could still see a hint of her shapely curves that were hidden from his view. The white of the garments she wore were the perfect complement to her developing tan and blonde hair. She looked healthy and relaxed—and as sexy as a woman could look fully dressed.

His body hardened at the sight. The more he watched her, the more he wanted her.

She stirred a large pot at the stove, then reached for a ramekin and placed a dollop of sauce inside. She dipped her finger into the contents, bringing it up to her lips to taste. His breath caught at the motion.

Moving to her side, he caught her hand and brought that same finger to his lips, taking it into his mouth, tasting the sauce mixed with the sweetness of Felicity herself. A strange shiver moved through his body at the whisper-soft feel of her finger against the roughness of his tongue.

"Delicious," he breathed.

A blush rose to her cheeks as she shot a glance at Haku. He continued moving about the kitchen, ignoring the two of them. "When will our guests arrive?" she asked as she drew her hand from Blake's grasp.

"In two hours." He stared down at her, at those parted lips that beckoned him. It had been so long since he'd had someone to share things with. Someone who filled an emptiness inside him he hadn't known existed before she entered his life.

Despite being around people every hour of every day, he hadn't realized how lonely he'd been until he looked into her wide, intelligent eyes. He'd been completely unprepared for her.

Her face was so close he could see the flecks of gold in her eyes. She stared at him without blinking, and he felt as if he could see straight into her soul—and it was a frightened, vulnerable place like his own. For the first time in his life, he considered giving her insight into his own life. He'd never trusted anyone enough to do that. His heart sped up. He stood there motionless, waiting while he considered what to do.

"Thank you for sharing the secrets of your success with me today. I know you didn't have to do that. I have a few ideas I'd like to implement at the Bancroft when I return to Seattle."

"You're welcome. Now, don't we have a luau to cook for?" The answering warmth in her eyes brought a grin to his face. A feeling of camaraderie clung to them. Something new and fragile had blossomed between them over the past few days, and he was loath to let the feeling end. He twisted toward the table beside him and picked up an abandoned apron from the stainless steel surface.

"How may I be of assistance?"

She arched a brow. "You want to help me cook?"

"My services don't come cheap."

She crossed her arms before her and gave him a level look. "Of course they don't. All right, what's this 'help' going to cost me?"

"A kiss."

She hesitated, looking across the kitchen at Haku.

"Don't mind me," the Hawaiian said with a smile. "I'll have my own payment later when I force you to fix me up with one of your good-looking friends from the mainland."

Felicity's smile broadened. "I'll see what I can do."

Humming a tune, Haku left the kitchen to go check on the pig roasting in the pit.

Blake curled his hand around the nape of her neck and anchored her to him. He lowered his head and his lips molded to hers, moving slowly and sensually. The kiss lasted forever and beyond. With each second, each flick of her tongue against his, Blake felt his need for her swell, until he thought he would burst from wanting her. Finally, with a groan, he pulled back, releasing her.

"Best bargaining terms ever," she said breathlessly against his cheek.

Invisible hands clutched his heart and squeezed at her words. He set her away from him even though he desperately wanted to pull her back into his arms. "And you're making me consider a career change as your prep chef."

She grinned and handed him a spoon. "Stir this while I get the other ingredients for the Huli Huli chicken."

"Okay, boss." He would do anything she asked of him, if it meant they'd get to the luau sooner and he could get her alone to indulge himself in her sweetness more fully.

◆ ◆ ◆

A soft breeze cooled the warmth from the day as Felicity sat among the crowd while Polynesian dancers entertained them with movement and fire, legend and mystery. The food they'd prepared had been well received by their guests who sat at their tables, watching the show. The rhythm of the Hawaiian drums matched the tempo of her heartbeat. Her body tensed as she fought the desire to tap her foot to the beat.

The heady sweetness of hibiscus lingered in the night air, seducing her every bit as much as the fire in Blake's eyes. All afternoon as she worked alongside Blake, she could feel herself changing. It was as if his very presence in her life brought the sunshine that had been missing for years, lighting all the cold dark places she hid from everyone else.

The music, the drum, the fire, the sweet scent of the night, all conspired against her, filling her with need. When the festivities were complete and Blake stood and reached for her hand, she didn't hesitate.

He brought her hand to his lips. His eyes locked with hers as he kissed each one of her fingers. He turned her hand over and allowed his lips to press against the inside of her palm. He let his lips linger just long enough for her to tremble at the intimacy of his touch. Her breath caught when he pulled back and, without a word, led her inside the hotel, up the stairs, and to their suite.

And willingly she followed.

In the privacy of their room, the beat of the drums remained in the echo of her heart, filling her with that same need, that same desire, that had to be quenched.

Blake stood facing her as desire leaped to life in his blue eyes. "I know you feel it, too. The rhythm. The magic."

She swallowed roughly and didn't deny the truth.

"I want to spend the night with you, in your bed, not mine. I want morning to come and for the two of us to wake there together. No seduction, no coercion. A choice we both made," he said, his voice deep and low.

"Yes," she whispered her response.

Then she was in his arms, and he was kissing her. His lean, hard body was pressing against her own. His kisses were warm and intimate and more fervent than usual as he lifted her in his arms and carried her to her side of the suite and on into her bedroom, before shutting the door and everything else out.

She took out her phone and turned it off. "No interruptions."

He smiled, took out his phone, and did the same. Then, leaving the world behind, they undressed each other slowly. She feasted on his body—his muscular chest, the strength of his arms, the flat belly leading downward . . .

She reached down to touch him, eliciting a groan of response. Emboldened by her success, she caressed his tender flesh until he laid her against the crisp sheets. She touched him in places she'd never explored before, caressed him until desire swept away both restraint and thought. Left only with sensation and feeling to cling to, her kisses grew hungrier, more demanding. His tantalizing assault left her senses reeling and her nerves skittering as she tried to urge him on.

But he was in no hurry tonight, even though the heat between them was palpable. His kisses went on as he explored every nuance of her body, as he left her senses whirling at the edges of that vortex of pleasured delight. He overwhelmed her senses and reduced her to mindless need, filled her with a craving that went past logic and straight to her core.

She arched into him, inviting his touch when he finally relented and settled between her legs. He tilted her hips beneath him and pressed slowly into her body until she felt his possession inch by inch, felt every nuance of his penetration stretching her, filling her, completing her.

He filled her completely, his gaze never leaving hers. His chest rose and fell with the force of his breathing as he slowly pulled out, then filled her again. The slowness of his movements sent her senses spiraling. She closed her eyes and gave herself over to the flames— burning, melting, as pleasure spilled through every glorious part of her being.

Blake cried out. The sound struck her to her very soul as pleasure racked them both and flung them into the waiting abyss. It might have been minutes or hours later when they floated back to Earth in each other's arms. As satiation dragged them down, Blake pulled her against his body and smoothed her hair from her face, staring at her as though for the first time.

"Neither of us can turn back the clocks on our past, but I need to know . . . after your anger the day before yesterday, I wondered, was it all bad? Do you not have any happy memories at all?"

She drew back, searching his face. Was he searching for information, or did he seriously want to know more about her? Her heart told her the latter, and she smiled and squeezed his hand, signaling to him without words that she, too, felt the connection between them. "There were happy times. Lots of them, despite being poor." Before the accident, there were memories of birthdays, picnics by the Sound, movies in the park . . . after the accident, not as many, but she was certain even then there were a few happy moments when she hadn't been hungry or worried.

He brushed his fingers over hers. "You flourished in spite of it, but you don't have to be so strong with me. I'll take care of you," he said, then started as though the words were a surprise even to him.

"I don't want to be taken care of," she said softly. "I want a partner. I want what my parents had—companionship and love. Even though they were poor, they always had everything they needed in each other." What she wouldn't give for a relationship like the one her parents had shared—where their laughter had filled the house no matter if they were doing chores together or cuddling on the couch. She'd been a witness to their love—an honest and true love. She wanted that for herself.

Blake pulled her closer, wrapping her in his warmth even as a shiver racked his body. "The saying that money can't buy everything is true, because my parents never got along. I always wondered why they stayed together. Uncle Vernon wasn't pleased the day my father came home from a weekend away, married to a woman he'd met only the day before. My mother was a wonderful person, but she was no one of importance. Uncle Vernon was furious that she would be the one to continue the Bancroft family line. He made no secret of that displeasure. I always assumed that was why he hated me."

"Hate is a strong word."

"What else can explain why he didn't want me with him after my parents died? He took me in for two weeks before sending me away. I never lived with him again after that."

"Maybe he sent you away because he was mourning the loss of his brother, or maybe he was regretful of the way he'd always treated your mother, or maybe you reminded Vern of himself at that age." She stopped talking as a smile warmed his face. "What?"

"That's one of the many things I love about you. You never see a fault in anyone." He leaned forward and kissed her. He didn't add any additional words to their conversation. In fact, he didn't say another word for a very long time. Instead, he spoke with actions in the way his hands drifted over her body.

And while he did, one word he'd said drifted through her thoughts: *love*. He'd said it so casually, the way so many other people did, as a more intense version of liking something. Yet those four letters didn't resonate with her that way. Was that what he'd meant, or did he mean something more?

And as she gave herself over to the pleasure he evoked, she couldn't forget the one thing that still stood between them—the ownership of the Bancroft Hotel. Their physical relationship changed nothing. In fact, it complicated matters even more, because the day was soon approaching where one of them would have to concede. Someone would win, someone would lose, and the casualty of that decision would be one or the other of them.

CHAPTER SIXTEEN

The next day, Felicity woke and slipped from the bed, leaving Blake still asleep. Last night she'd seen the pain in his eyes when he'd told her about his parents. And she'd seen that same look when he'd told her about Vern sending him away. Why had Vern kept his only living relative at a distance? He must always have been as disagreeable as he was to most of the staff at the hotel. The bigger question was why befriend her?

Felicity showered and dressed while Blake continued to sleep. She had to pack and get ready to return to the mainland. A part of her was sad to leave the splendor of the island behind. Yet if they stayed any longer, she feared what she might do when filled with emotion. Twice yesterday she'd almost given him the Bancroft despite her fears about what would happen to the staff.

She paced the sitting area of the suite, looking out the big picture windows at the breathtaking view of Poipu Beach below. The sun was just coming up and casting golden rays across the palms and tropical foliage, making the soft rain from last night look like sparkling jewels on the deep green leaves.

Rain she understood. Rain she was used to. It was best for her to return to Seattle and keep her wits about her until she could make a logical decision about how they would move forward with the Bancroft and . . .

She couldn't finish the thought. She wasn't certain if there was anything else for them past this trip. Blake had given her no indication of such a thing. Besides, he lived in San Francisco. She lived in Seattle. And while long-distance relationships weren't impossible, it wasn't ultimately what she wanted. She'd liked going to sleep in Blake's arms last night and waking up the same way.

For the first time in her life, something had been easy and spontaneous. But if Blake remained in her life, would anything ever be normal? They came from such different worlds. That was one thing she hadn't revealed to him last night, just how impoverished she had been. Not because she was embarrassed by her early poverty, but because she'd pushed those memories so deep, it was hard to pull them back without experiencing the same terror she'd gone to sleep with each night as a child.

Those memories were better off tucked deep inside.

"Morning, gorgeous." Blake came up behind her and slipped his arms around her waist, pulling her back against his chest. He kissed the top of her head and handed her her cell phone. "You left this in the bedroom."

"Thanks," she said, turning it on and nestling back against his chest.

"Did you sleep well?" he asked.

She turned in his arms to smile up at him. "Better than I can ever remember."

His eyes filled with pleasure. "The island does that to you."

"It was more than the island," she said, impulsively lifting up on her toes to kiss him. Her phone buzzed, indicating someone had left a message while it had been turned off. It buzzed again. Another message. Then again. And again. She pulled back out of his embrace and stared down at the screen. "I have thirteen missed calls." Eleven calls had been from Mary Beth and two from the assisted living facility where her father lived. A chill slid through her as she accessed her voice mail. Trying to be positive and not read anything into the calls, she quickly accessed her messages.

Felicity stood stock still as she listened. A desperate cry lodged in her throat.

Her father . . .

The words crashed through her brain and a great weight pressed down on her lungs. Through a distant, detached part of her brain, she heard Blake talking to her, but the words sounded far away, jumbled, until he reached out and took her by the shoulders. "Felicity?"

"I have to go home."

"What's wrong?"

"My father. They released him from the hospital this morning. Mary Beth took him back to the assisted living facility where he lives, but now he's gone."

His face paled. "Gone, as in missing or dead?"

"Missing," she said. "For the first time in sixteen years he walked out the door, and no one knows where he is."

Concern flashed in Blake's eyes a moment before he palmed his own phone.

Their time in Hawai'i was over. She had to go home, and as quickly as possible.

CHAPTER SEVENTEEN

While the luxury of Blake's plane was not completely lost on Felicity as they took off, the six-hour flight seemed endless. She sat in the padded leather seat in the main cabin, wishing with every mile that they would touch down in Seattle already.

She stared out the airplane's small oval window, seeing her own reflection in the Plexiglas. Her eyes looked like two smudges of black on an ashen canvas as she fought back tears.

Guilt swamped her. She never should have left her father so soon after his procedure. Even though the doctor had said there was very little that could go wrong and had encouraged her to take a few days for herself, she should have known that something would happen. She'd never had the kind of luck that others experienced.

The thought brought her up short. She couldn't really say that, not after what Vern had done for her. His gift of the hotel and the restaurant had started her down a different path. If anything was to blame, it was her own inability to afford better care for her father.

Felicity sat in her seat, unable to move, her stomach tightening. She'd talked with Mary Beth twice before the plane had taken off, trying to reassure her friend that she wasn't to blame. She'd also talked with the assisted living facility to learn her father had slipped out of his room and out of the facility while the staff had been changing from the night to morning shift. They'd reviewed their security tapes and had witnessed him walking down the back stairs and out the door, heading south. Every spare employee at the facility was out combing the streets of Seattle for her father. Because of her father's medical condition, the police had been alerted and the twenty-four-hour waiting period for a missing person had been waived. They were doing what they could to find her father, but was it enough? She squeezed her eyes shut. Beside her, Blake talked on a satellite phone. She'd given him permission to call in his own people to help aid in the search.

Where was her father?

Blake got off the phone, and she knew a moment of hope until he shook his head, confirming her worst fears. "No one can find him. I've hired two detectives and their teams to find where he's gone. By the time we touch down, we'll know something."

Felicity drew a deep, steadying breath. There was no time for fear or panic. Later she could fall apart, once they'd found him and figured out what was wrong. Her father needed her to be strong.

Blake knelt before her and drew her into his arms, holding her close. A shudder moved through her. "We'll get there, and everything will be okay."

If only that could be the truth.

When the plane's wheels finally hit the tarmac and the door of the cabin was pushed aside, Blake reported that the detectives had found her father's location. "He's in a house in Seattle. I have the address. They say he's unharmed. He's simply waiting there for something."

"What house?"

He told her the address, and her stomach plummeted. Why would her father go back to the one place she'd worked so hard to escape? "Hurry, Blake, please? He's at the trailer park where I grew up."

Without saying anything more, Blake guided her down the air stairs and to a waiting car. Peter sat behind the wheel. He nodded to her a moment before he fired the engine and drove off the runway at Boeing Field. For a moment, she wondered how the driver could be behind the wheel so quickly when he had also been on their flight, but she gave up questioning Blake's abilities several days ago. He had the resources to move mountains if he wanted to. Finding her father so quickly was proof of that.

As the car sped toward South Seattle, Felicity tried to push away the weight of her guilt without much success. When they pulled up in front of the dilapidated single-wide trailer, she hopped out. Only when she approached the detectives waiting in the yard, did she slow down. She looked past them to see her father sitting on the porch with his legs crossed, staring into the distance.

At her approach, he turned toward her, and Felicity's heart faltered. Tears streamed down his cheeks. It wasn't the tears that sent a shudder of both fear and hope through her, it was the spark of awareness that lit her father's eyes.

Felicity couldn't breathe as hope built. "Dad?"

His mouth worked, but no sound emerged. Yet it was more of a reaction than she'd seen in him since the accident.

Answering tears leaped to her lashes. She moved to her father's side. Gently, she placed a hand on his cheek. "I'm here, Dad. I won't leave you alone again." Other than being covered with dust, he looked as he always did, except for the light of awareness in his eyes.

Her tears spilled onto her cheeks. "It's me, Dad, Felicity."

Blake knelt beside her and touched her shoulder. "Let's get him out of here."

The tender look in his eyes stole her breath. "Okay."

Blake scooped her father up in his arms. He staggered for a moment from the weight, but made his way to the car. "To the hospital," he said to Peter when her father was settled in the car between them.

"No," Felicity interrupted. "Take him to the Bancroft. I want him with me."

Without a word of objection, they headed to the Bancroft Hotel in record time. They managed to get her father in the front door and into a transport chair, then up to her suite. There, Blake once again lifted the older man from the chair and settled him on the gold and black contemporary sofa.

"I called the paramedics. They're just outside the door, waiting to check him out," Blake said.

She nodded, then stepped back, allowing the medical professionals to make the determination if her father was well enough to remain at the Bancroft. When they were done checking his vitals as well as his surgical site, they gave her the okay to keep him with her. She was reluctant to put him back into the assisted living home he'd escaped, for fear that painful memories lingered there as he remembered what had happened all those years ago. Why else would he have gone back to the house if he wasn't remembering? His brain was starting up again.

Felicity's heart wrenched at the coiled emotions in her father's eyes—pain, acceptance, fear, gratitude. Again, she placed a loving hand to his cheek and smiled. "I'm glad you're with me again, Dad."

His lips quivered, then the corner of one pulled up in a half smile. "Alligator," he said, the word brittle and dry as he forced it out.

Unbridled joy filled her. "After a while, crocodile," she echoed in the phrase he'd said to her every time he left her. Yet he wasn't going away this time. He was here to stay, of that much she was certain.

He said nothing more. It was as if that word cost him most of his energy. He nestled back against the sofa, spent.

Felicity sat beside her father until his eyelids grew heavy and his breathing settled into a slow, even pattern before she moved away.

"You sure he wouldn't be better off in the hospital?" Blake asked.

"No. The EMTs cleared him, and something good is happening here. I don't want to go backward. It's best just to keep him safe and see where this leads. If he does need to go back there, we're close enough for safety's sake."

"You know best."

She hoped she did. Felicity turned her head to watch her father. His breathing was slow and easy.

"Why was he in the hospital?"

Felicity stood and motioned for Blake to follow her to the opposite side of the room. She didn't want anything to wake her father, or worry him. "My father hasn't said one word since my mother's death, not until today." She'd told Blake that much, she might as well tell him the rest. "He had a procedure I paid for with money I saved by moving into the Bancroft. An experimental procedure that was supposed to kick-start his brain."

"Looks like it worked," he said softly.

"Yes," she responded, her throat suddenly tight.

"What happens now?"

She shrugged. "We see what he remembers and get him therapy to help pull out the rest."

"Will it return him to normal?"

"Doubtful, but just the return of some of his speech is more than I'd ever hoped for."

Blake was silent for a long while before he spoke again. "What's next for us, Felicity? Where do we go from here?"

He couldn't be asking her what she thought with that statement. "You mean with the hotel?"

Again, he hesitated. "Of course, what else is there to discuss? Did I convince you of anything in Hawai'i?"

She looked over at the sofa, to her father sleeping there. "I need time to think about things, Blake. This is a big decision for both of us."

He nodded, then turned and left, shutting the door silently behind him.

Taking a seat in the chair opposite the sofa, Felicity looked up at the ceiling and released a soft, nervous laugh as she pondered her options with the hotel. She played out every scenario that came to mind, trying to determine how she and Blake could both win when it came to the Bancroft.

Could she keep the restaurant and give him the hotel? He'd said before that he intended to tear much of the hotel apart. Did that include the Dolce Vita? And if the hotel were under construction, would her clientele still come to dine as they had in the past?

Plus, that solution wouldn't solve any of the problems with her staff. If Blake took over the hotel, they would most likely lose their jobs. And she knew most of them didn't have any savings to carry them through until they found new ones. If new employment were even possible.

What if she sold the property back to him for the million dollars he'd offered her? Could she use all that money to establish a salary fund for her furloughed employees?

But if she kept the Bancroft and the restaurant, things would remain exactly as they were—everything, that was, except her heart. All she'd ever wanted for herself and her father was a normal life, job, house, and family.

Normal did not include owning a restaurant, living in a hotel, or having an extremely pleasant physical relationship with a billionaire. There was nothing normal about any of that. The irony was that she wasn't sure she'd know what to do with normal. Or if she even wanted that anymore.

She liked the extraordinary feeling of owning her own restaurant and hotel. Added to that, nothing would make her happier than to see a spark of awareness in her father's eyes each day when he woke. Then there was Blake. Nothing about him was normal, or easy, or as expected. And she liked him that way.

Since she was trying to be brutally honest with herself, she and Blake had no future together in any of the scenarios she'd thought out. How could they? They were two very different people. They came from two different worlds, miles apart.

Blake might have lost his parents when he was a young man, but he'd had a safety net in his uncle Vern, even if the two of them hadn't gotten along. Money could buy things that she'd only dreamed about when she was growing up.

She'd allowed herself to be vulnerable in Hawai'i. She'd let him sway her with his wealth and his passion for the environment, she'd even given in to the man's seductive pull, but there was one thing left to cling to, and that was the promise of a future for herself, her father, and all the other people she now employed.

The future was what mattered.

◆ ◆ ◆

Later that night, Mary Beth knocked on the door of Felicity's suite. "Can I come in?"

A welcoming smile on her face, Felicity stepped back and let her friend in.

"I'm so relieved you found your dad."

In a hushed voice Felicity said, "Me, too." She waved her hand toward the man sleeping on her sofa.

"Where did you find him?"

"At our old house."

Mary Beth narrowed her eyes on Felicity. "I shudder to think how he went all that way alone. But he looks okay. Is he?"

Felicity nodded. "He spoke to me."

Mary Beth drew a startled breath. "The procedure worked. Oh, Felicity, this is so exciting. Everything you've ever hoped for is coming true."

An eerie chill went up Felicity's spine. "Don't say that."

"Why not?"

"Because every time someone says something like that, the opposite comes true."

Mary Beth arched a brow at that. "Not this time. I heard Blake rushed you back here like a man possessed."

"Out of a sense of obligation for taking me away. He had no idea my father was in the hospital."

"Are you serious?" Mary Beth shook her head. "Is that what you think? Do you really not see the way the man looks at you?"

"He's a businessman who is making a business agreement with me. Nothing more."

Mary Beth's gaze narrowed on Felicity. "Tell me you finally gave in to that man in Hawai'i."

Felicity nodded.

Mary Beth raised her hands toward the sky. "Finally, she listens to me." Then with less drama she added, "I'm glad. I think the two of you would be good together in more ways than one."

Wild longing tore through Felicity. A part of her desperately wanted Mary Beth's belief in her and Blake to be true. Felicity wished she could tell Blake how much she cared about him. She ached to say the words, but doubted he'd want to hear those feelings. He'd had plenty of opportunities to tell her his own feelings in Hawai'i, but he hadn't. Not directly, anyway. She'd been the one to read into his words.

The hotel was all he'd ever wanted from her.

"Why did you stop by?" Felicity asked, trying to force her thoughts in a different direction.

"To see if you want to help with dinner tonight at the restaurant. Marie volunteered to come sit with your dad if you do."

Felicity frowned. "I don't know. I'm hesitant to let him out of my sight now that he's back and remembering."

"How about if, when he wakes up, Marie comes down and sits with him in the restaurant. He'd be close."

"All right," Felicity relented. "When he wakes up. I could use the distraction."

Mary Beth smiled. "Yeah, it must be tough having to think about a man like Blake all the time. Really, Felicity, I think you have the wrong impression about why he's still here. If he wanted to, he could have brought his lawyers into this battle days ago. Instead, he's the one trying to negotiate."

"He offered me a million dollars for the hotel."

Mary Beth's eyes widened. "That's a lot of money."

"The building and the businesses within are worth more than that."

"What's your relationship with Blake worth to you?"

Felicity stiffened. "I have no idea what to believe anymore when it comes to that man. Is he the best thing that has ever happened to any of us, or the worst?"

Mary Beth tilted her head, studying her with a mixture of hope and resignation. "I think you know the truth, if you'd only be willing to acknowledge it."

Felicity's throat closed up at the quiet observation. She didn't like the turn this conversation was taking. It was getting entirely too personal for her. "Blake will show his true colors soon when we must make a decision about the Bancroft. Of that, I have no doubts."

"There might just be a happy ending for all of us because of Blake, especially for you," Mary Beth said with a smile.

Felicity bristled. "I wouldn't count on it. I'm not sure happy endings exist outside of fairy tales."

"Well, maybe it's time for that to change," Mary Beth said, fixing her friend with a look of sheer determination.

CHAPTER EIGHTEEN

"You look happy," Mary Beth said as she moved past Felicity to deliver a fresh batch of focaccia to be sliced and served to their guests.

The door between the restaurant and the kitchen flapped open as Casper entered, revealing a quick glimpse of Felicity's father. He sat at a table in the restaurant with Marie who coaxed him to eat the cioppino Felicity had just sent out for his dinner. On the other side of the kitchen, helping Michael with prep, was Blake. He looked so at ease in her kitchen now, like he belonged there. Felicity allowed herself a satisfied smile. "I am happy. As weird as it seems, everything is going better than it ever has for me. I could get used to this."

No sooner had the words left her mouth, when the door opened again revealing two uniformed police officers. Felicity's body flushed hot then cold as she stared at the two men. What were they doing here? She and the policemen stared at each other for a second before she moved away from the pass-through window and said, "Can I help you?" in what she hoped was a steady voice.

The older of the two uniformed officers stepped forward. "We're working a case, ma'am. We need to speak with Blake Bancroft."

All the voices of her crew died, and the staff members turned to stare at the men as they made their way toward Blake. The only sound in the kitchen was that of sizzling meat. Instinctively, Felicity's eyes moved to where Blake stood beside the prep table.

"Thank you, ma'am, we'll take it from here."

They moved past her to Blake. "Are you Blake Bancroft?" the older officer asked.

"I am," he said, his eyes narrowing on the two men before him. "What's this about?"

"Is there somewhere we can talk privately?" the older officer asked.

Blake's jaw set into a hard line. "Not until you tell me what this is about."

"You've been named as a person of interest in the assault of a young photographer named Jack O'Conner."

"Who?" Felicity asked, coming to Blake's side.

Blake's gaze softened momentarily at he turned to her.

The younger officer responded, "We have a witness who saw you leaving the scene of the attack, and we found your fingerprints on his camera—a camera that was used a few times to bash him over the head."

The photographer from Hawai'i? The one Destiny had sent to capture pictures of her and Blake?

Blake remained silent as he reached inside the pocket of his pants, withdrew his cell phone and placed a call. "Marcus, send my legal team to the Bancroft Hotel immediately. Thanks." He hung up and returned his cell phone to his pocket. "As soon as my lawyers arrive, we can talk about whatever you want."

The young officer paled, but the older man stepped forward and signaled for Blake to walk before him. "We can take you in to the station, if you'd prefer."

"No," Felicity objected. "You can talk in my office." She moved in front of Blake. "Right this way." The four of them made it as far as the doorway of the restaurant before two men with cameras rushed forward, snapping pictures, one after another. And standing off to the side, but instantly recognizable by the bright color of her hair, stood Destiny Carrow.

Felicity froze. Destiny. Photographers. This could not be good for either her or Blake.

"Come on," Blake said as he slipped his arm around her waist, turned her face in to his chest, and hurried them both across the lobby and down the long hallway toward the business office. Once she and the officers were inside, he shut the door with a resounding click.

Felicity collapsed into a chair, expelling her breath in a rush. "Was Jack O'Conner the photographer who you talked to in Hawai'i?"

"You heard that?" he asked frowning, studying her face.

She nodded.

"So you did know the victim?" the older officer asked.

"We met briefly," Blake replied, dispassionately.

The words were devoid of concern, yet the presence of the policemen in her office, along with the fact that Blake had called his lawyers caused her heart to palpitate. "Is the man okay?" she asked.

"He's hurt pretty badly." The gravity of the young officer's tone sent her heart beating even faster. "He's in Harborview right now in critical condition."

"This has to be a mistake," Felicity said, ready to defend Blake. "Why would Blake do something like that?"

The older officer shrugged. "It happens all the time with photographers and celebrities." He turned his gaze on Blake. "Where were you last night at ten forty-five?"

Blake stood, leaning against the wall, with a look of cold indifference on his face, saying nothing. Why wasn't he defending himself?

"Blake was with me last night," she said, her tone overly loud in the quiet of the room. Wasn't he? She suddenly questioned herself. He'd left her alone in her hotel room after the paramedics had examined her father. Did that mean he didn't have an alibi? Even so, she knew that Blake didn't do it. If he'd gone back to his room, then all she had to do was give the hotel's security tapes to the police to prove Blake hadn't left the hotel again after they'd brought her father home.

"Felicity, say no more until my lawyers arrive," he instructed in a calm tone like he'd had to put up with this kind of situation more than once in his life.

In silent dread, she snapped her mouth closed. The sound of her heartbeat filled her ears as they waited another ten minutes simply staring at one another.

When the door of her office opened once more, three men in expensive suits entered the suddenly overcrowded space. One of the men moved to greet the officers. One made his way to Blake's side. The other came for her. "We'll take things from here, ma'am." His gaze was alarmingly sharp as he motioned toward the door. "You can wait outside."

She looked over at Blake. He nodded and offered her the hint of a smile as she moved into the hallway. The door of her office closed behind her. She stared at the wooden door as her mind began tormenting her with all kinds of vague, disastrous possibilities.

"Looks like Blake's in some serious trouble."

Felicity turned to see Destiny.

"Why are you here?"

"I'm waiting to see what happens now," Destiny said. "That's what good reporters do—they watch, listen, and anticipate."

Felicity's stomach felt as if it were being squeezed in a vise. "Will you do something for me, Destiny?"

"Depends." Destiny raised a perfectly sculpted brow in an unspoken question.

"Go away and leave things alone."

Destiny shook her head, her red hair spilling around her shoulders. "I can't do that."

Felicity frowned at the woman before her. "We used to be friends. What happened?"

Destiny's face went blank. "It's really nothing personal. I just needed to move on."

"That's a lie, and you know it. What's really happening? How did you know the police were coming to talk with Blake? If I thought you capable of such a thing, I'd say you set this up. The friend I used to know wouldn't have done something so cruel."

The barb must have struck a nerve, because Destiny stiffened. "You have no idea what it's like to want something so desperately that you'd do just about anything to get it."

Felicity met Destiny's gaze. "You've met my father. You know that's not true. What do you gain from all of this, Destiny? You said you were desperate. Desperate for what? There has to be a reason. You're not the self-sacrificing type."

Destiny bristled. "I've changed."

"I'd find that easier to believe if you weren't the cause of Blake's latest troubles."

"I'm not the cause," Destiny countered, then pressed her lips together as though forcing herself to say nothing more.

"But you know who is."

"You know." Destiny straightened, then glanced down the hallway as though searching for a way to end their conversation. "I think I'll take you up on your suggestion to leave. After all, I have a story to write." She moved quickly down the hall and out the front door.

Felicity was tempted to follow her onetime friend to see what she would do next, and perhaps who was the "cause" she'd referred to only moments ago. But she couldn't leave, not during the dinner rush. But there was one person who might be able to help. She reached for her cell phone and re-called a previously dialed number.

The call was answered in one ring. "Hello, Felicity. How can I help you?" Peter, Blake's driver asked.

"Are you parked out front?"

"As usual."

"Do you see a red-haired woman leaving the building?"

After a slight pause, Peter asked, "Miss Carrow?"

"That's her."

"She's getting into a taxi."

If Peter could follow Destiny to see where she went or whom she talked to, he might discover some information they could use to help Blake get out of his current situation with the police. "Any chance you could follow her and see where she goes? It's really important, Peter. Blake's in serious trouble, and Destiny might be the reason why."

"You'll look after Blake while I'm gone?" he said, his voice suddenly strained.

"Consider it done."

"I'll call back as soon as I know something." Peter hung up.

The same moment she ended the call, the door of her office opened and the two policemen came out. With a nod to her, they headed down the hallway. Blake's lawyers came out next, and after promising to call him in the morning, they followed the policemen until only she and Blake remained.

In that endless moment, their gazes met and held. She had an almost overwhelming desire to go to him and fold him in her arms, but she held herself back. "Are you okay?" she asked, breaking the spell between them.

"I didn't assault that man."

"I know. I'll have Edward pull the security tapes from the hotel that will prove you were here last night. You were here, right?"

He nodded. "Don't worry, Felicity. My lawyers will take care of everything."

She prayed he was right.

Blake stood and came toward her. "Have you been standing out there the whole time they were questioning me?"

She nodded. "I had company. Destiny followed me here."

"Ah, yes. I saw her in the lobby," he replied, his eyes intent on Felicity's face.

"While we were out here talking, she said something that makes me believe she's up to something."

He quirked an indifferent brow and said, "I suspected as much from the first day we met."

"I hope you don't mind, but I asked your driver to follow her when she left here. Who knows, maybe he'll discover something."

The warmth in his gaze told her he was pleased. His manner was relaxed, in spite of all he'd been through in the last half hour. "It's the tail end of the dinner rush. Are you still needed in the kitchen?"

"I'm afraid so."

"Then let's head back." He turned toward the lobby, then stopped, hesitating, no doubt remembering the photographers that waited there.

She reached for his hand. "Come with me. There's a back way. I have no interest whatsoever in giving those photographers any more fodder than they already have."

He tightened his hand around hers, giving her a conspiratorial smile. "I couldn't agree with you more."

◆ ◆ ◆

Blake and Felicity were alone in the kitchen two hours later when Peter called back. "What have you got?" Blake asked after Felicity turned the phone on speaker so they could both hear.

"Destiny went to Harborview to visit someone named Jack O'Conner in the ICU. Then she went to the *Seattle Gazette*'s headquarters. I saw her meet Reid Fairfax in the lobby, before they both got into the elevator. That's as far as I could go," Peter explained.

"Reid's Destiny's editor," Felicity replied. "She probably met up with him to tell him about the story she intends to write to accompany the pictures that were taken of you with the police."

"Where are you now?" Blake asked his driver.

"Outside the building. I didn't want to hang out in the lobby and look suspicious. I'm no detective."

"You did great, Peter, thank you. Stay there, and just keep an eye on things. I'm going to call my detectives to come and relieve you. They'll be there soon." Blake hung up the phone.

"You're excited." Felicity's gaze was on his face.

"We've finally got a break. The pieces of the puzzle are finally starting to come together," Blake said.

"What do you mean?"

"So you remember the picture we found in the book in my uncle's hotel room?"

She nodded.

"I learned today that the man with my grandfather in that picture was Byrne Fairfax. Reid Fairfax's grandfather and a former partner in one of my family's early businesses. Destiny is the link we've been waiting to find."

"How is she involved?"

"I don't know. That's for my detectives to figure out." He could see that she needed him to try to make sense out of why Destiny had turned on her. He only hoped when this was through that she would have the answers she needed. Just as he hoped he would have his about his uncle. The kitchen was clean, everything put away. He held out his hand. "It's been a hell of a day. Why don't we go check on your father, then go to bed?"

She looked at him inquiringly. "Together? Are you sure that's wise?"

Nothing he'd done since coming to Seattle had been wise, but he knew he didn't want to be apart from her tonight, wise or not. He slipped his arm around her waist. "How about we take the stairs?"

She smiled. "Follow me."

◆ ◆ ◆

Back upstairs in the new two-bedroom suite Felicity had moved herself and her father into earlier in the day, she said good night to Marie. She thanked the older woman for taking her father back upstairs, then staying with him while she and Blake had been occupied with the police. On silent feet Felicity crossed the living area, standing at the doorway of her father's room, watching him sleep. It had been quite a day, but in the end, her father was safe, and Blake was with her.

She shut the bedroom door and moved to the light. Flicking it off, she pitched them into darkness. Only the light of moonbeams seeping through the window illuminated the room, though she didn't need any light to locate Blake. All her senses seem to lock in on him, helplessly drawing her into his arms.

He folded his arms around her, pulling her against his chest. She could hear the sound of his heart, beating in tempo with her own, telling her he was every bit as affected by her presence as she was by his. She didn't want to dwell on any of the reasons why he wanted to be with her tonight. Tonight she would have him for herself. There was no other outcome for them.

Darkness. Heat. Blake.

He lightly brushed his lips against her throat. A primal shudder went through her. With the darkness enveloping them, her other senses sharpened, and she could smell the woodsy scent that would always remind her of Blake.

"You are so hard to resist. You always have been," he whispered against her hair.

"Then don't resist."

"Felicity," he said, his tone suddenly serious. "We have to decide about the hotel."

"We will, but not tonight. This moment has nothing to do with the future. This moment is you and me, right here, right now."

"And tomorrow?" he asked.

"All that matters is now. You and me." Tonight she wanted to set aside all the decisions that would need to be made and seize this moment with both hands. She moved against him, blatantly inviting him into blissful forgetfulness with her, demanding his attentions in return. Tonight they would both hold back the tide of what tomorrow would bring, bury that sense of something dreadful approaching that grew more intense every day they spent together.

Tonight she wanted to set it all aside and know only their passion for each other.

"Come with me," he said, leading her toward the bed in the other room. A mindless rush of pleasure flooded her senses, bringing the sound of his voice into sharp focus. She held onto the languid tone, reveled in it, as he slowly removed her clothing. Her own fingers trembled with desire as she peeled his clothing from him and tossed it to the floor. With no more barriers between them, he flipped the covers back, lay down, and pulled her down beside him.

He was all heat and power in the darkness as he lowered his head, slowly, until his breath washed over her lips. But he didn't kiss her then; instead his lips lowered to the base of her throat, to a freckle on the arch of her collarbone, then lower, to her breast. His mouth closed on her nipple. Heat flashed through her, the muscles of her stomach clenched. And while he explored her with his mouth, his palm swept down her back, pressing her to him, then sliding lower, over her hip, to grasp her bottom and angle her hips to his.

Beneath the silver light of the moon, he molded his hard length against her most intimate core. The sensation of his warmth, his strength, his arousal, overpowered all else, working its way into her memory. Never again would she be able to separate the silvery glow of the moonlight from him, never would she want to. She trailed her hands slowly over his body, savoring the feel of his sinewy strength. She dipped her hand down between their bodies and touched his arousal with a boldness that surprised even her. His body pulsed, throbbed, making her burn all the hotter. "I want you, Blake," she whispered against his lips. She wanted more of him, more than he'd ever given to anyone else before.

He took her lips then, in an achingly slow, devastatingly thorough kiss as he moved over her. Her weight stole her breath as she wrapped her legs around his hips. A thousand bright shivers of expectation hovered between them as he entered her, his warm, throbbing presence filling her fully. With slow, deliberate thrusts, he moved within, coaxing a response from her. She arched against him, meeting his thrusts, and gasped as each stroke that sent her further and further into a space in time where only sensation and promise existed.

That promise gathered momentum and overtook all else, until an urgency born of flesh and fire and consuming desire burst within. His thrusts came harder, deeper, faster. She moved with him, their bodies mingling as they rushed headlong into the flood of sensations that surged through every fiber of her being. She tightened her legs around him, pulling him closer, never wanting to let go.

He plunged into her with a final thrust as deep as life and breath could take him, and the world splintered into hot arcs of pleasure as the promise was fulfilled. That moment of exquisite pleasure extended. Deep within, her womb contracted, clutched, and held him, before satiation claimed her and all her senses surrendered to glorious, drugging bliss.

They lay like that, a tangle of arms and legs, beating hearts and ragged breathing as the world drifted down around them again.

He nestled against her. "Felicity, we are good together."

His voice was deep and caressing. And the way he said her name made it sound so beautiful. She had always hated the formal name her parents had given her. But now hearing it from his lips, she loved it, loved him.

She loved him fully, as any woman could love a man.

Felicity sat up, forcing Blake to relinquish his touch. *We are good together.* The words echoed through her mind. She could not deny she felt the same way. She was part of him now, just as he was part of her. Nothing had ever seemed more natural than being in his arms, having his hands caress her skin, having his lips on her lips.

But at what cost to her or to her employees? Did she love him enough to give up the hotel and restaurant? Did she love him enough to sacrifice the lives of every employee at the Bancroft Hotel? Did she love him enough to put her father's recovery at risk?

Even if she did, would she then resent him for denying her those things? How would they ever build a relationship on that? Felicity drew a steadying breath and turned to face him, looking into the startling blue depths of his eyes. She had to ask the question, even though she feared his answer. "Where does this leave us, Blake?" she asked, her voice raw.

He looked away, closing his emotions off to her. "You said all that mattered was you and me."

"I did."

"And you wish for something different now?"

"I want you and the Bancroft and security for my employees. I want it all."

He reached for her hands as a flicker of sadness crossed his face. "I know about wanting it all, but neither of us can have that. Either you or I have to change our minds about what we want from this hotel, and from each other." His features softened. "If you're worried about taking care of your father, I can help you."

"Absolutely not," Felicity burst out. "Please, Blake," she implored, realizing how ungrateful she must sound. "At least leave me some pride. I can't accept your money. I won't be beholden to you, or anyone, in that way." She'd made it this far on her own.

He nodded and released her hands. "So where does that leave us?" He echoed her question. "Right back where we started?"

"No, Blake," she said softly. "We are both different now. I'm stronger, and your heart is bigger than it used to be."

"Felicity, I—" He stopped himself before he could continue. Instead, he leaned down and pressed a kiss to her forehead. "You're right," he said tenderly as he pulled her back into his arms and once again gathered her against him. "Let's wait and see what tomorrow brings."

Tomorrow. The word held both a hopeful and ominous tone. Moments ticked by as he looked into her face, his eyes dark with promise. Then, as a slight smile curved his lips, he bent his head and kissed her. It was an achingly slow, devastating kiss that sent them right back to the bliss and forgetfulness they found in each other.

CHAPTER NINETEEN

Watery sunlight filled Felicity's room at the Bancroft Hotel the next morning. As she woke, she rolled over to find Blake was gone. Fumbling for the clock by the bedside, she was alarmed to see it was almost eight o'clock. She shook off the sensual miasma that still lingered deep inside her from their lovemaking last night and got out of bed. After checking in with Hans to find he had everything covered for the restaurant, she took a quick shower, then got dressed.

Entering the sitting room of the suite, she found her father in a chair by the window. She was thrilled to see he'd moved himself from the bed to the chair. The procedure on his brain was definitely causing changes to occur. "Good morning, Dad," she said cheerfully as she kissed him on the cheek.

At her approach, he turned to her with clear eyes and a smile. He remained quiet. He'd said nothing more than that single word two days ago. But that one word was enough for her to see him as the father she used to know instead of the stranger who had taken his place years ago.

"I've arranged for your therapist to meet you here today, and I've hired a nurse to stay with you while I take care of some business." She'd had to use the rest of her savings to do so, but that had covered the expenses for the next two weeks—plenty of time for her and Blake to determine the fate of the Bancroft Hotel.

Since Hans had things covered at the Dolce Vita, Felicity decided to check in with the Seattle Historic Preservation Program to find out where her petition was in the process. She could call the lawyers and have them check in for her, but she felt like doing something herself. Action always made her feel more in control of her goals. But before she headed there, she needed a cup of coffee. She would have preferred a cup from the Starbucks on the corner, but a quick glance outside from the lobby told her the local reporters were still there, waiting for, as Destiny put it last night, "something to happen."

If she wanted coffee, she'd have to get some downstairs with the rest of the hotel staff. Taking the elevator to the ground floor, she headed for the staff break room. The gathering place was unusually quiet for this time of the morning when all the housekeeping and restaurant staff seemed to congregate in the same place.

The smell of burnt French roast coffee wafted through the room. The tables were empty, their cheap tan-colored plastic surfaces littered with only a few earthenware mugs with black coffee stains around the rim. Felicity smiled. Her employees were not unlike so many other Seattleites who loved their morning brew.

Hans sat alone at the back of the room reading the *Seattle Gazette*. As soon as he saw her, he hurriedly folded the paper and tossed it onto the table. "Felicity," he greeted. "What brings you down here?"

The headline on the front page jumped up at Felicity.

Billionaire and Lover Questioned in Assault

Below the headline were two separate articles and two pictures. One of the pictures was of Blake being escorted through the lobby by the police. The other was of her pressed intimately against Blake, wearing nothing but his shirt.

Mechanically, she reached for the paper.

"You haven't read the newspaper this morning?" Hans asked, attempting to snatch the paper away.

Felicity avoided his grasp. "No, I haven't."

Hans grew silent, suddenly nervous. The slow, soft whirring of their breath became the only sound in the room.

She looked down at the byline at the top of each article: "Story by Destiny Carrow." Obviously that was what Destiny had done when she'd gone back to the *Seattle Gazette*'s offices last night.

A knot of fear tightened Felicity's stomach. And she knew the color had seeped out of her cheeks as she read the article about Blake first. It contained a great deal of lurid speculation about why he was questioned for the assault of a photographer that still remained unconscious at Harborview. Destiny didn't outright accuse him of the crime, but she might just as well have, considering the conjecture she'd used in the article.

But there was one paragraph in the article that chilled Felicity to the core. Destiny described an argument Blake had had with his father the day before his parents died. She described the scene with the coins. His father's concussion. The coroner's report, stating the cause of the accident might have been due to that very concussion.

He'd told no one but her about that incident.

So how had Destiny found out?

"Oh my God," Felicity said in a strained voice. He'd think she told her onetime friend.

"It will blow over," Hans replied.

No, she doubted it very much. Blake would hate her for this, regardless of her innocence. "People will believe the worst, before they seek the truth about a man as rich as Blake."

Almost afraid of what she'd find in the article about her, Felicity started reading. When she was through, it was no longer fear, but anger that made her fingers tremble. Destiny had claimed she'd wanted to be a serious journalist. If that were the case, these articles were a poor example of her skill.

The second article not only exposed Felicity's impoverished beginnings, but it painted her as a desperate woman, willing to do whatever it took to climb her way up the social ladder. In the pictures accompanying the article, she did look like a social climber aboard the fancy yacht. Hysterical laughter bubbled up in Felicity's throat. She clamped her teeth together to keep the sound from slipping past.

She and Blake had both been played for fools. Before she could launch into a tirade, her cell phone rang. A look at the screen told her it was Blake.

"Hello?"

"Have you seen today's newspaper?" he asked. His tone was flat, but not accusing.

"Yes," she said hesitantly.

"Where are you?"

"At the hotel."

"Stay there. I'm sending Peter to get you. Meet him in the back alley behind the kitchen."

Before she could agree or object, he hung up.

"I'm sorry, Felicity," Hans said softly in the silence that followed. "I had no idea about your past."

The pity in Hans's voice hit her like a fist to the gut. Hot tears stung her eyes. She dashed the tears away with the back of her hand. "Don't pity me, Hans. I worked hard to leave that past behind." She made her way toward the door, her need for coffee forgotten.

"And you have." The sous-chef stood, blocking her way before she reached the door. "No one here who reads the article about you will be anything but proud of what you've overcome. In fact, it explains why you're so passionate about your Hungry Hearts program."

Felicity shifted her gaze to the wall, trying to gather herself.

"Are you okay, Felicity?" Hans asked.

"I'm fine," she said, forcing her chin up and squaring her shoulders. "Will you cover the restaurant tonight?"

"Of course," Hans replied. "If there's anything else I can do—"

Before he could finish the sentence, Felicity moved past him. She clenched the newspaper in her hands as she kept moving toward the hotel's lobby. Five days ago she had been the happiest she'd ever been in her life. Vern had given her the greatest gift she'd ever received. After years and years of scraping by, of sacrificing, she finally had something that could give both herself and her father the future she'd always dreamed of.

Her gaze drifted to the picture of her and Blake. She'd been so happy in that moment, too—wrapped in his arms, with nothing between them but their mutual attraction. Or so she'd thought.

Felicity turned the paper over, hiding the picture of her and Blake from her view as she made her way to the alley. Vicious lies and grotesque innuendos—that was Destiny's idea of what it took to get ahead in the newspaper business? Perhaps in the tabloids.

Raking her hair back from her forehead with her fingers, Felicity tried to consider what to do. Surely Blake had a plan. That's why he'd sent for her, wasn't it?

She paced the back alley for fifteen minutes until Peter arrived. After a short car ride through Seattle, they arrived at the Columbia Center off Fifth Avenue.

"I'll let you out here," Peter said, stopping in the loading zone in front of the skyscraper. "Blake's waiting for you in his attorneys' office on the sixty-third floor."

◆ ◆ ◆

Felicity knew the moment she saw Blake that something was different. The gentle man who'd held her in his arms last night was nowhere in sight. He stood, as did the man at his side, when she was ushered into an elaborately appointed meeting room with a highly polished mahogany table in the center of the room.

"I'm glad you could join us," Blake said, motioning for her to sit in the chair opposite the handsome older man next to him. "Felicity, this is my lead counsel, Marcus Grady. Marcus, Felicity Wright." His voice was pleasant enough, but his face gave no hint of his mood or emotions.

Marcus greeted her, his dark eyes assessing. At a nod from Blake, he removed a sheet of paper from the stack before him and slid it across the table to her. It was a newspaper article from a paper many years ago with the same picture he'd showed her of his grandfather and Byrne Fairfax, Reid's grandfather.

"Byrne was my grandfather's partner. He was removed from the board of trustees by my grandfather and fired from what was then called B&F Industries. The minutes from the trustee meetings report that they could prove he had embezzled more than a million dollars from the company. Back in the forties that was a lot of money."

"It's a lot of money even now," Felicity said, realizing her perspective and Blake's were radically different.

Blake and Marcus shared a glance she didn't understand, but before she could question them, Marcus continued. "We found a witness who is willing to testify that Reid was the one who assaulted Jack O'Conner. The police are on their way to arrest Reid right now."

"Why would Reid try to blame you for the crime?" she asked, but she already knew. Destiny had reported in her article that this wasn't the first time Blake had been questioned by the police. Once he'd had to fight off an intruder in his hotel room, another time he'd been attacked as he stepped out of his car. Both times, the attackers were found beaten in an alleyway. Jack O'Conner was Reid's third attempt to ruin Blake's reputation. Although this time, with Destiny's help, he'd taken it further than ever before by exposing Blake's fear that he'd caused his parents' deaths and painting a picture of him for the world of an angry and violent man.

Felicity's heart hammered wildly in her chest as she tried to capture Blake's eyes. He kept his gaze averted. "You don't think I had anything to do with this, do you?" she asked in a pained voice.

He stiffened at the question, and, when he brought his eyes to hers, she could feel this unspoken accusation like a knife to her heart.

In silent protest, she shook her head and stood, coming around the table toward him.

"I wouldn't do that if I were you," he warned softly.

She stopped cold, her mind registering the physical threat in his voice, refusing to believe it, her gaze searching his granite features.

"Blake," she began, trying to formulate an explanation, but the words died before they were spoken, frozen by the blast of contempt in his eyes.

He was closing himself off again, protecting himself from being hurt. It didn't matter if she was innocent or guilty, he didn't care. He'd already locked her out of his heart in an effort to stop himself from feeling any more pain.

"I love you," she continued bravely, putting her own emotions out there for him to see. "You have to listen to me."

"No, I don't," he said icily. "We had a business arrangement that is now concluded. I trusted you with intimate details of my life, and you used them against me."

Felicity shook her head. "That's not true. I—"

"It was you and me in the rooftop garden, Felicity. No one else. You told me you'd do anything at all to make sure you kept the Bancroft. I should have believed you."

Felicity swallowed roughly at the look of betrayal in Blake's hard blue eyes. "I would never do anything to hurt you like that, Blake. You have to know that."

"I don't know anything when it comes to you and me, other than that you want something that isn't yours. If you won't willingly give it up, then it's time for me to take it from you. Marcus, you're up."

The older man's dark eyes filled with remorse as he slid a packet of papers toward her. "Felicity Wright, Blake Bancroft is serving you with papers . . ." Marcus continued, but the words he spoke jumbled together in her brain. The room swam before her eyes as she blindly felt for a chair, then dropped into it, suddenly boneless.

Pain gripped her. She clenched her eyes shut, as if blocking out the light would make this last wound hurt less. It didn't. Memories of her and Blake, playful and carefree in Hawai'i, merged with her unspoken hopes and dreams until they became a tangled, useless coil of burning pain.

What a fool she had been, falling in love with him. For a short time, he'd actually made her believe she deserved to be loved, to be happy, that good things could happen to her. He'd shined a light upon her and she'd reached out of the darkness for the warmth that he offered her. But now that light was gone, and she was back where she'd started.

Alone.

◆ ◆ ◆

Blake tore his gaze from the love in Felicity's eyes. He didn't believe it was real. He couldn't allow himself that luxury, not when everything he'd worked for over the past few years was at stake. He had been forced to take irrevocable steps to banish Felicity from his life. Felicity or, if she was to be believed, someone else had exposed his deepest secrets to the world, only reinforcing in the public's mind the truth about who he was. He prayed for blessed numbness to seep over him, to spare him any more pain. But numbness didn't come, just the hard, cold reality that he had always believed—that he was unworthy of love.

Across the table, Felicity's gaze met his. For a heartbeat her bright brown eyes searched his with such an aching need that it made him hurt all the more. Her face went ashen as he stood and headed for the door, leaving her alone with Marcus. That final look of sadness on her face tore through him. He'd been a fool to let things go this far. He'd started this game knowing the consequences and sacrifices that would come in the end. Bancroft Industries was his life. There was no room for anything more. As he approached his waiting car, he growled his frustration, making Peter jump.

"Everything all right, sir?" the startled driver asked.

Blake doubted anything would ever be right again once he returned to his old life in San Francisco, a life without Felicity. "I'll be fine. I just need a minute." Sliding into the car, Blake shut the door. The sound resonated deep in his soul.

"Take me to Pioneer Square, please. There is something I need to do before leaving town."

"No problem, sir." Peter started the car and whisked Blake away from the Columbia Center and Felicity.

"Damn you to hell, Uncle Vernon," Blake breathed as they made their way through downtown Seattle. Even from the grave, his uncle had wounded him by bringing Felicity into his life.

CHAPTER TWENTY

The next day Felicity sat in her office, attempting to go over the hotel's accounts, but the numbers jumbled before her eyes. No matter how hard she tried to focus her thoughts, the task eluded her today. She looked out her office window only to see summer rain rolling down her windowpane.

She quickly averted her gaze. The rain reminded her too much of the tears she tried so hard not to shed. Blake Bancroft was gone from her life. She should be happy about that. Instead, it felt as though she might never be happy again.

A light tap on the door interrupted her thoughts. Edward stood there, framed by the doorway, a look of concern etched on his face.

"What's wrong?" Felicity asked as a sense of foreboding came over her.

"There is a man—a Mr. Marcus Grady—here to see you," he said. "He says he has papers he must hand you personally."

Blake's lawyer wanted to serve her with yet another lawsuit? Felicity went pale. "Did he say what sort of papers they were?"

Edward's eyes slid away, his face harsh with sorrow. "They're from Mr. Bancroft."

The world reeled as Felicity tried to stand. What would he do to her now?

"I can tell the lawyer you left," Edward said, coming to Felicity's side, offering her a supportive hand.

Felicity stiffened. "It's okay, Edward. He can't hurt me anymore. Tell Mr. Grady to meet me in the Dolce Vita in five minutes."

In those five minutes, Felicity tried to run through every possible reason that Blake could sue her yet again. Was it because she'd applied for historical protection? Was he upset that she still lived on the premises with her father? Was it because she used the hotel's kitchen for purposes other than feeding paying customers? She had absolutely no idea what to think as she hesitantly approached the man she'd met yesterday.

When she entered he stood and greeted her. "Greetings, Felicity. How are you?" His tone was cordial, friendly even, confusing Felicity all the more. He didn't wait for her to answer his question as he pulled out a chair at the table he'd been sitting at and encouraged her to sit down. "I'm sure you're surprised to see me, especially after our—"

"I'm sorry," Felicity interrupted. "If this is about the lawsuit, I think you should talk to my lawyers at Vetter Douglas."

He gave her a radiant smile. "This is about a different matter. Blake asked me to deliver these papers to you." He slid a thick manila envelope across the table toward her. When she hesitated to touch it, he said, "Go on. Nothing harmful in there."

Silently she opened the envelope and read the first page of the packet of papers on top. It was the property deed to an old building in Pioneer Square. The second stapled packet was official paperwork for a nonprofit agency called Hungry Hearts, complete with a logo of a saucepan with a heart suspended above it. A headache banged to life behind her eyes. "I don't understand," she said, more confused than ever.

"It's a gift from Blake. He bought you a building and filed paperwork on your behalf, establishing your Hungry Hearts program as an official nonprofit entity."

Felicity suddenly found it hard to breathe. "He bought me a building?"

"He's also engaged an architect who specializes in remodeling the interiors of historic buildings to plan out the space for a new cooking facility and dining area. He's contracted a construction company known for their preservation work to start the buildout next week. And he's included a sizable donation in a bank account set up for the nonprofit to outfit the facility with state-of-the-art equipment."

She couldn't stop the tears that shimmered in her eyes. "But he was so angry with me yesterday. And he's suing me over the Bancroft. Why would he do something so . . ."

"Kind?" Marcus supplied.

Felicity nodded.

Marcus leaned back in his chair. "Between you and me?"

She batted at her cheeks with the back of her hands and nodded.

"I've known Blake a long time. I've never seen him as happy as he's been over the last week, or as angry over what he presumed was your betrayal."

"I didn't betray him. I would never tell Destiny Blake's deepest secret. I don't believe he was responsible for his parents' deaths. It was a sad coincidence. Nothing more."

Marcus smiled. "I've told him that same thing for years."

"The accident also explains why he thinks Vern abandoned him, isn't it? He's let himself believe Vern blamed him."

Marcus grinned. "I knew I liked you."

Instantly she sobered. "Blake wouldn't listen to my explanation. He's shut me out." Felicity bit her lip, trying to force back sudden tears.

"I'd say what he's done for you today is a good sign that eventually he'll come around."

"What he's done is nothing short of miraculous."

Marcus nodded. "That's it. You keep believing in miracles, and don't give up on him yet."

Keep on believing in miracles? How could she not?

After Marcus had left, Felicity moved from the dining room into the one place in the hotel that brought her a sense of peace: the kitchen of the Dolce Vita. The restaurant wasn't open yet for lunch, and she was all alone.

No matter what chaos ensued in her life, cooking always calmed her, made her feel more in control. A few simple ingredients could be combined in many different ways to create any number of things. Knowing exactly what this moment called for her to create, she lit the stove and reached for a tall-sided pot.

She filled the container with salted water and set it to boil. Once that was done, she pulled a saucepan down from the rack overhead and set it over a low flame while she gathered butter, flour, milk, cheese, spices, and her favorite pasta to prepare the only dish that might make her feel as though Blake hadn't ripped her heart out: her specialty, macaroni and cheese.

Lost in the process of making a roux, Felicity's thoughts returned to the one man she couldn't seem to extricate from her brain no matter how hard she tried. She added spices to the butter and simmering milk, letting the flavors mix. The mustard and bay leaf were her secret weapons, and the reason no one else could replicate her dish's unique taste unless she revealed her recipe to them. Without much thought to what she was doing, she assembled the rest of the dish until she placed it in the oven to bake. Fifteen minutes later, she took it out and set it on the counter.

And all the while, she kept thinking back over what Marcus had said . . . to wait for Blake to come around.

Her attention returned to the kitchen at the sound of footfalls in the hallway. Her heart sped up and nearly stopped when the doors separating the kitchen from the dining area opened. It wasn't Blake who stood there. It was her father, escorted by Mary Beth.

"Dad?" Felicity started toward him, then stopped, noting the steadiness of his steps and the clarity in his gaze.

Mary Beth greeted her with a smile. "I stopped by your room to give the nurse a break. I thought we'd find you here."

"Are you hungry, Dad?" She didn't expect a reply.

He smiled.

Her chest tightened at the response. Cheered by his progress, Felicity grabbed two stools from the corner and placed them near the prep station. She signaled for her father to sit on one, Mary Beth on the other. Felicity gathered three plates and three forks from the rack and set them on the table before her father, Mary Beth, and herself.

She pasted on a bright smile and dished them each a scoop of the creamy pasta. "Do you remember the first time I made macaroni and cheese? What a disaster. I got cheese all over the kitchen. I spilled so much on the burners, I had to open all the windows to air the house out."

"Are you okay?" Mary Beth asked, interrupting Felicity's rambling.

"I'm fine," Felicity said, perhaps a bit too brightly.

Mary Beth gave Felicity a sideways glance. "You're way too perky, and I know you too well. What's happened?"

Felicity released her breath in a rush. "Blake gave me my heart's desire." At her friend's questioning look, she explained about Blake purchasing a building for her and not only establishing her Hungry Hearts nonprofit, but funding it as well.

Her father sat back and looked at her as though he'd been tracking their entire conversation. He brought his hand to his heart and thumped his chest. When she continued to stare at him with a curious expression on her face, he frowned and thumped his chest again.

Felicity took a stab at interpreting the motion. "I love you, too, Dad."

Her father shook his head, his agitation growing.

"Come on, I think we should take you back to your room."

Felicity moved around to her father's side. He brought his hand up to cover her heart. "Alligator," he said for the second time.

It was the way they'd always said goodbye to each other for as long as she could remember. "Oh, Dad," Felicity said, folding him in a hug. "I wish I understood what you were saying."

Her father shook his head and once again tapped her heart.

Mary Beth reached for her plate of macaroni and cheese and scooped the gooey mixture onto her fork. "I think your father knows a lot more than he can communicate. I swear he's telling you to trust your heart with Blake."

Her father visibly relaxed, and Felicity could only assume it was because Mary Beth had guessed correctly.

"There's too much between us," Felicity said, her tone raw, aching. "The only way things could ever work out is if I gave up the hotel. Are you asking me to give up the hotel?"

He didn't answer. He simply reached for the plate she'd set before him. He lifted the fork to his mouth, chewed, then smiled.

Silence stretched between them until finally Felicity released a pent-up sigh. "I know what I need to do."

Her father said nothing. He simply took another bite of the macaroni and cheese before him. Pride shone in his eyes.

Felicity ignored her food as her thoughts centered on Blake. He'd come into her life so unexpectedly. He'd been an adversary who became a friend and then a lover. As they grew closer, he filled the dark spaces in her soul, the parts she'd never exposed to anyone else. With his gallantry and charm he'd swept her off her feet and made her fall in love. Hopelessly and completely.

She'd always thought love would solve all her problems, that when she fell in love no one and nothing could ever hurt her again. But she'd been wrong.

Love hurt her in places even hunger and poverty hadn't touched. But even so, her heart belonged to Blake. Emotion swelled in her chest. He did not need to buy her love with expensive gifts or luxurious vacations. He had won her heart with nothing but his smile and his gentle touch.

She drew a shaky breath, one filled with infinite hope, and she knew exactly what she had to do.

CHAPTER TWENTY-ONE

A week ago, Felicity would rather have walked across hot coals than enter the headquarters of the *Seattle Gazette*. Yet, here she was, standing in the lobby about to give Destiny Carrow the news story of the year.

As if thinking about her had conjured her up, Destiny came toward her in reception, stopping before her onetime friend. "What do you want?" Destiny asked with barely concealed contempt.

Felicity straightened. "Is there somewhere private we could talk?"

"I doubt you have anything I would want to hear."

Felicity struggled to keep her tone light. "It concerns Blake Bancroft and the Bancroft Hotel, but if you're not interested . . ." Felicity turned toward the door.

She took three steps before Destiny called, "Wait."

Felicity looked back over her shoulder. A frown marred Destiny's flawless features.

"Come with me. We can talk in here." Destiny led her to a room not far away. She waved Felicity into a chair, then folded herself into the one opposite her. The newly promoted reporter crossed her long legs and fixed her interviewee with a hard stare. "This better be worth my time."

"It will be," Felicity replied, "but before we get to that, I need to ask you something." Before Destiny could object, Felicity plunged ahead. "How did you find out about Blake's deepest fears? He told me in confidence."

Destiny smiled. "I followed you and Blake around all over Seattle. When you came back to the hotel, I decided to book a room. After that, I had access to all levels of the hotel, including the rooftop garden. You and Blake thought you were alone, but the walls can have ears, especially at night and with a listening device. It was easy enough to hear what you said."

"Eavesdropping is illegal."

Destiny shrugged. "Sue me."

Felicity's gaze narrowed. "Blake just might."

Destiny's face paled. A moment later she released a long, tired sigh. "What have I done to you and Blake? To myself? I'm a better person than this . . ."

"Yes, Destiny, you are."

"What if I printed a retraction?"

"I'd say it was a start," Felicity conceded. "But I guess I'll never understand why you allowed yourself to be manipulated by Reid in the first place. Was this new job really worth your own integrity?"

"I thought so at the time." Destiny paused, then brought her gaze to Felicity's. "I'm sorry about my terrible review of your restaurant. Every word of it was untrue. I'm also sorry that I put a job ahead of our friendship. It was wrong of me to do that, I realize now."

A look of remorse shadowed Destiny's eyes. Felicity knew the reporter well enough to acknowledge the words were sincere, even if they might have been motivated by the reality of Reid going to jail. Felicity dug deep inside herself, forcing the anger over Destiny's actions away. Being mad at Destiny for making it look like she had betrayed Blake wasn't going to help any of them move on with their lives. She dredged up the words she knew she must say. "I forgive you."

Destiny's eyes widened. "Why? I don't deserve that."

Saying the words made Felicity feel lighter. Forgiveness was the right path to take. "Can we start over, Destiny?" Felicity asked, ready for a return to at least a measure of the closeness they once shared. "No more secrets between us, no more hurt feelings, and definitely no more jealousy."

An odd expression came over Destiny's face. "You would trust me again after what I did to you and Blake?"

"I'm willing to give it a try. Are you?"

Destiny nodded, then sat forward as if she suddenly remembered why Felicity was there. "So what's your news?"

Felicity allowed herself a small smile. This was the Destiny she knew, the one she'd been friends with. Perhaps there really was hope for that again. Drawing a breath, Felicity said, "I'm giving the Bancroft Hotel and the Dolce Vita back to Blake. There will be no court battle. I'm walking away."

"Why?" Destiny asked, her tone an octave higher.

Felicity paused for a long moment as she considered telling Destiny the truth; that she loved Blake more than she wanted the hotel or the restaurant; that sometimes you had to let go of something to find your way to something else. But the eager look on Destiny's face dissuaded her. She didn't trust her old friend with her heart just yet. She barely trusted herself. "Because I found another way to protect my employees."

"Which is?" Destiny asked.

"Do you want my story or not?" Felicity said, with a hint of annoyance.

"Oh, I want it." Destiny grabbed her phone. "Do I have your permission to record this?" she asked a moment before initiating a recording app.

Felicity agreed.

"You'll give me the exclusive?"

Felicity smiled. Yes, this was the Destiny she used to know. "Of course, that's why I'm here."

"Then it looks like we have a story to break, my friend."

◆ ◆ ◆

A week later, Blake paced across his luxurious office on the seventieth floor of Bancroft Towers in the heart of downtown San Francisco. He clutched an unopened letter that had been hand delivered by his own lawyer, Marcus Grady.

"Have you read the newspaper lately?" Marcus asked.

"No. I have no desire to read anything more about the sordid details of my love life or anything else. I've a business to run."

"Yes, and lives to ruin," Marcus replied, his voice laced with uncharacteristic sarcasm.

"What's that supposed to mean?"

Marcus raised a brow. "Aren't you going to read what Felicity wrote in her letter?"

"No," Blake replied, studying his friend's angry face instead.

"Read it," Marcus demanded, wearing an expression he usually reserved for his toughest clients.

Blake frowned as he ripped the envelope open and withdrew a piece of white linen stationery embossed with the Bancroft Hotel emblem of a shield bearing the letters B and H across the top. "So she wrote me a letter," he said without reading the words.

"Would you like me to read it for you?" Marcus said, standing and plucking the letter from Blake's slack fingers.

> *My dearest Blake,*
> *When you love someone, you have to be unselfish*
> *enough to give them what they want. There is no need to*

go forward with your lawsuit. The Bancroft Hotel and the Dolce Vita are yours to do with as you desire. As owner, you will have the right to withdraw any historical protection the building has received.

Your gift of the building and establishment of a nonprofit for the Hungry Hearts program was the kindest thing anyone has ever done for me. The program is doing so well, and sponsors are flooding to donate. I've even been able to hire all my former employees into secure positions with Hungry Hearts as soon as you are ready to take ownership of the hotel.

And if it helps you to know, Destiny overheard us talking on the rooftop. She's the one who betrayed your secret, not me.

I hope you are well and that life brings you much happiness. My most sincere thanks for your gift, and I wish you only the best in your future endeavors.

Always yours,

Felicity

"Sweet, huh?" Marcus scoffed. "Proud of yourself? Stealing a hotel away from someone who needed the money a whole lot more than you."

"This was never about money."

"No?" Marcus asked. "You could have fooled me." He slapped the letter on the desk beside the two of them. "Open your eyes, Blake. That girl was the best thing that ever happened to you."

Blake refused to react to Marcus's anger. His mind was still fixated on the first words she'd written. "*When you love someone . . .*"

"How do you live with yourself sometimes? You forced her into a corner and she folded, exactly like so many of your business opponents do. It's all yours. Everything reverts to you at midnight tonight. My compliments to you on another acquisition, but at what price?"

Having said his piece, Marcus stalked out the door, leaving Blake behind to stare at the handwritten letter.

At what price, indeed. A heartbeat later he picked up his cell phone and dialed Peter. "Have the plane readied, then pick me up. We're flying to Seattle tonight."

CHAPTER TWENTY-TWO

It was dusk when Blake entered the Bancroft Hotel. He searched the familiar lobby, and when Felicity wasn't there, he moved to scan the restaurant, expecting at any moment to see Felicity's platinum-blonde hair and enchanting face as she talked with her patrons. Instead, he came face to face with the hotel's manager.

"Come to gloat?" Edward said, glowering at him from behind the maître d's desk.

"Where's Felicity?"

He crossed his arms over his chest. "She's gone."

"Gone for a walk, or left the hotel for good?" Blake needed the man to be specific as uncharacteristic desperation threaded his veins. She couldn't be gone. Not yet. Not until he'd had a chance to talk with her, to explain.

Explain what? What a fool he'd been? That he should have trusted her?

Her laughter rang through his mind. A memory of Felicity wearing only his shirt and standing on the deck of the yacht with the wind gently tossing her hair slammed through him, bringing a white-hot slash of pain to his chest. He tightened his fists so hard the nails bit into his palms. He tried to think about something else, without success.

"Please, Edward. I need to speak to her. Tell me where she is." The words were not a demand. They were the plea he meant them to be.

The hotel manager's steely gaze softened somewhat. "How do I know you won't hurt her more than you already have?"

"You don't. None of us has that kind of insight into the future. Where is she?" he repeated with calm determination.

"She made me promise not to tell you."

"A hint then, anything."

Edward shook his head, and his eyes hardened to steely gray. "I keep my promises."

Blake frowned, even though he understood and respected the man for his loyalty. Felicity, he'd learned from their time together, did that to people. She earned their trust and their respect by giving the same things back. "I understand," Blake said as he turned and headed from the hotel. Absently, he walked right past Peter and the car, heading down the street. He wasn't even sure where he was heading until he caught sight of the gray-green water of Puget Sound.

With only the creamy yellow light of the street lamps to guide him, he walked along the waterfront. Felicity had said she came here when she needed to think. Perhaps the salty air and the quiet lapping of the waves against the piers would provide answers or at least bring him solace.

He headed toward the bench she'd said she liked, when he saw her and her recognizable platinum blonde hair, shining beneath the light of the stars overhead. She'd come back to this place to think. He held tight to the hope that her thoughts were of him, but that might be wishful thinking.

He stood there for a time, simply watching her, allowing his pulse to settle, gathering the nerve to do what he'd come to do. As he stared out at the water, he wondered how two people who'd shared such intimacy were supposed to find their way back to each other.

"Felicity?" The word was carried away by the breeze. The only movement in the night became the ceaseless rhythm of the waves slapping against the dock. The wind picked up and pushed the waves harder against the pilings. The noise covered his approach.

It wasn't until he stood beside the bench that Felicity started. "Blake, you scared me!"

"May I?" he asked, motioning to the open seat beside her.

She nodded, and he slipped onto the bench. "How did you find me?" she asked, watching him warily as she clenched and unclenched her fingers.

"I followed my feet, and they led me here."

She smiled faintly. Her eyes lifted to his, filled with an emotion he'd never seen there before. One she'd never let him see as fully as she did now. *Love.*

"Did you mean what you said in your letter to me?" he asked.

"About giving you the hotel and restaurant?"

"About loving me?" he asked with a raw ache in his voice. He watched her with an almost unbearable sense of desperation. He'd never wanted anything as badly as he wanted her to say the words he longed to hear.

She blinked up at him. Her eyes appeared as luminescent as if the stars danced in their depths. "Yes, God help me, I meant it."

In that moment, he put a name to the emotion he'd been fighting for so long. It was love. That knowledge filled him with both wonder and fear. Did he truly deserve to feel something this big? The answer was surprisingly a resounding yes. The guilt he'd been carrying around with him since his parents' deaths eased, and he breathed easily for the first time in a very long while.

"How's your dad? I read that his therapy is progressing and that he's saying an occasional word."

"You read the articles?"

"Not at first, but eventually I was so desperate for the sight of you that I read them all, many times."

"That will make Destiny happy to hear she has at least one reader." Felicity laughed. The sound filled him with a satisfaction that had been missing in his life every day that he'd been separated from her.

"She has many more readers than that, I'm sure. I liked the article she wrote today about the Bancroft's acceptance into the Seattle Historic Preservation Program."

Her smile was apologetic. "I knew they would approve the Bancroft for acceptance, and I apologize if it makes your tasks with the hotel harder from this day forward, but the hotel deserved to be honored for her past."

"I agree." He reached out and cupped her cheek. "How did you ever stay so optimistic in spite of your past?"

"I'm pretty stubborn."

He shook his head. "No, you're a good person, and every day that I spend by your side makes me strive to be more like you."

"Is that why you started the Hungry Hearts program?"

"You started it. I'm simply a donor." He slipped his arm about her shoulders.

"You're my very best donor, then," she said, leaning against him.

"I like the sound of that." Warmed by the feel of her body against his, he stared up at the night sky, feeling as though he'd been given the greatest of gifts this night. He reached for her hand, held it in his own with uncertain fingers, afraid that this moment might soon blow away in the cool night breeze just as his words had. If she vanished from his life, he'd be left with nothing. He'd waited his entire life for this moment without really knowing it.

"You're trembling," she whispered as she returned her gaze to his.

"You do that to me."

She tightened her fingers around his and scooted closer.

Wrapped in silence as they watched the moonlight dance upon the water, Blake realized tonight Felicity had given him back his dreams. With her, anything seemed possible, even those things he'd never allowed himself to want. A family. Children. A wife.

She turned to him and her eyes searched his briefly, then to his surprise she stretched up and lightly kissed him on the lips.

He responded, touched by her sweetness, her warmth.

When they came apart a moment later, she pulled back with a smile. "We should make our way back to the hotel."

Blake stood, then helped her up. Hand in hand they walked slowly back to the Bancroft, neither one of them wanting to end the moment, but knowing they had no choice. He had yet to say the words he'd come to Seattle to say. He had to wait until the time was right, until he could wrestle away the last of her reservations.

He had to convince her, not with words but with action, that he loved her. To show her that with every moment they'd been together, every time they'd made love, she'd become more entrenched in his soul until he was no longer certain where he ended and she began.

Blake smiled into the darkness. He knew exactly how to make that happen.

◆ ◆ ◆

Two days later, Blake was nearly ready to implement his plan. He'd blocked off the entire seventh floor of the Bancroft Hotel, refusing to let anyone but himself in on his secret. He'd cleaned the big, open room until it smelled like fresh lemons and sparkled like the midday sun.

Grateful he'd learned early in his career as a manager how to install light fixtures, he'd hung twenty-six vintage 1900s chandeliers from the ceiling. He'd reworked the units to run on LED bulbs, and now nearly two thousand twinkling lights cast a soft golden glow about the large room. Blake turned around slowly, inspecting it all. Everything had to be perfect.

Earlier today, he'd decorated the ceiling above the chandeliers with ivy and white roses that hung down as though suspended in midair. The entire room looked magical, exactly as he'd hoped it would. He checked his watch. He had ten minutes more until his guests arrived.

The day could only be more complete if Felicity decided to stay with him forever. He faced the biggest challenge of his life: one where he stood to lose everything, or win it all. There was no in between. Blake straightened his Armani suit and ran a suddenly nervous hand through his hair. It was time to find out what her decision would be.

At precisely six o'clock, the doors of the elevator opened and Felicity stepped into the room. When she came forward, he greeted her with a single white rose. He paused, feeling more than a little breathless as he took in the sight of her. Her hair hung loose about her shoulders, curling at the ends. She'd worn the dress he'd picked out for her, an iridescent white silk. The fitted bodice clung to the lines of her body, accentuating every feminine curve. At the hips, the skirt flared out in a graduated fullness until it draped against the floor.

His gaze traveled back up the length of her body to come to rest upon her face. "You're beautiful."

"What's all this about?" Her cheeks flushed pink.

His hand cupped her face. "Do you trust me, Felicity?"

She leaned in to his palm. "With my life."

"Then trust me now. All will be well. You'll see."

◆ ◆ ◆

Blake withdrew a single folded sheet of paper from the inside pocket of his suit. "I have something for you," he said as he handed the paper to her.

She opened the paper, then gasped. She met his gaze. It was the deed to the Bancroft Hotel. "Why?"

"Because a wise woman I know taught me an important lesson. She said, when you love someone, you'll sacrifice anything for them."

She stared at him, feeling dazed.

"I don't know what to say? I never imagined . . ."

"Name anything in the world you want, Felicity, and I'll give it to you," he said thickly. "No strings attached."

His words were like a balm to her soul—a soul that had gone too long without the warmth and security she'd always wanted and had never hoped to find. "The only thing I've ever wanted is you."

Blake smiled, slowly, the blue of his eyes peaceful and calm. "Marry me."

Felicity's throat grew tight as her gaze passed over the decorations strewn about the chamber. Suddenly everything became clear. She looked down at the gorgeous dress Blake had sent to her room. White was what a bride wore on her wedding day when she married the man of her dreams.

Felicity drew a steadying breath, trying to hold at bay the moisture that pooled in her eyes. She wanted a lifetime of the fullness, the sweetness, the all-consuming joy she'd experienced when Blake had held her in his arms at the railing of the yacht. She'd wanted those precious few moments to stretch out forever. It was in that moment she knew she wanted a lifetime with him. "For how long?"

His brow puzzled. "You want to negotiate?"

She held her breath, needing him to say the words.

"Forever. Is that long enough?"

She nodded. "Will there be a prenuptial agreement?"

He shook his head as he gathered her closer. "I told you I'd give you anything. That includes everything I own, everything I am. There will be no prenuptial agreement. Now or ever."

She couldn't keep the smile from her face. "I'd be an idiot to refuse you, wouldn't I?"

"I'd have to say yes."

"Okay," she whispered. "I'll marry you." The moment she said the words, an incredible sense of rightness came over her. Before she could say anything more her father, her employees, and her friends spilled out of a room that was normally used for catering purposes.

Tears burned at the back of Felicity's eyes and finally spilled over as everyone she cared about came to congratulate her and Blake. Each person who came to greet her offered her a rose, until she held a huge bouquet in her hands.

The heady scent of roses filled the room, making her dizzy with a kaleidoscope of happiness, contentment, and love. The emotions tumbled through her, bringing joy one moment, awe the next. Her heart surged with humility and pleasure and hope for a future with the man she loved.

When her arms were full, the guests laid flowers at her feet, until she was surrounded by a sea of fragrant petals and greens. Through tear-filled eyes, Felicity looked up at Blake when he, too, came to stand before her.

"Why?" she asked, not bothering to disguise the joy that rode through her.

"You said you liked roses better than any flower," Blake replied. He reached for her hands, folding them in his. "I love you, Felicity, for now and for always. I don't want you to give up your dreams. I simply want a chance to share them with you."

"My dreams are here in Seattle. What about your job . . . the hotels . . ."

"I can do my job just as easily from Seattle as I can anywhere in the world. The only thing I require is you."

For endless seconds she stared at everyone gathered around before returning her gaze to Blake. Her heart leaped. Never had she felt as loved as she did right now. And in that moment every fear of loneliness she'd ever had slipped away, never to return.

"Felicity?" Blake asked, placing a finger under her chin, he brought her gaze back to his. "Marry me right here, right now, in front of our friends and family?"

She could only nod as her heart filled to overflowing.

In a sea of roses, they stood together and joined their lives. She stared down at the ring he'd slipped on her finger, laughing and crying at the same time. The center diamond was absurdly big and surrounded by a ring of smaller diamonds. The ring was dazzling, no doubt expensive, and very bright. "It's so big. You shouldn't have . . . We could feed a small country with the money you spent on this ring."

He grinned. "We'll keep that as an option if we need it someday." He pulled her close as the minister stepped before them. "I wanted the world to know you're mine. You are mine, aren't you, Felicity?"

"Always."

The word had barely settled between them when he kissed her firmly, telling her more clearly than words how fervently he loved her in return. She savored the moment as the scent of roses surrounded her, and wondered exactly when her dreams had become reality.

EPILOGUE

One year later, on the anniversary of Vern's death, Felicity opened the door of the high-tech mansion she shared with Blake and her father in the Madison Park area of Seattle. A lanky deliveryman handed her two slim envelopes, one addressed to her, one addressed to Blake. She thanked him, abstractedly, as she noted the unmistakable handwriting on the labels even though a forwarding sticker had been slapped over part of the address.

"Blake?" Felicity called as she headed toward the room where she'd left him only moments ago.

"What's wrong?" In three strides Blake was in front of her, standing so close she could smell his woodsy cologne and see the bright blue of his eyes. She had to tip her head back to look up at him, finding comfort in the certainty of his gaze.

"These arrived. They were postmarked two days ago in Seattle." She held out the envelope addressed to him and could tell the moment he recognized his uncle's unmistakable script.

"He wouldn't?"

Felicity's heart raced. "We won't know unless we open them."

In unison they broke the seals. Felicity reached inside and removed another smaller envelope. She broke that seal and pulled out a single sheet of stationery with the Bancroft Hotel crest at the top.

Blake followed her example.

"What does yours say?" Felicity was almost afraid to ask what mischief Vern had sent them from the grave.

Blake's expression softened as he read the message. "The future I wanted for you is here. I apologize for my methods, but I learned long ago that you were not one to take advice, mine or anyone else's. I did love you in my own odd way, and as I grew older, I didn't know how to mend the rift between us. I want you to be happy and to carry on the Bancroft name." Blake paused and smiled. Contentment shone in his eyes. "And yours?"

"If there's one thing I know about my nephew, he never could resist a challenge. I hope he'll challenge you for the rest of your long and happy lives." She looked up to meet Blake's smiling gaze. "He planned this all along. He gave me the hotel so that it would lead us to each other."

Sorrow shadowed her husband's eyes as he set his note aside and took her in his arms. "My only regret is that my uncle didn't live to see he got exactly what he wanted." Blake's hand slid to her abdomen, to the barely discernable bump there. Inside her, deep inside, something fluttered. *Life.* They'd found out a month ago that they were expecting.

Felicity covered Blake's hand with her own and offered him a smile filled with all the love in her heart. "He knows. I'm certain of that."

"In his own strange way, he did all this to see us happy," Blake said, bringing his lips to hers in a heart-melting kiss that communicated his love.

When she surfaced from the seductive pull of his lips, Felicity reached out and took his hands. She laced his fingers through her own. "I'm so grateful Vern brought you to me through the ownership of the Bancroft Hotel." Which they now both shared.

CULINARY TREATS TO YOU FROM GERRI RUSSELL

Braised Celery with Onion, Pancetta, and Tomatoes

    2 pounds celery

    1/4 cup extra virgin olive oil

    1 1/2 cups onion, sliced very thin

    2/3 cup pancetta, cut into strips

    3/4 cup plum tomatoes, either fresh or canned, coarsely chopped with their juice

    1 teaspoon salt

    1 teaspoon pepper

Directions

Cut off the celery's leafy tops, saving the leaves for another use, and detach all the stalks from their base. Use a peeler to pare away most of the strings, and cut the stalks into three-inch pieces (cutting on the diagonal looks nice). Set aside.

Put the oil and onion in a pan and sauté over medium heat. Cook and stir the onion until it wilts completely and becomes a light gold color. Add the pancetta strips.

After a few minutes, when the pancetta strips lose their flat white uncooked color and become translucent, add the tomatoes with their juices, the celery, salt, and pepper, and toss thoroughly to coat well. Adjust heat to cook at a steady simmer, and put a cover over the pan. After fifteen minutes, check the celery. It should cook until it feels tender when prodded with a fork. The longer you cook the celery, the softer and sweeter it becomes. If, while cooking, the pan juices become insufficient, refresh the celery mixture with two to three tablespoons of water. Or, if the pan juices are too watery, uncover, raise the heat, and boil the juices away.

◆ ◆ ◆

The Bancroft Peach Bellini
    2 ripe peaches, seeded and diced
    1 tablespoon freshly squeezed lemon juice
    1 teaspoon sugar
    1 bottle chilled Prosecco sparkling wine

Directions

Place the peaches, lemon juice, and sugar in the bowl of a food processor fitted with a steel blade and process until smooth. Press the mixture through a sieve, and discard the peach solids in the sieve. Place two tablespoons of the peach puree into each champagne glass and fill with cold Prosecco. Serve immediately.

◆ ◆ ◆

Hawaiian BBQ Short Ribs
    1 package pork spare ribs
    4 tablespoons of your favorite brand of dry rib rub
    1 cup light brown sugar

2 cups Welch's Essentials Orange, Pineapple, Apple Juice Cocktail
1 16-ounce can chunked pineapple, with its juice
4 tablespoons light yellow mustard
1 cup Hawaiian BBQ sauce

Directions

Sprinkle both sides of the spare ribs with dry rib rub and light brown sugar. Marinate in foil for almost twenty-four hours.

When the meat is finished marinating, prepare the grill, and add a pot of water to keep the air inside the grill moist. Cook the ribs for three hours on indirect heat, uncovered. Flip meat occasionally.

Next, lay the ribs on two layers of foil and pour the pineapple juice over the top. Add pineapple chunks. Finally moisten with the orange, pineapple, and apple juice cocktail. Wrap tightly and cook for two more hours.

Remove the ribs from the foil. Reserve the pineapple and some juice. Coat the ribs with the yellow mustard and Hawaiian BBQ sauce, and let it cook for one more hour, directly on the grill. Turn the meat occasionally.

Serve decorated with the reserved pineapple.

◆ ◆ ◆

Huli Huli Chicken

3 to 4 pounds chicken wings, thighs, and breast pieces
1/4 cup frozen pineapple juice concentrate
1/3 cup white wine
1/2 cup chicken broth
1/4 cup soy sauce
1/4 cup ketchup

1/4 teaspoon powdered ginger or a pinch of fresh ginger

1 to 2 drops Worcestershire sauce

Directions

Wash chicken parts and pat dry with paper towels. Mix all sauce ingredients in a bowl, and brush the mixture over the chicken parts. Grill over barbecue for about forty minutes. Turn and baste with the sauce until the chicken is done. Serves ten to twelve people.

◆　◆　◆

Felicity's Macaroni and Cheese

4 cups (1 pound) elbow macaroni

5 tablespoons unsalted butter

4 cups milk

1/2 medium onion

4 cloves garlic

1 bay leaf

3 sprigs fresh thyme

1 teaspoon dry mustard

2 tablespoons flour

2 cups grated cheddar, plus 1 cup in big chunks

1 cup sharp white cheddar cheese

1/2 cup grated parmesan

Kosher salt and freshly ground black pepper

Directions

Cook the macaroni in a large pot of boiling salted water until done, about five to seven minutes. Drain and toss it with two tablespoons of butter; set aside.

Heat the oven to 350 degrees.

Coat a large baking dish with one tablespoon of butter, and set it aside. Mince the onion, and crush the garlic cloves. Pour the milk into a saucepan, and add the onion, garlic, bay leaf, thyme, and mustard. Warm over medium-low heat until the milk starts to steam, about ten minutes. Remove from the heat, and let the flavors infuse while you make the roux.

In a large pot over medium heat, add two tablespoons butter and the flour. Cook, stirring, for about two to three minutes; don't let the roux color. Remove the bay leaf from the infused milk and add to the roux, whisking constantly to avoid lumps. Cook, stirring often, for about five minutes until the sauce is thick. Remove from the heat and add one half of the grated cheddar, one half of the sharp white cheddar, and one half of the parmesan; stir until it is melted and smooth. Taste and adjust seasoning with salt and pepper.

Pour this mixture over the macaroni, add the chunks of cheddar, and mix until well blended; put this in the prepared baking dish. Sprinkle the remaining cheeses evenly over the top. Bake until the top is golden and crusty, about twenty-five to thirty minutes.

ACKNOWLEDGMENTS

No book is ever written in seclusion, and this book is no exception. I am so grateful to Pamela Bradburn, Teresa DesJardien, Karen Harbaugh, Ann Charles, and Joleen James for cheering me on, sharing advice, and reading the early drafts. You are all so special to me, and I don't know what I would do without you.

A special thank you to Nancy Northcott for sharing her legal knowledge with me at random odd hours of the day and night, and to the staff at the Regency Newcastle. I've learned so much from you all about what quality assisted living can do to celebrate the sunset years of life.

Special appreciation also goes to my Amazon Montlake team, especially Kelli Martin, Maria Gomez, and Krista Stroever. Thank you from the bottom of my heart for sharing your time, talents, and enthusiasm for this story. You all push me to be a better writer, and for that I am grateful.

ABOUT THE AUTHOR

Photo © 2011 Barbara Roser

Award-winning author Gerri Russell has done it all when it comes to writing; she's worked as a broadcast journalist, newspaper reporter, magazine columnist, technical writer and editor, and instructional designer, which all finally led her to follow her heart's desire of being a romance novelist.

Gerri is best known for her adventurous and emotionally intense historical novels set in the Scottish Highlands. *Flirting with Felicity* is her debut contemporary romance.

When she's not reading, writing, or researching, Gerri is a living history reenactor with the Shrewsbury Renaissance Faire. A two-time recipient of the Romance Writers of America's Golden Heart award and winner of the American Title II competition sponsored by *RT Book Reviews* magazine, she lives in Bellevue, Washington, with her husband and children. You can find reviews, excerpts, historical tidbits, and links to Facebook and Twitter on her website at www.gerrirussell.net.